Who's hunting whom?

Lon's receiver crackled to life.

"Major, this is Taw. The raiders have changed course, almost due east. I can't see the lay of the land clearly. I don't know if this is where they're going or if they're just crossing to the next valley."

Lon answered, "Hold up for a minute, Taw. Give them plenty of room before you follow." Lon pulled his mapboard out and unfolded it. "I don't see any clearing big enough for a ship to extract them." He zoomed in on a section. "Maybe five miles southeast, along that creek. Taw, if you don't see which way they turn, hold back. Let's see what they're up to."

Five minutes later, Lon got his answer when Taw called again. He could hear a heavy firefight in the background.

"They suckered us, Major!" Taw yelled, "We've got raiders on three sides!"

Lon cursed under his breath, turned to his company and barked, "Let's *move*!"

MAJOR

RICK SHELLEY

ACE BOOKS, NEW YORK

MAJOR

This is a work of fiction. Names, characters, places, and incidents are
either the product of the author's imagination or are used fictitiously,
and any resemblance to actual persons, living or dead, business establishments, events, or locales is entirely coincidental.

An Ace Book / published by arrangement with
the author

PRINTING HISTORY
Ace edition / December 1999

The Penguin Putnam Inc. World Wide Web site address is
http://www.penguinputnam.com

Check out the ACE Science Fiction & Fantasy newsletter
and much more on the Internet at Club PPI!

ISBN: 0-441-00680-9

ACE®
Ace Books are published
by The Berkley Publishing Group,
a division of Penguin Putnam Inc.,
375 Hudson Street, New York, New York 10014.
ACE and the "A" design are trademarks
belonging to Penguin Putnam Inc.

PRINTED IN THE UNITED STATES OF AMERICA

10 9 8 7 6 5 4 3 2 1

To
Amanda Howell, RN
for making a terrifying experience
worthwhile
Amazing

MAJOR

The year is A.D. 2814. The interstellar diaspora from Earth has been in progress for seven centuries. The numbers are uncertain, but at least five hundred worlds have been settled, and perhaps well over a thousand. The total human population of the galaxy could be in excess of a trillion. On Earth, the Confederation of Human Worlds still theoretically controls all of those colonies, but the reality is that it can count on its orders being obeyed only as far as the most distant permanent outpost within Earth's system, on Titan. Beyond Saturn, there are two primary interstellar political groupings, the Confederation of Human Worlds (broken away from the organization on Earth with the same name, with its capital on the world known as Union), and the Second Commonwealth, centered on Buckingham. Neither of those political unions is as large or as powerful as they will be in another nineteen decades, when their diametrically opposed interests finally bring them to the point of war. In the meantime, humans who need military assistance, and do not want the domination of either Confederation or Commonwealth, have only a handful of options. Those who can afford it turn to mercenaries. And the largest source of those is on the world of Dirigent. . . .

Angie Nolan had blue eyes and blond, almost white, hair that was naturally curly. In two days, she would be ten months old. So far, Lon had been able to see no resemblance in Angie to either her mother or her father, though he tried, diligently.

Captain Lon Nolan finished dressing his daughter after a diaper change, then picked her up and carried her back to the living room, talking softly to her the whole time. Though he kept the words simple, he never resorted to the gibberish of "baby talk."

"It'll be a miracle if she ever learns to walk, the way you and Junior carry her around all the time," Sara Nolan said when she saw them. There was a smile on her face, though; this was an old joke between her and her husband. Sara stood in the doorway between kitchen and living room. Outwardly, she looked little different to Lon than when he had first seen her, more than eight years before. Even now, there were times when Lon could not believe his memories of that evening. They had gone from being strangers to being engaged to be married in only a couple of hours. The precipitous nature of their courtship had led some to predictions of disaster, but that clichéd "love at first sight" had not only survived, it had also grown with each passing year. There were tiny lines at the corners of her eyes now, and she wore her red hair shorter, but that was the extent of the changes that Lon noticed.

Lon, Junior, was sitting on the floor, too near the entertainment console, as usual. He was seven years old and looked very much like his father. Junior looked toward his mother as if he were ready to contradict some part of what she had said, but he saw the smile and turned back to his program instead.

"She'll have plenty of time for walking," Lon said, carefully setting the girl on the floor next to her brother. She immediately climbed onto Junior's lap and made herself comfortable, ready to stare at the show on the console with him.

"Angie walks pretty good already," Junior said then, shifting her so he was more comfortable. The boy had never exhibited any jealousy at the arrival of a sister. He doted on her nearly as much as their parents did.

"Go wash your hands for supper," his mother said. "It'll be ready in two minutes."

It was a Saturday evening in early October, a mild autumn in Dirigent City. A third of the Dirigent Mercenary Corps was off-world on contract. Lon's unit, Company A, 2nd Battalion, 7th Regiment, was near the top of the lists for both company- and battalion-size operations. The next contract, the next trip away from Dirigent, might be no more than days—weeks at the most—away. That made Lon's time at home, evenings and weekends, all the more precious to him. After eleven years in the DMC, he no longer looked eagerly forward to the next chance for contract pay. Even if a mission did not involve combat, it still kept him away from his wife and children, and that was hard, beyond what the extra pay for off-world service was worth to him.

The battalion had been back on Dirigent for seven months this time around. The men had gone through their regular stints of training and planetary defense duty, getting in furlough time as possible, and had just gone back to a training schedule. For Lon that generally meant a five-day workweek, eight to five, little different from any other working man on any developed world. Night exercises were rare. The only regular interruption to the routine was the one night out of twelve when he drew duty as battalion officer of the day. His last turn at that had come the previous Sunday.

Angie sat in her high chair between her parents at the kitchen table. Lon, Junior, sat across from his sister. Living quarters for married captains and lieutenants did not include a separate dining room. Those were reserved for senior officers.

When everyone was in place, Lon said grace. He had never been particularly religious, but he had rarely questioned the existence of a God, and Angie thought that it was important to show a good example for the children. When possible, they even attended services at the nearest chapel on base together. At times like this, Lon found that there was little pretense in his open prayers. He looked around at his family and thought how lucky—how blessed—he had been in life. *It couldn't be better*, he thought.

Junior carried most of the conversation during supper. He talked about his day—the shows he had watched, his "adventures" playing, and what Angie had done. Every day seemed to bring some new accomplishment for the infant, and that amazed the boy.

Lon listened and watched in fascinated amusement. He could not recall ever being as exuberant as his son. He could not really recall being that young himself. There was only one passage in the boy's talk this evening that bothered Lon. In the course of one tale, Junior said something that started with "When I grow up and join the Corps . . ." Lon felt the frown settle across his face before he could mask it, but Junior did not notice.

"There are other things besides being a soldier," Lon said when he got a chance.

"But I *want* to be a soldier, just like you," the boy said, and he went on with his story.

I hope you change your mind, Lon thought, no longer really listening to the narrative. *You're smart, even smarter than I was at your age. There are lots of other things you could do with your life*. Junior had started reading when he was just a little past his third birthday, and he tested in the top percentile of children his age. Lon had never seriously questioned his own career as a soldier, and the desire to follow that vocation had started when he was perhaps no older than his son was now. Lon did not like to admit it, even to himself, but the thought that his son might someday join the Corps made him anxious.

"He'll change his mind a thousand times over the next ten years about what he wants to be when he grows up," Sara told Lon when they were alone for a moment after supper. Junior and Angie were in the living room again. Lon was helping his wife put dishes in the washer. "Children are like that." She had seen the strained look on Lon's face when Junior talked about wanting to be a soldier.

"I hope so," Lon whispered. "But I wasn't. I set my mind on being a soldier when I was about Junior's age and never wavered. All I ever wanted to be was a soldier." That phrase nearly brought a shiver to him. It hadn't been easy. He had lost his chance at becoming a soldier on Earth when the top students in his class at the North American Military Academy were earmarked for the federal police and the task of containing the millions of idle poor who lived in the city areas known as circuses. He had left Earth to escape that career of intentional brutality, heading for the mercenary world of Dirigent . . . a lifetime ago. "And here," Lon continued, "one way or another, the entire planet revolves around the Corps. It's impossible to escape the influence."

"It *is* what we do," Sara said. "Without the Corps, Dirigent wouldn't amount to much." She kissed Lon on the cheek. "And it's too soon to worry about what Junior's going to be when he grows up, anyway. It'll make you old before your time." She started the washer, then led Lon toward the living room. When Lon was home, Saturday evenings were for the family.

Junior chose the show they watched that evening, not

the rarest of events. This one was an adventure about a handful of people stranded on some world dominated by gigantic dinosaurs and dragons, searching for some fabulous—and improbable—artifact. The plot had more holes in it than a target after a long day on the rifle range, but that never bothered Junior. And his father could tolerate it. The vid was full of unintentional humor. The adventure was nearing its incredible climax when a red light on the status line at the bottom of the screen started blinking to signal an incoming call.

"I'll get it in the kitchen," Lon said.

He closed the door between the two rooms to shut out the sounds of dragons and dinosaurs, then keyed the accept button on the complink. The screen came to life instantly. Major Matt Orlis, adjutant for 2nd Battalion, was calling from his office.

"Lon, we need you at regimental headquarters as fast as you can make it," Orlis, Lon's predecessor as commander of A Company, said.

"A contract?" Lon asked.

Orlis shook his head no. "Are you alone there?"

Lon nodded yes.

"There's been a problem, in 3rd Battalion. You will be sitting as one of the officers on a general court-martial."

Lon felt his breath catch. "What's the offense?"

"Murder."

2

By the time Lon had changed into uniform, there was a car waiting outside to take him to regimental headquarters.

"You're not going out on contract, are you?" Sara had asked as soon as he got off link and headed through the living room toward their bedroom.

"No, not a contract," he said, not stopping to talk. Sara followed him into the bedroom. Once the door was closed behind them, Lon told her what little he knew.

"Murder?" she asked.

"That's what Matt said. I'll let you know as soon as I know anything I can share," Lon promised. He was already out of his civilian clothes and reaching for a fresh uniform from the closet.

Murder. No one in the DMC had been charged with that crime in all the years that Lon had been on Dirigent.

"Will you be late?" Sara asked as Lon affixed the oval pips of a DMC captain, red enamel and gold, to the lapels of his uniform shirt.

"I have no idea if I'll even get home tonight," he said. "I don't know how complicated this is going to be." In the DMC, a court-martial panel was assembled as early in the process as possible. They oversaw the investigation by the military police and judge advocate, charged with protecting the rights of victims, witnesses, and the accused—as well as with finding the truth. Lon had sat on two special courts-martial—one step below a general court-martial in numbers and in the maximum sentence they were allowed to impose—in his years as an officer in the DMC.

Lon was slipping on his dress boots when the doorbell rang and Sara went to answer. It was the driver sent for Lon.

"Sorry to have to roust you out on a Saturday night, Captain," the driver, a corporal from regimental headquarters, said.

"Not your fault, Corporal," Lon said as the driver held open the door to the ground-effect vehicle for him.

They did not discuss the case. Lon knew no more than what Matt Orlis had told him, and he knew better than to ask. Nor did the driver volunteer any information. The ride to 7th Regiment's headquarters took less than ten minutes. Several other vehicles were parked in front of the building, and there were more lights than usual on inside.

An MP standing watch just inside the main entrance directed Lon to the office of the OD, the officer of the day. The door to that office was standing open. Major Orlis, now the executive officer for 2nd Battalion, was the regimental OD.

"Sorry to spoil your weekend, Lon," Orlis said, getting up to return Lon's salute and to shake hands. "But this is a bad one. I can't tell you more now. We're still waiting for two more members of the court-martial. I'll brief you all at the same time. It shouldn't be long."

"Where do I wait?" was the only question Lon asked, though there were several others he wanted to have answered.

"Conference room just across the hall. There's a fresh pot of coffee going in there, or there was ten minutes ago."

Lon nodded and went to the other room. There were two officers already in there, sitting at the oval conference table, across from each other. Major Tefford Ives was the executive officer of the regiment's 1st Battalion. Near fifty and unlikely to advance any higher in the Corps, Ives nodded a casual greeting to Lon and gestured at the empty chairs. Lon needed a few seconds to recall the name of the other officer, Captain Dave Gowers from 5th Regiment. Lon could not recall what battalion or company Gowers belonged to. Lon got coffee and sat at the table.

"Orlis say how much longer we've got to wait before we find out what's going on?" Ives asked after Lon was seated.

"Just that it shouldn't be long, Major," Lon said.

The next officer arrived almost on Lon's last word. Captain Wallis Ames commanded 2nd Battalion's B Company, and had ever since Lon had joined the battalion. He was past sixty years of age, steady but unremarkable as a combat leader. And less than two minutes later, the final member of the court-martial panel was escorted into the room by Major Orlis.

"Gentlemen," Orlis said, "Colonel Johan Ellis will be the president of this court-martial." The officers sitting at the table had all stood to attention as soon as the commanding officer of 12th Regiment entered the room.

"Please sit, gentlemen," the colonel said as he went around the table to sit at the center of one of the long sides. "Let's save the formalities for when there are others present."

"Coffee, Colonel?" Lon asked. He was closest to the chair that Ellis took.

"Thank you, Captain, yes."

Matt Orlis waited until Lon had fetched coffee for the colonel, then moved to a position across from Ellis, but remained standing a couple of paces from the edge of the table, where everyone could see him without straining their necks.

"Colonel, gentlemen, you have been convened to sit as a general court-martial," Orlis said, part of the ritual required for the empanelment. "The convening authority is the General, Herman Rodrigues."

Lon closed his eyes for an instant. The General himself was the convening authority, and the president of the court-martial was a full colonel. Those two items were enough to tell him that the case was one in which the sentence might be death if the suspect—whoever he was—were convicted.

"The accusing officer is Lieutenant Colonel Jack Draco, commanding the Corps' military police detachment," Orlis continued. "The defendant is Private Kalko Green, A Company, 3rd Battalion, 2nd Regiment. The charge is willful murder, the specification that Private Green did, on or about sixteen-fifteen hours, October seventh, 2814, willfully murder Platoon Sergeant Holfield O'Banion of C Company, 3rd Battalion, Third Regiment, in Dirigent City, at the civilian establishment known as the Purple Harridan."

Lon did not recognize the name of either the defendant or the slain man.

"Captain Knowles, the officer in charge of the investigation, is waiting for you to join him at the scene of the crime," Orlis said. "Your transportation is waiting. There is only one formality left before you depart, Colonel, gentlemen. Major Rice from the judge advocate's office is here to swear you in as members of the court-martial."

The formality took less than a minute. Then Major Rice escorted the five members of the court-martial out to a waiting floater, a large vehicle that could have comfortably seated twice as many. The driver was a sergeant, as was the armed guard who accompanied him.

There was no talk during the ride into the section of Dirigent City known as Camo Town, the area that existed to serve the off-duty desires and needs of the soldiers who were the backbone of the world's economy. Bars, brothels, gaming arcades, restaurants, cheap hotels, and various other establishments lined the streets of Camo Town. Lon stared out the window at his side, but he was not really looking at the passing scenery. The thought that one member of the Corps had murdered another—if the allegation was true—was too disturbing. Lon tried to tell himself not to make guesses about what might or might not have happened. Before hearing the facts, that would be presumptuous. But he could not entirely restrain his mind. The accused killer and the victim had not been part of the same company, or even the same battalion. Unless one or the other had transferred, that might indicate that it was not a duty grudge carried off base. Beyond that . . .

It's been a long time since I was in the Purple Harridan, Lon thought, and that almost brought a smile to his face. *Or the Dragon Lady, or any of the other places we used to go.* Phip Steesen, Janno Belzer, and Dean Ericks had been his usual companions—an age before, it seemed now. When Lon had first joined the Corps, they had been in the same fire team, unofficially assigned to steer Cadet Nolan through the process of adjustment. The four of them had done almost everything together, been compared with more regularity than any of them liked to D'Artangan and the Three Musketeers. But that couldn't last forever, even though they had been nearly inseparable. Janno had married a waitress from the Dragon Lady, then resigned from the Corps for civilian work. Lon had won his officer's pips, then promotion to captain . . . and a wife. It was the latter more than the other considerations that had put an end to his jaunts into Camo Town with friends and comrades. Phip and Dean were still in the Corps, still in A Company. Phip was a platoon sergeant now, and Dean a corporal, a squad leader who would earn his own sergeant's stripes before much longer. The four men were still close friends, but time and circumstances had forced the relationships among them to change. It was not the same as it had been back in . . .

"The good old days," Lon whispered very softly.

The Purple Harridan had been closed for the investigation. Two MPs stood at the main entrance, their look of formal menace enough to ensure that passing soldiers gave them a wide berth. Some crossed to the far side of the street to avoid coming too close. Lon assumed that the other doors would be similarly guarded.

Inside, the loud music had been stilled and the strobing lights switched to constant—normal—illumination. Several more MPs stood around, making sure that nothing was disturbed and that the potential witnesses—staff and customers—did not leave the premises prematurely. An MP captain came over to Colonel Ellis and saluted. Ellis returned the salute.

"Colonel Ellis is president of the court-martial, Captain Knowles," Major Rice said. "These other officers have been empaneled to sit on the court-martial."

"Has the accused been assigned representation yet?" Colonel Ellis asked. "His attorney should be present for this."

"That would be me, Colonel." A man in civilian clothes moved away from the others at the bar and approached the newly arrived group. "Tim Isling, attorney-at-law." He nodded but did not offer to shake hands.

"Counselor." Ellis returned the nod. "If you have no objections, we might as well begin the tour of the crime scene."

Captain Knowles started reporting. "At sixteen-fifty-five hours today, our office received a call from the Dirigent City police, reporting that there had been a murder committed at this location, that they had responded and found that both victim and accused assailant were serving members of the Dirigent Mercenary Corps. They requested that we dispatch personnel to accept responsibility for the investigation. My team responded immediately, arriving here at seventeen-eleven hours.

"I accepted custody of the accused, Private Kalko Green, and gave the investigator from the city police a receipt for him and formal acknowledgment that the Corps accepted responsibility for the investigation. The victim, identified as Platoon Sergeant Holfield O'Banion, had been pronounced dead by the medical emergency response team. The body was still in place when we arrived. Once we had taken holographs and accounted for physical evidence on and around the body, it was removed to the base's medical center.

"If you will follow me, gentlemen, I will show you the crime scene now." Knowles led the way to the back barroom of the Purple Harridan, a somewhat smaller room than the front bar.

Lon noted a table with a broken leg, tipped over, the leg itself lying nearby, covered with stains that he assumed were blood. There were other signs of a struggle in the room, though that was not exceptionally uncommon in the Purple Harridan.

"According to the witnesses we have interviewed so far," Captain Knowles said once everyone had a chance to look around the room, "Private Green first accosted Sergeant O'Banion at approximately fifteen-thirty hours. Several other soldiers, apparently friends of the accused, managed to pull Private Green away. Several people said that they thought that Private Green and his companions left the establishment at that time. No one recalls, with any certainty, seeing the accused here during the next twenty to twenty-five minutes. At approximately sixteen-ten hours, though, Private Green reappeared, coming over to the table where Sergeant O'Banion was sitting. According to witnesses, Green started shouting at the sergeant, then pushed the table over onto him. When Sergeant O'Banion got to his feet, he was immediately assaulted by Private Green. At some point in the next minute or two, one leg was broken off this table. Private Green grabbed the leg and repeatedly struck Sergeant O'Banion with it, knocking him to the ground, and continuing to use the table leg as a weapon to batter the sergeant's head until several other people, soldiers and members of the establishment's staff, managed to pull Private Green off and subdue him."

"Have you interviewed all of the witnesses to this fight, Captain?" Mr. Isling asked.

"We have interviewed all of the witnesses who were present when the municipal police arrived on the scene. Any witnesses who might have left between the time of the fight and the arrival of the first police are unknown to us. We are making efforts to discover if such witnesses exist, and to identify them.''

"You have verified the identities of those witnesses you know about, and informed them that they may be required to respond to additional questions by myself and the court?'' Isling asked next.

"Yes, sir,'' Knowles said, "as required by both the civilian and military justice codes. A list of names and addresses, along with a transcript of preliminary evidence from each, will be available to you and to the court as soon as we conclude our work here.''

When Major Rice and the members of the court-martial left the Purple Harridan, Tim Isling went with them. The next stop for the bus was the medical center on the DMC base. The group was expected. The medical examiner had the body of the dead man laid out on an autopsy table.

"My preliminary examination shows that the deceased died from massive blunt instrument trauma to the head,'' the doctor reported, pointing out the grossest injuries. "The skull was fractured repeatedly, and there was severe hemorrhaging within the brain. Death would have occurred very rapidly.''

"Have you tested the blood and stomach contents yet for alcohol or other foreign substances?'' Isling asked.

"Blood samples have been taken and are being tested now,'' the doctor said. "The contents of the stomach will be tested during the autopsy. All procedures will, of course, be recorded, and the record will accompany my report. This should all be available by oh-eight-hundred hours tomorrow.''

"Thank you, Doctor,'' Isling said.

Colonel Ellis nodded, then turned to the other officers with him. "If any of you have any questions . . . ?'' he prompted. No one offered any.

Next the group went to the guardhouse, where they finally saw the accused, Private Kalko Green. The private was escorted into a conference room where Major Rice, Mr. Isling, and the members of the court-martial panel were seated. Two MPs flanked Private Green, whose hands were cuffed in front of him.

"You are Private Kalko Green, A Company, 3rd Battalion, 2nd Regiment, Dirigent Mercenary Corps?" Colonel Ellis asked.

"Yes, sir."

"You have consulted with your attorney, Mr. Tim Isling?" Ellis asked next.

Green glanced at the civilian before he answered. "For about two minutes, sir."

"Understand, Private Green, we do not sit in judgment of you now. Your trial has not yet been scheduled. You may, if you wish, make a statement or offer evidence you feel has not been addressed by the investigating officers at this time. You are not required to do so, and you may consult your attorney in private before deciding whether you wish to speak now. Is that clear?"

"Yes, sir. It's clear. Mr. Isling told me I should say nothing at this time."

"You have been advised by counsel," Colonel Ellis said, nodding. "I must inform you that the decision is still yours. You are not required to abide by the advice your attorney gives."

"I guess I'll do what he says, sir," Green said.

"Very well. You may go now," Ellis said, and the two MPs escorted Green out of the room. Ellis turned toward the attorney then. "Counselor, is there anything you would like to say to us at this time? Either officially or off the record. If convicted of the charge of willful murder, your client could well face a sentence of death by hanging. I will extend every possible consideration to you in your defense of him."

"I believe I should wait until I have time to study the report of the investigators and the testimony of the witnesses before I say anything specific, Colonel," Isling said. "I assume that the court-martial will be held Monday?"

"As I told your client, it has not been scheduled yet, but—providing the investigating team gets all of its data submitted in time to provide you with the mandatory twenty-four-hour notice—my guess is that it will indeed be held Monday."

After Isling left the room to consult with his client, Colonel Ellis permitted himself a short sigh. "Well, gentlemen," he said, looking around at the other members of the panel, "I believe there is no more we can usefully do tonight. I suggest that we meet at fourteen hundred hours tomorrow to go over our preparations for the trial of Private Green. I also suggest that each of you review the pertinent sections of the court-martial manual before we meet tomorrow. This is an ugly business, gentlemen, so we must be especially careful that we make no errors.

"Major Rice, if you would be so good as to have our transports come here to take us home?"

The children were in bed, asleep, when Lon finally got home. It was nearly eleven o'clock. Sara was still up waiting, reading—or pretending to read. She was still holding the hand-reader when she met Lon at the door. She had heard the staff car drive up.

Lon gave her a tired kiss, then put his arms around her and rested his head on hers.

"Was it bad?" Sara asked.

"Gruesome," he said.

"Do you want to talk about it?"

"No. I don't even want to think about it. I've got to go back in for a meeting tomorrow afternoon, and the court-martial will probably be held Monday."

"Anyone we know involved?" Sara asked.

Lon pulled his head back and shook it. "You might as well go on to bed, dear. I've got to study the court-martial manual tonight. It's going to take a while."

"Why not sleep now and do your studying in the morning?" Sara asked. "You look as if you've had all you should tonight."

"Can't take the chance. Besides, it's going to be some

time before I can even think about sleeping.'' *And getting through the night without seeing that body laid out on the slab in the autopsy room will not be easy,* he thought, but he would not say that to Sara—or anyone else.

''Want me to fix you something?'' Sara asked.

This time, Lon shook his head more vigorously. ''I can fix myself coffee later, if I want it. Just go on to bed. The kids will have you up early in the morning.''

Lon had first studied the court-martial manual of the DMC while he was an officer-cadet. As in the army of the North American Union, back on Earth, there were three possible levels of court-martial—summary, special, and general, in order of increasing severity. A summary court consisted of one officer, and the most severe punishment it could impose was thirty days' imprisonment and discharge with prejudice from the DMC. ''Discharge with Prejudice'' deprived a soldier of all pay and allowances, and the right to vote or to hold any government job for the rest of his life. A special court consisted of three officers and could impose a year's imprisonment, plus the same sort of discharge. A general court was made up of five to seven officers and had no limits on the punishment it could impose, up to and including death or life imprisonment.

The manual had sections dealing with each type of court-martial, and procedural instructions for every stage in the process. ''During the investigative phase, it is the responsibility of the court-martial panel to ensure that the civilian or military police adhere to proper procedures, to protect the rights of victims and accused, and to order any steps necessary and permitted under law to determine the truth.''

We're in that stage of the case now, Lon thought, turning away from the complink monitor he was using to read the manual. *Any steps necessary and permitted under law*—if the case required it, they could even order a suspect questioned under truth drugs that could not be circumvented. A defendant was not permitted to refuse such questioning, but could request it if his lawyer thought it might help his case.

Lon scanned some sections and read others very closely. He was not concerned with memorizing anything. There would always be a law officer, a lawyer from the judge advocate's office, present to help with details and procedures. Lon assumed that Major Rice would continue to serve that function.

In general, the procedures were not much different from those Lon had learned at The Springs, the military academy of the North American Union. The prosecuting attorney would begin with his case, evidence and witnesses. The defense attorney had the right to cross-examine witnesses and object to evidence. Then he presented the defense case, evidence and witnesses. The prosecutor could cross-examine and so forth. And the members of the court-martial could also directly question witnesses for either side.

Lon fixed himself coffee but got little enjoyment from it, even after he seasoned it with just enough whiskey to give it flavor. After two sips he set the cup aside and forgot it.

When he finally closed the manual and blanked the complink screen, Lon simply stared at the blank screen for more than a minute. *I'm going to have to vote on whether or not to hang a man,* he thought.

He slept very little that night.

3

Sunday's meeting of the court-martial panel consisted largely of listening to reports from the military police who had questioned people who knew the dead man and the accused, trying to determine what had occasioned the assault. They also formally called the start of the trial for Tuesday morning at 0900 hours.

"More than the required notice," Colonel Ellis told the defense attorney. "It gives the MPs and yourself more time to find and question people who knew both individuals."

"Thank you, Colonel," Isling said. "We shall be ready."

After Isling left, Major Rice spent twenty minutes explaining the procedures for the beginning of the trial, and answered questions from several of the members of the court. It was nearly five o'clock, 1700 hours, before Lon got home.

"It's been twenty years since a DMC court-martial sentenced a man to death," Lon said. He was sitting at the table as Sara set it for an early supper. Angie was taking a nap while Junior played outside. Once in a while, his parents could hear him whooping through whatever game he was playing. "I wish I didn't have to be involved this time."

"You don't know yet that you'll do that," she said, watching him more than what she was doing. The way he had moped about since coming home worried her. It was so unlike him. "You haven't heard all of the evidence yet."

"No, but I can't imagine any extenuating circumstances that could result in a conviction for less than willful murder—certainly not in acquittal. Too many people saw the killing, and the witnesses are unanimous in saying that Green was the aggressor. And if we convict him, we'll have to vote on whether to sentence him to death or something less."

Sara wasn't sure what else she could say. She had watched the news reports the evening before and earlier Sunday afternoon. Normally she didn't bother with crime news, but this was clearly affecting her husband.

"Why don't you see if Angie's ready to wake up?" Sara suggested. "Supper will be ready in ten minutes. And call Junior. Tell him to wash his hands."

Not even the exuberance of the children could pick Lon up out of his funk. But that could not slow Junior and Angie. After supper, Lon went into the bedroom alone for a time. He simply sat on the edge of the bed, leaning forward, his arms resting on his thighs, his mind as nearly blank as it could get. He wasn't in there for long before Sara came in.

"Junior asked, 'What's wrong with Daddy?' " she said when she sat next to him. She rested her hand on one of his. "Lon, you've got to quit beating yourself over the head with what *might* happen. You tossed and turned all last night. You look like hell now. You're not doing anybody any favors."

"I know," Lon said, almost in a whisper. He did not lift his head or look at Sara. "I've seen death before, all too often. I've given orders to men, knowing they might die as a result. But this is different. Right at this minute I don't much enjoy being a soldier."

"There are five of you on the court-martial. You'll listen to the evidence. You'll decide whether the man is guilty or not, and vote on the sentence. Then the General will review everything and decide whether to uphold the verdict the court imposes or reduce it. It doesn't all rest on your shoulders. Anyway, think about the other man, the one who was killed."

He sighed, almost theatrically, then straightened up and looked at her. "I know. I know. I'll be okay. I just need a few minutes alone to get myself together. You go on back out with the kids. I'll be out shortly."

After Sara left the bedroom, Lon continued to sit for several minutes, then got up and went into the bathroom. He stared at himself in the mirror. There were dark circles under his eyes, and his face looked more drawn than usual. He ran cold water in the sink, then splashed water on his face several times before shutting off the faucet and drying his face and hands.

"I'll use a sleep patch tonight to make sure I get some rest," he promised his reflection.

Eight hours of sleep did help, but not as much as Lon had hoped. There had been no restless dreams in the night, but the nightmare was still there when he woke. He was up at six in the morning, ready to head in to his headquarters by seven. A shuttle service operated for married officers and their families. Lon only had a five-minute wait for the small bus, and a five-minute ride to the edge of the regimental parade ground. Reveille was long past. Some of the men were already returning from breakfast, ready for the next formation, at 0800 hours. Lon needed a moment to recall what A Company's schedule held for the day. The men were due to spend the entire day at the rifle range.

Good, Lon thought as he walked across the parade ground toward the building that housed A Company's offices and headquarters staff. *Nothing I really have to be present for.* There was another meeting of the court-martial scheduled for the morning, and there was no telling how long it might take—perhaps the rest of the day.

Lead Sergeant Weil Jorgen was in the company orderly room when Lon arrived. Weil had been promoted nearly four years earlier after his predecessor had been transferred to regimental headquarters.

"Morning, Weil," Lon said.

"Morning, Captain." Weil got to his feet and followed Lon across to the commander's private office. "I hear you've drawn court-martial duty, sir."

"Yes, and you know I can't discuss the case," Lon said.

"I know, sir. Looks pretty calm for us the next couple of days, though, rifle range today and squad tactics tomorrow," Weil said. "No need to worry about us while you're, ah, occupied."

Lon smiled, briefly. "Tebba and Harley here?"

"Yes, sir, up in the coffee room. Should I get them?"

"No, I'll go up there. I need the exercise."

"I'll have the manning reports ready by work call," Weil promised as Lon left the office.

Tebba Girana had been commissioned from the ranks just days after Lon had been promoted to captain, following the Aldrin contract eight years before. He now led the first two platoons of A Company. The other two platoons were under Lieutenant Harley Stossberg, who had won his lieutenant's pips two years ago, on Kepler, after doing his stint as an officer-cadet under Tebba's tutelage. Girana had been in the Corps since before Stossberg was born.

The two lieutenants were sitting and sipping coffee, scarcely aware of each other's presence. Tebba was leaning back, staring out the window. Harley was just staring, perhaps at the ceiling. Stossberg was the first to notice Lon's arrival. He stood immediately, not *quite* jumping to his feet. He was barely twenty-one years old, and three hard combat contracts had not yet robbed his face of a look of youthful naïveté. He had soft blue eyes and rosy cheeks that always made him appear as if he had just come in from the cold.

"Good morning, Captain," Harley said. "Can I get you a cup of coffee?"

"Sit down, Harley," Lon said. "You've been at this too long to still be acting like a cadet." There was humor more than censure in Lon's voice. The young lieutenant was still so infernally *eager*. But it was impossible to dislike him.

"Captain," Tebba said, getting to his feet more slowly—making it seem that he was stretching rather than showing proper military courtesy. "I heard you got stuck with trying the murder."

"Yes, and you know that's all I can say," Lon said.

"I assume you're going to be busy on that and not paying much attention to us here until it's over," Tebba said.

"Yes, so you two will have to keep things going at least the next couple of days. That makes you in charge while I'm gone, Tebba. Try to keep the beaver here from blowing a fuse."

"I'll slap a tranq on him if I have to," Tebba said, grinning at Harley.

The younger lieutenant showed no annoyance at the ribbing he took from the others. After two years, he was more than used to it. At times he seemed to revel in being the butt of such jokes.

"I'll be here for formation this morning," Lon said after pausing long enough to be sure that Harley did not have one of his rare rebuttals. "Tomorrow morning as well, if I can."

Lon got a cup of coffee and sat on the edge of the table to drink the brew. Tebba asked Harley about his weekend, and Harley replied at some length. Lon scarcely listened. His mind had drifted inside itself again, going to something near a trance state to avoid thinking about the court-martial of Kalko Green.

Five minutes before it was time for the morning regimental formation, Lead Sergeant Jorgen knocked on the door, opened it, and reminded the officers of the time.

"Let's get to work," Lon said, getting off the table. "You two better check with your sergeants and find out what's going on." He waited until the lieutenants had left, then poured himself another half cup of coffee and drank it quickly. He did not need to head outside quite yet.

That afternoon, once the work of the court-martial panel was finished for the day, Lon went to the regimental gymnasium and worked out for an hour, pushing himself as hard as he had when he was half as old. In high school and the military academy on Earth, Lon had been a distance runner, his best time for the mile nine-tenths of a second short of the world record, which had continued to improve while his times had started to fade. Now fifteen pounds heavier than he had been at his racing peak, Lon's times were markedly slower, but he remained in top physical condition. An officer in the Dirigent Mercenary Corps did not dare allow himself to get out of shape. Combat made no allowances for desk duty, and the DMC rigidly enforced physical standards for all its personnel. Even the colonels who sat on the Council of Regiments had to meet those standards each year.

Lon ran two miles on the indoor track. The standard he set for himself was eight minutes and fifteen seconds for the distance. That was enough to make him press himself carefully. After he took a final lap to gradually relax, he did twenty minutes on the weight machines, working his upper body, then did fifteen minutes swimming laps in the pool in the next room. By the time he had taken a hot shower and dressed again, he was feeling pleasantly exhausted, his mood improved by the physical exertion, as it usually was. The entire time Lon had exercised, he had not once thought of the trial starting Tuesday morning.

At home that evening, he was more nearly his usual self, playing with the children, helping Junior with his studies, spoiling Angie relentlessly. After the children were in bed, Lon and Sara sat together on the sofa in the living room, cuddling gently while music played on the entertainment center.

"If you're still on-planet then, do you think you'll be able to take a week's leave so we can go visit my folks for Christmas?" Sara asked.

"I'm afraid there's not much chance I'll be home for Christmas this year," Lon said. "We're too close to the top of the small-unit lists. If I am, though, I'll try. I might only be able to get a couple of days. You and the kids can go for longer, though, whether I'm here or not."

"You might have a short contract and be back before then," Sara suggested.

He chuckled. "Always the optimist, aren't you."

"Of course," she agreed, nestling her head against his shoulder. She never let him see the *I have to be, I married a soldier* thought that always came when they talked about him going on contract. And she worked very hard to keep him from ever seeing how much she worried about him when he went on a combat contract. She was a Dirigenter, and Dirigenter women had been sending their men off to battle for centuries.

"One of these years, maybe we'll draw another stint at the testing range and we can spend a little more time with your folks," Lon suggested.

"When I was talking to Mama yesterday, she said that Dad is looking forward to the day when they can retire and turn the pub over to us."

Lon couldn't help himself. He nearly convulsed with laughter, shaking loose from Sara in the process.

"I didn't think it was *that* funny," she said, watching him with amusement . . . and relief.

"I'm sorry," Lon said, wiping a tear from the corner of his eye as he fought to stifle the laughing jag. "I just had a mental picture of me pulling pints and you slaving in that little kitchen, and we both looked ridiculous."

"Lon . . ."

"Come here." He pulled her against him, hugging her tightly. "I know your father hopes to turn the pub over to us eventually. *Some*day, maybe ten or twenty years from now, I'll be able to see it. But I'm a long way from

being ready to retire from the Corps and move to Bascombe East and the rural life, hon. It's too alien to the
way I think now.'' He kissed her on the forehead. ''At
least I know you can cook as good as your mother.''

In the morning, Lon woke before five o'clock, more than
an hour before his alarm was scheduled to wake him.
The murder of Holfield O'Banion had invaded his
dreams, and shocked him from slumber. Lon got out of
bed before the last of the dream faded from his mind,
crossing first to the bathroom, then going out to prowl
through the living room and kitchen, trying to subdue
the lingering emotion that the vision of O'Banion's murdered body had left in its wake.

Nightmares were nothing new. Lon had too often been
visited by the ghosts of men who had died in combat.
Sometimes they came to chat about old times—and what
had happened since death had separated them. At other
times they just stood in Lon's mind and shook their
heads sadly, as if in anticipation of the day when he
would join them. It had been several years since the last
time Lon had felt compelled to seek counseling to deal
with those ghosts. He understood the why and how. But
this was different.

Lon had not known Holfield O'Banion in life.

And what about Kalko Green? he asked himself as he
stood in the kitchen and waited for fresh coffee to brew.
*If we sentence him to death, is he going to haunt me as
well?*

As soon as the coffee was ready, Lon poured himself
a cup and drank it as quickly as he could, not moving
from where he stood at the kitchen counter. Slowly, the
memories and the worries faded—as he concentrated on
coffee so hot it threatened to scald his tongue.

After he poured a second cup of coffee, Lon decided
to fix breakfast for himself. That was something new
that married life had taught him. He had come to the
point where he actually enjoyed bustling around the

kitchen, fixing an easy meal, or helping Sara prepare something more complicated.

"How long have you been up?"

Lon started, badly shaken. He had been so deep in thought that he had not heard Sara walk into the kitchen. He sucked in breath to cover the instant of shock and turned toward her. "I didn't hear you coming," he said.

"That bacon must be about burned," she said, nodding toward the stove. "It woke me from a sound sleep."

"I just turned it off," he said. "I was just ready to toss a couple of eggs into the pan. You want some?"

She shook her head. "I'll wait until later, after the kids have their breakfast and Junior leaves for school. You didn't answer my question."

Lon shrugged. "I haven't been up all that long. I woke and decided I might as well get up to stay. It wasn't worth going back to sleep for just another hour."

"An infantryman who doesn't think another hour's sleep is worthwhile?" Sara said in her most sarcastic tone. Lon shrugged again. "Nightmare?" she asked, more gently.

"Yeah." Lon turned to the stove again, pulled the bacon from the frying pan, and cracked three eggs into the hot grease.

"You want to talk about it?"

"No, it's okay now. A little coffee and a little cooking, that's all it took. Nothing serious."

She came across the kitchen to give him a quick kiss. "I'm going back to bed, then. *I* think another hour's sleep is worth something, even if you don't."

There was a light mist falling when Lon left the house a little before seven o'clock. There were patches of fog softening the autumn morning. Lon grinned as he walked out to catch the shuttle bus. It was perfect weather for squad maneuvers; the men would grouse all day.

Lon went to his company offices, talked with Weil

and the two lieutenants, but did not take morning formation. He watched that from the orderly room window, staying dry and warm, and drinking another cup of coffee—his fifth of the morning. The caffeine gave him a momentary edge, before the medical nanobots that guarded his health could neutralize it. Platoon sergeants reported to platoon leaders, who would normally have reported to Lon. Tebba Girana was in front of the company formation today, though, and he made the report to Lieutenant Colonel Hiram Black, the battalion commander, who reported to the regimental commander.

"The eternal ballet of the army," Lon mumbled. He watched until the regiment was dismissed, battalions and companies marching off to whatever work and training they were scheduled for that morning.

A moment later, Weil Jorgen returned to the office. He would spend the day there rather than out in the field with the men. While they practiced squad tactics, he wasn't needed.

"The weather forecast said it's supposed to be clearing up early, Captain," Jorgen said after he had hung his cap on the stand next to the office door, "but it sure doesn't look like it. This kind of mist can go on all day."

"No good training only when the weather's perfect," Lon said. "We sure as hell don't get perfect weather often on contract."

Jorgen chuckled. "That's a fact, Captain." He sat and scrolled through the day's notes on the calendar window of his desk complink. "This says you should be at regimental HQ by oh-eight-thirty, sir."

Lon nodded. "I was just waiting for the troops to get moving before I left." He paused, then said, "I'm not looking forward to any of this, Weil. I'd much rather be out in the rain with the men." Jorgen met his gaze. For an instant, the two men just looked at each other.

Then Jorgen nodded. "I know what you mean, Captain," he said, his voice deadly serious.

4

There were no spectators in the chamber. Only the members of the court-martial, Major Rice as law officer, the prosecutor, the defense attorney, and the defendant were in the conference room, which was only rarely needed for proceedings such as this. An automated recording system would provide a complete audio and three-dimensional visual record of everything that transpired.

The room's standard furnishings—a large round table with a number of complink consoles set in it—had been removed. The five officers who comprised the court-martial board sat along one side of a long table that had been placed parallel to the head of the room. Major Rice sat at one end of the table. Smaller tables were arranged for the prosecutor—Captain Eulie Tuk—and the defense attorney. Private Green sat with his lawyer, Tim Isling.

There was only one other chair in the room, centered between the head table and the other two, for witnesses.

Colonel Ellis, president of the court-martial board, sat at the center of the head table. Major Ives was at his right and Captain Gowers at his left. Captains Ames and Nolan were at the ends, the junior officers on the panel. Once they were all seated, Major Rice gestured to an MP at the door. Captain Tuk came in, followed a few seconds later by Mr. Isling and Private Green.

The MP, a company lead sergeant wearing pistol and baton on his belt, closed the door and stood at parade rest in front of it, a physical barrier to disruption.

Colonel Ellis opened a mauve portfolio in front of him

and studied the top paper for a moment. He glanced at Major Rice then, who nodded, and Ellis read the document authorizing the conduct of this court-martial, and naming the members of the court and the attorneys.

The next sheet of paper in Ellis's portfolio contained the formal indictment of Private Kalko Green. Colonel Ellis read that document with even greater care than he had read the first.

Green was not asked to plead guilty or innocent. There was no place for that in a DMC court-martial. In any case, the judge advocate's office had to present its evidence and prove its case. A guilty plea from a defendant could not be advanced as a cause for reduced punishment.

"Private Green, do you understand the charge that has been brought against you?" Colonel Ellis asked after he had finished reading the indictment.

At his attorney's urging, Green stood before replying. "Yes, sir, I understand the charge."

"Do you understand the sentences that this court can impose if you are convicted?" Ellis asked next.

This time Green faltered a little before he could get his answer out completely. "Yes, sir. That was explained to me."

As soon as Green sat and Ellis had asked both attorneys if they were ready to proceed, the first witness was called.

Lon tried to listen attentively to everything that transpired in the courtroom. He made occasional notes, despite the knowledge that complete transcripts and recordings would be available. The first witness was the civilian policeman who had reached the scene in response to the call, describing what he had found and what he had done in the first minutes. Other policemen, civilian and military, followed, describing what they had learned at the scene. The medical examiner described the autopsy and his findings. Other witnesses were called, one by one, people who had seen the altercation in the Purple Harridan.

Few of the interrogations lasted longer than fifteen minutes. The court broke for an hour, for lunch, at noon. By two-thirty the prosecution had rested its case. Then it was Mr. Isling's turn to present the defense.

"As stated in my witness list," Isling started, "Private Kalko will testify. I also have five witnesses to speak to the prior relationship between my client and the deceased, witnesses the prosecution chose not to include."

"Are all of your witnesses present?" Colonel Ellis asked.

"Yes, sir, those I have been able to locate. There may be several others who are currently on contract and out of my reach. And I know of one who might have shed considerable light on this matter who was killed on contract six months ago." He shrugged theatrically. "I do not believe that these additional witnesses would be crucial to the defense's case."

I guess not, Lon thought, careful to keep his face from showing any reaction. He was fairly certain of Isling's tactics. He had little choice but to try to show that Sergeant O'Banion had been a bully who had repeatedly made life miserable for Private Green—always off duty, since they had never served in the same company. There was little doubt that the court would be forced to find Green guilty of willful murder. All Isling could hope to do was to present enough evidence impeaching the character of the dead man to keep his client from the gallows.

Colonel Ellis nodded. "Very well, Counselor. Call your first witness."

Private Kalko Green was called. While Green was walking the few steps to the witness stand, Lon noticed for the first time how thin the private looked, as if he had not eaten in more than just the three days since the killing. He cheeks were slightly sunken. He walked with a hesitation. *There's fear in his eyes,* Lon thought. Green was sworn in and stated his name, rank, and unit for the record.

"Private Green," Colonel Ellis said before Mr. Isling could begin questioning his client, "I want you to understand clearly that this court will afford you every possible opportunity to defend yourself. To this point we have heard only the case presented by the judge advocate's office, the prosecution witnesses, and your attorney's cross-examination of them. It is your turn now. This court will not reach a verdict until it has heard all of the evidence."

"Yes, sir. Thank you, sir," Green said.

"Very well, Counselor. You may begin," Ellis said, glancing toward the civilian attorney.

Lon leaned back in his straight-backed chair, concentrating on the defendant's face. He would listen to everything Green said, and to the questions, but he wanted to see how the private spoke, and what his eyes did while he was talking. Already Lon had noticed that Green was far more composed than he would have expected. There was fear in Green's eyes, and in the small movements of his body, but there was still discipline.

"How long have you been a member of the Dirigent Mercenary Corps?" was Tim Isling's first question for his client.

"Seven years, sir, last June third," Green said.

"How many combat contracts have you been on?"

"Five, sir, and three training contracts."

"How long had you known Platoon Sergeant Holfield O'Banion?"

"All my life. We grew up in the same block in the Drafts," Green said.

"The Drafts? That is a residential quarter on the northwestern side of Dirigent City?" Isling asked.

"Yes, sir, for factory workers, mostly, and folks that live on basic maintenance."

Lon could not recall ever going through the Drafts, though he had heard the name. It was the closest Dirigent had to an urban slum, but it was still a far cry from the circus neighborhoods on Earth—the palest reflection.

"Tell the court about your relationship with Holfield O'Banion in the Drafts," Isling urged.

"Well, he was a couple of years older than me," Green started, hesitantly glancing first at his attorney and then at the officers of the court. "He was always bigger than me when we were kids, and sometimes he beat me up."

"How often did he beat you up?" Isling asked.

"I can't say how many times. A lot. You know, in memory, it seems like it was about every other day, but I know that can't be. But I doubt a month went by that he didn't at least take a couple of punches at me, or kick me, or something. All the way up until he joined the Corps. I think I was sixteen then."

"Did you see him in the Drafts after that?"

"Once or twice. He was in the Corps. He didn't come around much, I guess, or maybe I was just lucky enough to miss him."

"You joined the Corps when you turned eighteen?" Isling asked.

"Yes, sir. Three days after my birthday."

"Did you enlist in the Corps because Holfield O'Banion had?"

For an instant, Green appeared stunned by that question, as if he could not believe it had been asked.

"No, sir, of course not. I think maybe by that time I had almost forgot about O'Banion. I joined the Corps because I knew I was fit for it, and being a soldier seemed better than working in a factory or something like that the rest of my life. Being a soldier's the best work here unless you got the smarts to be a brain-boy— you know, a professional or a science type—and I never had that kind of smarts. And I knew it, early."

"After you enlisted in the Corps, you started to en- counter O'Banion again?" Isling asked.

"Yes, sir."

"Did he start picking fights with you again, beating you up?"

"Sometimes, yes, sir. The first time I saw him in

Camo Town, just a couple of weeks after I finished boot training, he pushed me into an alley and said he was going to show me I wasn't as hot as I thought I was, that I wasn't fit to wear the uniform. Well, I was just out of training, and feeling pretty good about being able to defend myself. In a fair fight, things might have been different, but he sucker-punched me, and I never got a chance to get started.''

"Is that the only time this sort of thing happened after you were both in the Corps?''

"No, sir. It wasn't usually as bad as that time, though, but he would give me a punch, sometimes follow me until he could get me where nobody would see.''

"Did you ever report this behavior to anyone in the Corps? Your own platoon sergeant, for example?''

Green looked down at his feet for a few seconds before he replied. "No, sir. I talked to a couple of the guys in my squad, but I never reported it. I couldn't prove anything. It would have been my word against his, and he was already a corporal the first time it happened. He set some kind of record for making corporal in his battalion, fastest anyone had ever done it. And he made sergeant almost as quick. Besides, he started threatening my family, said things would happen to them if I ever tried to make trouble for him. Said there might be a fire, an explosion, some night at my folks' home.''

"He threatened your family?''

"Yes, sir. That's what really led to the . . . trouble Friday at the Purple Harridan. He threatened my sister Jenny, and there was no other way I could make sure she was safe.''

His sister? Lon thought, leaning forward just a fraction of an inch. There had been no mention of a sister in any of the prosecution's evidence.

"Yes,'' Isling said. "Now we come to last Friday afternoon, Private Green. I want you to start by telling this court why you went to the Purple Harridan and what caused the argument you had with Platoon Sergeant O'Banion at about fifteen-thirty hours on Friday.''

"Yes, sir," Kalko said, straightening up a little on the stand. "My company was given Friday afternoon off because we won the Colonel's Cup for shooting the best overall score on the rifle range in the regiment for the third straight month. After noon chow we were off duty until Monday morning.

"Most times there's not a whole lot going on in Camo Town on a weekday afternoon. Not that many soldiers are off. I didn't know last Friday was different, that a lot of units were off. I made plans to meet several buddies at the Purple Harridan later in the afternoon, but I figured I'd stop by Outfitters and say hello to my sister Jenny and see if the family had anything planned for the weekend."

"Outfitters?" Isling asked.

"Yes, sir. That's a goods store in Camo Town—you know, a place that sells souvenirs and the sorts of odds and ends a guy might want to buy while he's doing the town, or gifts to send to folks, all kinds of stuff like that, even some civie clothes. My sister works in the replicator room in back, making sure they're never out of any of the stock items."

"Okay, thank you," Isling said. "Please, go on. You went to Outfitters to speak with your sister. . . ."

"Yes, sir. Jenny's boss is an all-right guy, retired from the Corps, I think. Least, that's what he says. He let me go through to the back room to talk with Jenny, but he said not to take too long 'cause they were busy and I shouldn't make Jenny get behind on her work.

"Almost the first thing Jenny said when I got back there was that she had run into O'Banion while she was out on her lunch break, about an hour earlier. Said he was stiff drunk then. He talked dirty to her, offered her money to have sex with him, and when Jen slapped his face and told him to stay away from her, he just laughed and told her to slap away, that if he decided he really wanted her, wasn't nothing she could do to stop him. Then he turned his back on her and walked away, laughing.

"Jen was crying when she told me that, and I got boiling mad. It was one thing for O'Banion to bother me all the time, but when he went after a young girl like Jenny, it was too much."

"How old is your sister?" Isling asked.

"She turned eighteen this February. Just out of school. Still goes to church regular, and believes."

"What did you do immediately after your sister told you about what Sergeant O'Banion had said to her?"

"I was mad, boiling mad. Right then, I couldn't hardly think straight I was so mad. I went looking for O'Banion, to tell him to stay away from Jenny, and that I would..." Green's voice had been rising, anger still clear in it over the way his sister had been treated. He stopped abruptly, though, and got a confused look in his eyes. His shoulders slumped a little.

"You were about to say?" his attorney prompted.

"I got nothing to hide," Green said. "I was so mad that I was ready to tell O'Banion I'd kill him if he ever touched Jenny. It was my little sister he was threatening."

"Go on," Isling said when Green went silent again.

"I asked Jen what was he wearing, where did she see him, and what way was he going. Then I went looking for him. I knew I'd find him someplace that served booze, so I started going in every place in the neighborhood. I got madder and madder the longer I thought about what he had said, and I had a drink or two to keep me going. It took me a while, but I found him at the Purple Harridan."

This time, when Green stopped talking, Isling remained silent, watching his client, the way the members of the court-martial board were, seeing the difficulty Green was having controlling his emotions even now.

"I went up to him. I guess I started by calling him a few names, and I told him what I intended to tell him. Almost. I said if he didn't leave Jenny alone, I'd fix it so he couldn't bother any innocent girls again, even if I had to get my whole squad along to help me. And more,

I guess. I don't recall everything I might have said, and maybe I just thought some of the things instead of actually saying them to O'Banion.'' He took a deep breath and let it out.

"A couple of guys from my platoon were in the Purple Harridan. I don't know if they saw me first or heard me, but they came over and pulled me away, took me outside. One of them slapped a killjoy patch on my arm but I ripped it off almost before it stuck. I told them what Jenny had told me, what O'Banion had threatened to do. They tried to cool me down, said they'd do what they could. We could all talk to the sarge together, get *something* done, but I knew better. I still didn't have any proof. It was just my word against his.''

"Your sister could have filed a complaint,'' Isling suggested. "You would then have been corroborating her report.''

Green shook his head a couple of times, looking down. "I couldn't put Jenny through that. I'm not sure she would have told anyone. She was too upset, too embarrassed by it.''

"What did you do next?'' Isling asked.

"I don't know just when, but I started walking along the street, away from the Purple Harridan. My buddies came with me for a bit, but I kept going and next thing I knew, they weren't around anymore. I didn't know where they went, back to the Purple Harridan, some other bar, or maybe back to base. I stopped walking and just stood there on the sidewalk, looking back the way I had come. I could still see the big sign out in front of the Purple Harridan, so I hadn't walked more than a couple of blocks. I stood there, not moving at all, and the anger started building again. I couldn't let it go. I had to go back and make damn sure O'Banion knew I was serious, that if he even went near Jenny again I'd dance on his face.

"Before I knew it, I was walking back toward the Purple Harridan, almost running. I could feel my face was red with anger. I wanted to make sure I got back before he could leave and go someplace else, or maybe go looking for Jenny right then because of what I had said to him before. I had to protect Jenny. I couldn't let anything bad happen to her.

"O'Banion was still sitting in the same place. He saw me coming and started laughing, as if I was the funniest joke he'd ever heard. That didn't help my mood any. I told him what I came to say, that he had better stay away from Jenny or else. He sat there smirking, and then he said . . ."

Green stopped abruptly and looked first at his lawyer and then at Colonel Ellis. "Sir, do I say it just the way he said it, or clean it up for court?"

"If you're quoting, use the exact words if you remember them," Colonel Ellis said.

"I remember, all right," Green said. "He said, 'I'm gonna go find your sister and fuck her up one side and then down the other. Then maybe I'll dump her for the jar dogs to play with.' " Jar dogs were not really dogs, nor did their heads closely resemble the jars that gave them the other half of their name. Jar dogs were one of the few wild carnivores left in the region of Dirigent's capital. Adult males reached two hundred pounds, females slightly more. They hunted as a family, adults plus adolescent cubs. Occasionally a family was spotted near the Drafts.

"I guess I really snapped then," Green said. He paused for a few seconds before he continued. "I threw myself at O'Banion, ready to beat him senseless right there. I don't remember much of the fight. I guess the table broke right at the start, when I jumped for him. I don't remember picking up the leg of the table. I don't remember actually using it. It wasn't really until people pulled me away that I was conscious of O'Banion lying there, his head all stove in, blood all around, and blood on the table leg they made me drop."

"I have no further questions for this witness," Tim Isling said.

"No questions," Captain Tuk said.

Colonel Ellis looked first to one side and then to the other, to see if any of the officers on the court had questions to ask. No one did. No questions were necessary.

Colonel Ellis recessed the court-martial until 0900 hours the next morning, Wednesday.

5

"We should reach an end to the testimony well before lunch tomorrow," Colonel Ellis told his companions before they left the room. Everyone but the five members of the court-martial had already gone, and the monitoring system had been deactivated. "I know you don't need to be reminded of this, but I have to tell you not to discuss the case with anyone outside this room, even among yourselves, while the case is still being tried. I believe we should meet here by oh-eight-forty hours in the morning."

Lon nodded and left the room. He walked out of regimental headquarters without really noticing anything around him. As if by habit, he turned toward the officers' club on the next street over. He was not a frequent visitor there, had not been since his wedding, but this day he did not even have to make the decision. He went in, sat at the bar, and ordered bourbon with water on the side.

The first drink went down in one long gulp. The burn of the whiskey in his throat finally brought Lon to something approaching awareness. He took some of the water and ordered a second drink.

I don't think I've ever needed *a drink before,* he thought. *Not like this.* Listening to Kalko Green talk about the events leading up to the killing of Holfield O'Banion had tied Lon's stomach in distressed knots. One question had started echoing in Lon's mind: *Would I have done any differently in his place?*

The knots had started when Lon had been unable to

convince himself that the answer was *Yes*.

The bartender set Lon's second drink in front of him. She was discreet, did not say anything about the way Lon had thrown the first measure of whiskey into his mouth. As long as an officer remained in control of himself and did not make a scene, nothing would be said. There was a ready supply of killjoy patches behind the bar. The closest any of the employees of the club would come to remonstrating with a patron would be to offer a killjoy along with a drink.

Lon did not notice that the bartender cast a sidelong gaze his way, waiting to see if the second drink went the same way as the first. It did not. Lon took a little water first this time, then a more refined sip of the whiskey. He savored the burning feeling as the whiskey warmed its way toward his stomach. He held off on the next chaser, to make sure that he missed nothing of the sensation. Before he took his next sip, Lon considered calling Sara to tell her that he would be staying at his office for the night, that he wouldn't be good company for her or the children until the trial was over. There was a cot in the room just above Lon's office. He could sleep there, and he always kept a change of clothing in an office cupboard for emergencies.

No, Lon decided after pondering the question nearly to the end of the second drink. *If I don't go home, I'll just drink myself silly. I don't want to do that, not tonight.*

The bartender tried to hide her relief when Lon signaled for the check and signed for his two drinks. She watched until he was through the doorway.

The remaining defense witnesses were questioned and excused by 1030 hours the following morning. Jenny Green had been the first to testify, and she needed forty-five minutes on the stand—more because she could not keep from crying than because she had so many questions to answer. She corroborated what her brother had said. The other witnesses testified about the abusive relationships Platoon Sergeant O'Banion had had with the Greens and with others.

The defense rested.

"The court will now retire to consider its verdict," Colonel Ellis announced. He stood, followed by the other members of the panel and by the others in the room.

It would have been much simpler for the members of the court to remain and have the others leave, but this was the way it was done in the DMC. They went to the floor above, to an office that had been cleared for their use. Electronic countermeasures were in place to prevent anyone from eavesdropping on the discussion. Major Rice would remain in the corridor outside, in case his advice was needed, but the deliberations were private, for the members of the court alone.

"Poor bastard," Colonel Ellis muttered, almost to himself, as the five officers were making themselves as comfortable as they could on the straight chairs that had been provided.

That's for sure, Lon thought, his eyes on the colonel.

Ellis looked around at the junior officers. "I don't see that there's much cause for it in this case, but the manual says that our votes are to be secret." He gestured at the table. "I see that slips of paper and pens have been provided. We might as well take a vote now. Guilty of willful murder, guilty of the lesser charge of manslaughter, or innocent—those are the choices we are permitted." Ellis was the first to reach toward the center of the table for paper and pen. The others quickly followed suit.

Lon stared at the square of paper in front of him for nearly a minute, hesitant to write what he knew he had to write. He closed his eyes for an instant, almost daring to wish that the choice would go away. When he opened his eyes, he wrote one word on the paper, shielding that word from the others with his hand.

Guilty. He glanced at the others, quickly, as if he feared discovery, a schoolboy afraid of being caught cheating on a test. *I know the standards of the Corps,* Lon thought. *I think I know how the others will vote.* His pen hovered over the paper, but he could not write the words "willful murder." He hesitated again, then took a deep breath and wrote the second word.

Manslaughter. Lon folded the paper over the words and pushed it a little away from him, then placed the pen carefully on the table and sat back. He put his hands in his lap, waiting.

"Captain Nolan, if you would be so good as to collect the ballots for me?" Colonel Ellis said after the last man had voted.

Lon gathered all five pieces of paper, even the one directly in front of Colonel Ellis, and gave them to the colonel together, then returned to his seat.

Colonel Ellis held the papers in his hand. "According to the procedural rules we operate under, a vote of five to nothing or four to one decides the question. If the vote is three to two, or split more completely among the alternatives, we will take time to discuss any portions of the case necessary, then take another vote."

He started opening the ballots. He glanced at each, then set it in front of him. The first two went together. The third went a little to the side. The last two went on the stack with the first two. Ellis stared at the papers for a few seconds, then looked up. There was no expression on his face.

"The vote is one 'guilty of willful murder' and four 'guilty of manslaughter,'" he announced. "I will not ask, and do not want to know, who voted how. That, gentlemen, should remain each man's secret. Captain Gowers, would you ask Major Rice to step in here for a moment?"

While Gowers got up and went to the door, Ellis carefully palmed the ballots and held them in his hand, below the table. Major Rice shut the door behind him when he entered.

"You wanted me, Colonel?" he asked.

"Please refresh our memories, Major," Ellis said.

"What would the possible range of penalties be if our verdict were manslaughter?"

You didn't say it is *our verdict,* Lon noted, as he had noted the way Ellis had concealed the ballots.

"The sentence could be anything from twelve to twenty years in confinement, and includes discharge with prejudice from the Corps and loss of all pay and allowances, sir," Rice said.

"Thank you, Major. That will be all. We will let you know if we need anything else." Ellis waited until Rice had left the room and the door was closed again before he put the five papers with the votes on them back on the table in front of him. They were well crumpled together now.

"In view of our previous vote," Ellis said then, looking at the other faces individually, "I would suggest that we choose a compromise figure rather than look at either extreme." He paused, as if waiting for anyone to argue that point. When no one spoke, he said, "I would offer fourteen years in confinement. Does anyone wish to argue in favor of a different figure?"

There was a lot of looking back and forth among the five members of the court-martial, but no one spoke.

"It might not be pure form," Ellis said, "but I think we can settle this with a show of hands. Those in favor of a sentence of fourteen years in confinement?"

Ellis was the first to raise his hand. There was very little hesitation around the table. Five hands were raised.

At least I'll be able to sleep tonight, Lon thought. He closed his eyes for an instant. His unexpected feeling of relief could scarcely have been greater had he been the defendant and his own life had just been spared.

The court-martial reconvened. Once the five officers were seated at the head table, Major Rice had the MP at the door call for the defendant and the attorneys.

"The defendant will rise to hear the verdict of this court-martial," Major Rice intoned after the opening formulas were completed.

Green looked at his attorney before standing.

He looks ready to pass out, Lon thought. In his mind, he echoed Colonel Ellis's earlier appraisal—*Poor bastard.*

Colonel Ellis stood. The other officers of the panel did likewise. So did the two attorneys. Major Rice had already been on his feet.

"Private Kalko Green, this court finds you guilty of the crime of manslaughter in the death of Platoon Sergeant Holfield O'Banion. Subject to review and approval by the convening authority, this court sentences you to discharge with prejudice from the Dirigent Mercenary Corps, loss of all pay and allowances, and a term of fourteen years in confinement, at such place as shall be determined by the office of the judge advocate."

Kalko Green very nearly did collapse when he heard "manslaughter" rather than "willful murder." His knees half buckled under him and he had to support himself on the edge of the table in front of him.

"You are remanded to the custody of the military police until the convening authority reviews this verdict," Ellis announced. "This court-martial stands adjourned."

6

Sara Nolan met her husband at the door. She had been watching for him. "Is it over?" she asked when she opened the door to let him in.

Lon gave her a kiss on the cheek before he said, "My part in it, at least." There was no need for him to ask what she was talking about. "The General still has to review and approve the verdict and sentence."

"Are they going to hang him?" Sara asked, her voice getting softer, apprehensive.

"No, we only found him guilty of manslaughter, fourteen years' confinement."

Sara closed her eyes for an instant, letting Lon guide her into the house. "I was so afraid you'd have to convict him of willful murder," she whispered. The killing and court-martial had been all the talk among the officers' wives in the neighborhood. Sara had been careful to just listen and not say anything, but the fact that her husband was sitting on the court-martial had not stopped anyone else around her from talking about the case. The consensus had been lopsided. Green would be convicted of murder and hung in front of Corps Headquarters.

"So was I," Lon confessed. "But that kid was as much a victim as the man he killed."

"In spite of that," Sara said, "the talk has been that the Corps couldn't tolerate a private killing a superior, no matter the justification, and that justice in the Corps was too rigid to permit anything less than hanging for a murderer."

Lon smiled. He was still caught in the feeling of relief

that had come when he discovered that the Corps wasn't quite that rigid. "If we had convicted him of murder, I'm sure that would have been the sentence, but we didn't."

Sara's next question was harder to answer. "How could a man like that sergeant be in the Corps so long, be promoted the way he was, and nobody find out how terrible a person he was?"

"I don't know," Lon said, shaking his head. "It shouldn't happen, but it did. Now, enough about that. It's all I've heard about all week. Where are the kids?"

"You know, I've been hearing some interesting things on the backyard net," Sara said that night as she and Lon were getting into bed.

Lon chuckled. "So what are the gossips doing now, handicapping the next election for General?"

Sara made a dismissive gesture with one hand. "We figured *that* out two days after the last election. Nembi of the First Regiment has a lock on the job unless he pulls something outstandingly stupid in the next six months. I was talking about something more important."

"More important than who the General is?" Lon asked.

"*I* think so. The talk is that for the first time in more than a century, the Corps is about to promote a man with under fourteen years of service to major. From what I hear, it could come before the first of the year. And I must say we've earned it."

"'We'?" Lon asked, trying without success to stifle a laugh. Sara hit him with her pillow.

"We," she said firmly. "Some of the boring chat I've got to put up with!" Then she started laughing, too. "I think it's serious, though. I can sense how things are going by who gets how friendly."

"Don't start making plans for the extra money yet," Lon advised. The Corps was always rife with rumor, but Lon hated to admit that the gossip Sara heard was often far more accurate than what he did. "Has the gabble gathering figured out when I'm going out on contract?''

Sara made a pouting face at him, then settled her pillow where it belonged. ''I haven't heard anything about that,'' she said.

''I guess the Corps is safe a little longer then,'' Lon said, turning out the bedside light. ''It can still keep a few secrets.''

Returning to duty in A Company the next morning felt almost like the start of a furlough for Lon. He even looked forward to wading through the inescapable backlog of forms and memos.

''They've changed the schedule 'round on us, Captain,'' Lead Sergeant Weil Jorgen said when Lon walked into the orderly room. ''Fourth Battalion of the 6th is going out on contract this morning, so headquarters has switched us into night-fire exercises tonight. The whole battalion.''

''That means the men are off at noon tomorrow,'' Lon said. ''Give 'em a long weekend.'' Weil nodded. ''Remind me to call Sara and tell her I'll be very late tonight.''

Weil grinned. ''Remember to call Mrs. Nolan and tell her you'll be very late, sir.''

Lon smiled and shook his head. ''Okay, I walked into that one. Don't take advantage of me just 'cause I've been gone a couple of days.''

''Who, me, sir?'' Weil asked, wide-eyed. ''But maybe it would be best to call her now, before we both forget.''

''You're right. Give me two minutes, then come on in and we'll start catching up on things. I know Tebba didn't tie any red tape together he didn't have to.''

Catching up on reports and the other necessities kept the two men busy for an hour after morning formation. When the last form had been keyed to battalion headquarters, Weil got up to go back to his desk in the outer office. At the door, though, he stopped and turned back toward Lon.

"Can I say something, sir, off the record?" he asked.

"Of course, Weil. What is it?"

"I know it's none of my business, sir, but I think the Corps should have given that kid a medal instead of sending him to jail. That O'Banion was a real bastard. Had no business being in the Corps."

"You knew him?" Lon asked.

"We had a run-in once, a lot of years back. I was a squad leader and he was just a recruit. I helped pull him off a kid wasn't much more'n half his size. In Camo Town. I guess maybe we should've turned him over to the MPs then, and maybe he woulda got bounced, but we didn't. If we had, this Green kid wouldn't be looking at fourteen years of bars and bad food."

"Don't let the 'could haves' eat at you, Weil," Lon said. "You couldn't know what would happen so many years later."

"Maybe I should have, though. This has been gnawing at me since I heard about the killing last Friday. I recognized O'Banion's name right away, even before I saw the ID holo of him on the complink. And I remembered the SOB, and thought about what we should have done. I couldn't say anything before now, though, not while you were on the court."

"No, I would have had to disqualify myself," Lon said. *Maybe I would have felt better then,* he thought, but he didn't say it. Weil obviously felt bad enough.

"I just had to get it off my chest," Weil said. He hesitated for two seconds, then turned and left the office.

When Lon left his office for lunch that day, he found Phip Steesen in the corridor outside the orderly room. Sergeant's chevrons still seemed to weigh heavily on Phip's arms. Responsibility had come hard for him. When Lon had told Phip that he was being promoted to platoon sergeant and given second platoon, a pained look had come over Phip's face. "What did I ever do to you to deserve that?" he had asked. "I know, you're getting back at me for all the times I ordered ale for you when you wanted lager.'' But then, Phip had said the same thing when he was promoted to corporal.

''What is it, Phip?'' Lon asked. ''If you're lurking around out here, you must have something on your mind.''

''Night-fire exercises, tonight?'' Phip asked. The two were alone in the corridor, so Phip left off any honorific. The friendship between them was as old as Lon's service in the Corps, but changing circumstances put some official strains on it. They were both careful to keep their personal relationship separate from the professional one. The tightrope was not always easy to walk.

''Not my doing, Phip. I take it you had hot plans for tonight?'' Lon grinned. With Phip, it was no longer just a hard night of drinking. He did less of that with each stripe he won. In lieu of that, he devoted himself to the ladies.

''And *what* plans!'' Phip said. ''But this sure puts a kink in it, if you know what I mean.''

''I know. Look at it this way. The company will be off duty early tomorrow and you'll have a long weekend to take the kinks out.''

Phip shook his head. ''Not with this gal. I've been trying to get a night out with her for weeks, and this was the only night she could make it.''

''I can give you a chit to see the chaplain,'' Lon suggested.

''No, thanks. Her father's a chaplain.''

''Well, offer to take her to chapel Sunday.''

''Me go to chapel?'' Phip's eyes got wide, as if Lon had just suggested something that violated the laws of physics.

Lon chose to eat in one of the snack bars rather than go to the officers' mess and face questions from his peers about the court-martial. Now that the trial was over and the verdict had been reviewed and approved by the General, it would be open season for questions—even if Lon and the other members of the court-martial still would not be able to answer them.

The men were working in the barracks, preparing for an inspection before going out to the firing range for the night exercises. The inspection would normally have been held on Friday, but the schedule change affected that as well. Lon would walk through the barracks later, with Lead Sergeant Jorgen. By that time the platoon sergeants and squad leaders would have made certain that they would find nothing out of place.

"Major Orlis called just after you went to lunch, Captain," Weil Jorgen said when Lon came through the orderly room. "And he called again ten minutes ago, said he didn't find you in the officers' mess. He'd like for you to come over to his office as soon as you can."

"He say what he wants?" Lon asked.

"No, sir, not a clue," Weil said.

"I guess I'll go now," Lon said, reversing course. "If he calls again, tell him I'm on my way."

I hope it's not about the court-martial, Lon thought as he turned toward battalion headquarters. *I'd just as soon forget that.*

Battalion headquarters was only eighty yards from Lon's office. Matt Orlis's office was on the ground floor, near the back of the building. His clerk, a sergeant, told Lon to go straight in, that the major was waiting for him.

"I've been trying to track you down for more than an hour," Orlis said when he saw Lon. "Come in and have a seat."

Lon nodded and went to sit across from Orlis. "What's up?" he asked.

"Officially, nothing. Yet. Until you get official notice, you don't repeat this outside this office. That will probably be first thing Monday morning, subject to change."

"A contract?" Lon guessed.

Orlis nodded. "A one-company job. The contract is for three months, training a constabulary militia. The world is Bancroft."

"Never heard of it," Lon said. He rarely knew the worlds they went to before the orders came. "Is this *just* training, or do they have a problem that needs put-down first?"

"As far as they're saying, it appears to be just training their people. They claim there is no serious current problem. Take that with a grain of salt until you can check it out for yourself, but if it's true, this should be a beer run."

"A beer run won't break my heart," Lon said. "I'd just as soon they were all like that."

"I'm afraid it means you'll be away from your family over Christmas, Lon. Sorry."

Lon shrugged. "We knew it wasn't very likely I'd be home for the holidays this year. Sara and I were talking about that just last week. We were too close to the top on both the company and battalion lists." Angie's first Christmas—Lon had missed Junior's first Christmas as well.

"If something doesn't come up for two companies while you're gone, the whole battalion might go out a company at a time. That fouls everything up."

Lon smiled. "Right now, I'd rather have it like that then to come back and head straight out again on a battalion contract. I'm not all that eager for contract pay anymore. Garrison pay is just fine."

The major laughed. "I know what you mean. Linda keeps telling me the same thing." Linda was Mrs. Orlis.

"One other thing," Orlis said when Lon got up to leave. "When you tell Sara you're going on contract, make sure she knows not to say anything to anyone else before it's official."

"Hell, Matt, she probably knows about it already; probably has my duffel packed. It seems she knows everything else in the Corps before it comes through channels."

Company A, Alpha, stood in formation, dressed for combat, before their barracks. The three other line com-

panies in 2nd Battalion were in front of their quarters as
well. The men did not wear packs or carry grenades,
rocket launchers, or other ancillary gear, but they were
in battledress with combat helmets, and each man had
his rifle slung over his left shoulder. Even the officers
carried their rifles. They, too, would be shooting for
scores that night. Ammunition would be dispensed once
they reached the firing range.

Lon had given the order to fall in and had taken manning reports from his lieutenants five minutes earlier,
then given the "at ease" order while they waited for the
other companies to finish lining up—and waited for
Lieutenant Colonel Black and his staff to come out of
battalion headquarters.

That afternoon, while making his inspection of the
barracks, Lon had heard some grousing over the switch
in schedule, over going out for night maneuvers at all,
but he had taken no official notice, and had managed to
repress any show of amusement until he was out of sight
of any of the enlisted men. The platoon sergeants would
do a good enough job of squelching complaints. He had
heard the lecture more than once himself, when he was
an officer-cadet, supernumerary in a squad in this very
company, junior even to the rawest private.

"You're infantry. The night is your friend. No matter
how good the night-vision gear your foe has, he still
can't see you as well as he would in the daylight. And
if you're going to operate at night on contract, you've
got to do a fair amount of your practicing at night."

It was not dark yet as the officers and men of 2nd
Battalion waited for the command staff. The sun was
slightly above the western horizon. But by the time the
men marched the five miles to the firing range they
would be using, it would be dark enough.

"I'll bet there's been a lot of bitching about hiking
out instead of riding," Lon said on a radio channel that
connected him with his two lieutenants. DMC battle helmets offered a variety of communications channels,
along with a head-up display that could show terrain,

position of both friendly and opposing forces, vital signs for subordinates, and so forth. The protection a helmet offered against hostile small-arms fire and shrapnel was almost a tertiary design concern.

"There's always bitching," Tebba said. "The only thing that keeps it under control is the fact they all know that the desk jockeys from HQ will be walking along with the rest of us."

Finally, at 1905 hours, the battalion commander and his staff, officers, and enlisted men came out of battalion headquarters and formed up. The clerks and drivers from the headquarters staff formed up to the left of A Company.

Lieutenant Colonel Black gave the command to fall in, which was repeated by each of the company commanders. The next order the colonel gave was "Report."

"Alpha Company all present, sir!" Lon said. The other company commanders reported in order.

"Left face," Black ordered. Almost as one man, the entire battalion pivoted to the left. "Forward . . . march!"

Lon and Lead Sergeant Jorgen walked at the head of their company with the company's headquarters squad. Lon was just to the right of the formation.

The battalion drew a few curious glances from off-duty soldiers, but everyone took regular turns at this. There were no catcalls from the gallery. Second Battalion turned right at the end of 7th Regiment's area, past the next regimental area and out to the unpaved road leading toward the firing ranges. The pace was not difficult, a moderate route step, not the quick march of the parade field. There were times when it felt too slow for Lon. He had to hold himself back, because if he started moving faster, his company—and the rest of the battalion—would do the same. Once the battalion was away from the buildings and on the country lane, Lon moved farther to the side and stopped to watch his company hike past him. Then he jogged back to his place at the head. It offered a change of pace, a different strain on lungs and legs. It was enough.

Along the way, Lon monitored the radio channels his men had available, randomly checking to make certain that there was no extraneous talking. His men were, mostly, good about sound discipline, but alone in the privacy of a helmet with a tinted faceplate, men *could* get careless, especially if they thought they would not be overheard.

The hike to the firing range took almost precisely an hour. The range safety team was already in place, manning three towers behind the firing line and ready to walk back and forth behind the shooters on the ground. An ammunition truck waited with cases of ammunition for the slug-throwing rifles, and power packs for the beamers.

"We'll take ten before the firing starts," Lon told his sergeants and lieutenants. "I believe everyone knows where the latrines are."

Lon and his two lieutenants headed toward the center tower, where Colonel Black was conferring with the range safety officer, RSO, a captain who had absolute authority on the range—his orders superseding even those of a lieutenant colonel or colonel. The officers from the other line companies were also heading in that direction.

"No surprises," Black told his officers when everyone had gathered and he had finished his initial conference with the RSO. "Captains and above fire first, then the lieutenants and lead sergeants. Next the headquarters detachment and the platoon sergeants from the line companies, then we run a company at a time through the course. Beamers in the last three slots to the right. Questions?"

Unsurprisingly, there were none. Day or night, this was routine.

The range was one of the simple ones, pop-up silhouettes spaced from fifty to four hundred yards out from the final firing positions in each lane. Each man would

fire first standing, then kneeling, prone, and from plascrete foxholes, twenty rounds in each position, half single shot, and half in short bursts.

The RSO lifted the faceplate of his helmet and looked
out across the range. "I think about another ten or
twelve minutes and it will be dark enough, Colonel," he
said, looking to Black.

Lon checked the timeline on his own helmet's head-
up display and barely noticed Black nodding. "We'll be
ready when you are, Captain," the battalion commander
told the RSO.

A few minutes later, Lon found himself in lane six,
counting from the left, waiting. He had four magazines
for his rifle in a pouch hung from his web belt. His rifle's
bolt was back, showing that there was no round in the
chamber, and no magazine attached. There were still a
couple of minutes left before the time the RSO had set
for starting. Lon stood easily, holding his rifle at port
arms, waiting for the command. He used the time to start
breathing shallowly and regularly, working to stay calm,
relaxed. Firing on the range was no mere formality.
Marksmanship was one of the essential skills for a soldier, a survival skill. The day a soldier could not meet
the high requirements of the DMC was the day he
stopped being a line soldier. If he stayed in the Corps
at all, it would be in one of the ancillary, noncombat
services.

"This is the range safety officer." The voice sounded
directly against Lon's ears, through his helmet radio.
"From this point on, you will obey only my commands
or those of the safety officers immediately behind the
firing line, and you will obey those commands
instantly." The voice was matter-of-fact, accepting authority routinely, even over senior officers.

"Make certain that your safeties are in the 'on' position."

Lon tilted his rifle to look directly at the selector
switch. It was where it was supposed to be. The RSO

waited fifteen seconds, more than long enough, before he continued.

"Gentlemen, lock and load."

Lon held his rifle in his left hand and picked a magazine out of the pouch on his belt, sliding the clip crisply into position, feeling the snap, then testing to make certain that the fit was tight. Then he ran the bolt, sliding the first round into the rifle's chamber.

"Remember, gentlemen, keep your weapons pointed downrange at all times. If your rifle jams and you cannot clear the jam on the first attempt, you will immediately return the safety to the 'on' position and request the assistance of a safety officer over this channel.

"Ten rounds, single shot, from the standing position," the RSO continued. "Ready on the right . . . ?" There was a pause while he waited for a response from the safety officers on that side of the range. "Ready on the left . . . ?" Another pause.

"Gentlemen, set your selectors for single fire and assume firing position."

Lon moved the switch while he stepped into position and started scanning the lane in front of him.

"Begin!" the RSO said, and Lon watched for the first target to pop up.

It was not a game. Targets sprang up at random, controlled by a computer. There was no effective way to anticipate where the next one would be. Each target remained visible for six seconds. The shooter had to react, aim, and fire in no more than five seconds to make sure that the target would still be up when the bullet reached it. Motion had to be smooth, to avoid throwing off the aim. Lon worked hard not to jerk the muzzle of his weapon from one target to the next. Spot, track, aim, then squeeze the trigger. Working at night, with the night-vision gear that was part of DMC combat helmets, did add one complication: The targets did not show as clearly as a live enemy would. The temperature difference between the target and its surroundings was minimal, which meant that the infrared half of the dual system gave little help. Shooters had to rely on visible-light enhancers. At times it could be almost like shooting at ghosts.

When the last target went down, Lon's head-up display flashed the result: ten targets, ten hits. Later, he would be able to go back over each run to see where he had hit each target, vital area or not, and the length of time he had needed for each hit.

There was only a short pause before the second phase at the first position. Each man had ten rounds left in his magazine. Three targets would come up, and remain visible for the same six seconds. The object was to hit each target three times. If you hit the first two targets three times with as many shots, you tried to put the last four into the final target. That required an extremely delicate touch on the trigger.

"Set your selectors at automatic fire," the RSO instructed, and Lon complied. "Begin."

On automatic fire, the rifle had a tendency to move up and right. Compensating for that, and trying to fire three-shot bursts, made this part of the test much more difficult. Lon scored nine hits of ten shots, and he had loosed four rounds at the middle target.

The officers on the range moved forward to the next positions and went through the same sequence each time, finishing up in the foxholes.

"Remove magazines and check to make sure the chamber of your weapon is clear," the RSO ordered. "Wait in position until a safety officer clears you to move back."

With only captains and above on the line, it did not take long for one of the safety officers to come to Lon, kneel next to the foxhole, and inspect the rifle to make certain that there was no round in the chamber and that the safety was properly on.

"You're clear, Captain," the safety officer, a lieutenant, said.

Lon got out of the foxhole and jogged back to where

the rest of the men waited, ten yards behind the first firing positions.

"Not bad, Captain," Phip Steesen said when Lon joined him. "I was watching. Seventy-seven out of eighty. Guess you haven't lost your eye yet."

"Gives you a mark to aim at, anyway," Lon said.

"Might just beat you tonight," Phip said. "I still get out at night once in a while."

"Just be sure you make your numbers so you don't have to come out Saturday and retest," Lon challenged. The requirements were tough. A man had to hit thirty-five of the forty targets presented during the single-shot portions and ten of the twelve offered during automatic fire. If he failed at either, he would receive two additional chances—Saturday and Sunday, when he would rather be off duty. If he still could not make his numbers, he would be detached for two weeks and sent to a remedial training company for daily firing drills. If that did not do the job, the soldier was finished serving in a line company, which meant an end to the higher contract pay rates.

For the rest of the battalion's time on the range, Lon was a spectator. He monitored the shooting of his lieutenants and noncommissioned officers directly. The results posted by the rest would be reviewed by squad leaders and platoon sergeants. Anyone who failed, *if* anyone failed, would be flagged by the range computer, directed to the man's commanding officer.

It took until after one in the morning, 0100 hours, for the entire battalion to finish. No one in Lon's company failed to make the minimum numbers, and twenty shot perfect scores for the night. Including Phip Steesen.

"You did that just to show me up," Lon charged before the battalion formed up for the march back to barracks. "You haven't shot a perfect score in five years."

Phip chuckled. "It's a dirty job, but . . ." He didn't bother to finish the cliché.

7

Sara Nolan woke when her husband got into bed. She glanced at the bedside clock and saw that it was nearly three in the morning. "What time do you want to get up?" she asked around a yawn.

"The usual," he said, getting under the sheet and making himself comfortable. "Morning formation's at the regular time. We just get off at noon."

"Should be the other way around. Take the morning off and work the afternoon," Sara suggested, not really paying attention to what she was saying. She was starting to slide back toward sleep already.

"Tell the General. By the way, you'd better figure on visiting your parents with the kids over Christmas. Without me."

For perhaps ten seconds, that did not register on Sara's conscious mind. When it did, she half rolled toward Lon. "A contract?" Sleep receded.

"This is still unofficial, so don't tell anyone until the word comes down next week, but yes, three months, strictly a training contract."

"When?" Sara propped herself up on one elbow, facing Lon, who had closed his eyes and was looking for sleep.

"Soon, sometime next week probably. I'll tell you more when I find out."

Lon was asleep in less than three minutes. Sara needed considerably longer.

• • •

Although it was a chore, Lon did wake within minutes of his usual time in the morning, just ahead of the alarm. He sat on the edge of the bed longer than usual, eyes scarcely open, yawning broadly. It would have been so wonderful to flop back down and return to sleep, but . . . He stretched, then finally got to his feet. It was that movement that woke Sara.

"Already?" she asked, squinting toward the clock. "It can't be. I just got to sleep."

"Already," Lon mumbled, too softly for her to hear.

Lon spent rather longer than usual in the shower, finishing with a hard blast of cold water to help shock his system to full alertness. Sara had put on a robe and gone to the kitchen to start breakfast. By the time Lon had showered and dressed, the meal was waiting for him.

"You'll be home shortly after noon?" Sara asked while he ate. She had not cooked anything for herself.

"As far as I know," Lon said. "You know, we could take the weekend to pop over to Bascombe East to see your folks. Catch a shuttle this afternoon and come back Sunday evening."

"Pull Junior out of school at noon?" she asked.

"I think he can survive it," Lon said. "He can finish his lessons during the flight, while I catch up on my sleep."

"Will we be able to get seats on the shuttle to Donnelly at such short notice?" Bascombe East was too small to have any scheduled flights. They would have to land at the nearby town of Donnelly and rent a floater or take a cab the twenty miles to the village where Sara's parents lived.

"Call and see," Lon said. "I don't recall the shuttle to Donnelly ever being booked solid. When you know, don't forget to call your mother and clear it with her."

Sara's brow knitted into a frown as she tried to discover if there were any other reasons to object, or problems that might have to be surmounted. *And* to force herself to remember everything she would have to do if they were going to take a trip on such short notice.

"I'll pack a bag for you," she said, not looking at Lon. "And I'll call and tell you what arrangements I can make."

It all kept her too occupied to remember to ask Lon more about the coming contract until after he had left.

Lon dozed for five minutes on the ride in to the regimental area. It was a trick most combat veterans mastered early in their careers. Being able to catnap was essential, for the sake of sanity if nothing else. Sometimes it was the only way to get any sleep at all, occasionally for days on end. But he woke before his stop, and it was unlikely that any of the other officers on the floater even noticed that he had slept.

The morning after night-fire exercises could be counted on to be quiet—sluggish, even. Probably half the battalion would have skipped breakfast, choosing an extra thirty minutes of sleep over food. No one would press anyone too hard through the morning. Only the inertia of any military system mandated the morning work formation at 0800. The men would be put to cleaning the barracks and their gear. There would be no training or extraneous work—fatigue—details. Rifles had been cleaned as soon as the battalion returned from the firing range in the middle of the night. That was always a priority. Weapons rated higher than the men who carried them.

It was five minutes before eight when Lon entered the orderly room. Weil Jorgen was already at work, but it appeared as if he had just started his morning routine. Most days, he had everything ready for Lon a half hour earlier.

"It's mornings like this I really hate, Captain," Weil said when he looked up and saw Lon. "When I woke, I was dreaming about retiring and raising geraniums for the next fifty years—and getting twelve hours' sleep every blessed night."

"You'd be smoking those geraniums in six months," Lon said, smiling. The lead sergeant just grunted.

"Come into my office for a minute, Weil." Lon glanced at the clock. They had little more than a minute before they would need to turn to for the morning formation.

In Lon's private office, he closed the door. "Tell the platoon sergeants that the inspection this morning needs to be thorough. If we come back after the long weekend and have orders to ship out on contract in three hours, I want us to be ready."

Weil raised an eyebrow.

"We're at the top of two rotas, Weil," Lon said. "A contract could come up at any time."

"I'll see to it, Captain," Weil said. He had been in the Corps long enough not to ask questions. If Lon had wanted to tell him more, he would have. "We've been keeping on top of things the past two weeks. Unless anything was damaged last night and I don't know about it yet, we've replaced everything that might be even marginally unserviceable. And the armorers have already been alerted to give all the weapons a close look this morning."

"Right. There's the call for formation. Let's not keep the colonel waiting."

It was not surprising that 2nd Battalion was the last to be in position for the regimental formation that morning. Lon was still receiving manning reports when the regiment was called to attention. The tardiness was overlooked; each battalion received the same courtesy the morning after night exercises.

After the men were released to their day's work, Major Orlis came over to A Company and called Lon aside.

"It's official, Lon. You can tell your men the company will be leaving on contract Monday afternoon. Contract briefing for you and your lieutenants will be Monday at oh-nine-hundred. For now, you can tell the men it's Bancroft for three months, training their people."

Lon nodded. "How firm is that three months?"

Orlis smiled. "As firm as it can be. You'll have authority as contract officer to accept an extension if they ask for it and the, ah, conditions are right. But since they say there is no military threat requiring our assistance, there shouldn't be much question of an extension. But don't go promising the men anything certain.''

''I understand, Major.'' Lon saluted and Orlis returned it, then turned and headed toward battalion headquarters.

Lon's two lieutenants were still standing on the parade ground, together. They had watched the conference between Lon and the battalion's executive officer but had been far enough away that they could not overhear. Lon went to join them.

''We go out on contract Monday afternoon,'' he told them, then gave them the little information he had. ''We'll know more Monday morning. I'll have Weil gather the platoon sergeants and squad leaders and tell them. Five minutes after that, every man in the company will know. You two might check the databases to see if we have anything on Bancroft.'' It was not until then that Lon realized that he had not checked that himself after Orlis first clued him in on the coming contract. *Maybe I'm slipping,* he thought. *Used to be, I'd have checked the DBs within minutes.*

Weil Jorgen came over to Lon just after the lieutenants left. ''Give them five minutes to get the men started working, Weil,'' Lon said, ''then tell the platoon sergeants and squad leaders I want to talk with them in the dayroom. And you.'' He watched Weil blink, then added, ''Major Orlis just gave me the word. We go out on contract Monday afternoon.''

The pool and snooker tables in the dayroom were both covered. The drink machine was clean. When Lon entered with his lead sergeant at his side, the noncoms already in the dayroom came to attention facing the door.

''Make yourself comfortable,'' Lon told them. ''This will only take a minute.'' Weil had not given anyone advance notice what the captain wanted to talk to them about, but all of the sergeants had been in the Corps long enough to at least suspect that the topic might well be a contract.

It did not take even a minute for Lon to tell them the little he knew. "Pass the word along to your men. The lieutenants and I have our contract briefing at oh-nine-hundred Monday. As soon as we get back from that, I'll give you more. Since this is supposed to be strictly training, we'll pack garrison undress greens as well as battledress and fatigue uniforms. Make sure everything is ready for contract when you inspect this morning." He looked around, meeting the gaze of each of his noncoms before he asked, "Questions?"

There were none at the moment. Questions would come later.

When he got back to his office, Lon used his complink to connect to the DMC's encyclopedic data files to search out what the Corps knew about the world of Bancroft. A note showed that the entry had last been updated the previous afternoon, with data supplied by a representative of the Bancroft government. Those data were all tagged, to indicate the level of reliability—much lower than data researched directly by Corps intelligence. Lon knew what the innocuous tag really meant: "Don't believe a word of this until you confirm it first-hand."

He had just started reading the short file when Sara called to tell him that she had made the arrangements for their trip to Bascombe East.

"I hope you're going to be ready right at noon," she said. "The connection is a bit tight. The only other flight isn't until this evening. We'll get a cab and pick you up at the southwest corner of the regimental area. The return flight leaves Donnelly Sunday evening at eight. Okay?"

"Perfect," Lon said, smiling at the camera over his complink terminal. "I'll be out at the corner at noon, waiting."

"I decided to keep Junior home all day instead of picking him up later. That saves a good half hour. He's excited about going to see Gramma and Grampa."

Lon leaned back as his smile grew. "It should be a fine weekend," he said. "Autumn's always the best time of year at Bascombe East."

"I'll let you get back to work. I've got a million things to do before we leave. Love you."

"Love you," Lon echoed before she blanked the link.

Lon got up and went out to the orderly room. Weil Jorgen had just returned from some chore. "If anything comes up that needs me over the weekend—and I sincerely hope it doesn't—I'll be at my in-laws in Bascombe East. We're leaving right at noon and won't be back here until after nine o'clock Sunday night."

"I'll pass the word to battalion, Captain," Weil said. "Since we're going out on contract Monday, they're letting us shut down our orderly room for the weekend. Any calls will be routed to the OD at battalion."

"I'll talk to Major Orlis then, have him shunt anything that doesn't absolutely require me to Lieutenant Stossberg." *Harley will* love *that,* Lon thought with an amused grin.

"I'll make sure the lieutenant knows too, sir," Weil said.

Lon shook his head. "I'd better handle that myself."

The conversations with Orlis and Stossberg ate up a few minutes. Lon spent more time signing forms that Weil queued up on his complink, then went back through the file on Bancroft. At 1100 hours Lon called Lieutenant Girana to the office.

"I'm going to be out of town until Sunday night, Tebba, leaving in about forty-five minutes. Anything comes up over the weekend, battalion will call Harley, but you might want to make sure the OD at battalion can track you down if necessary. And let Harley know where you'll be. We don't want to throw him into a panic."

Tebba grinned. "Harley's not that raw anymore, Lon. It's been ages since he pulled a 'Chicken Little' act. I broke him in good, you know that. Besides, he always seems to know where to find me, even when I don't want him to."

"Just to be safe. Since he knows we're going off-world Monday, he might get a little anxious. I'll be in East Bascombe until late Sunday."

"Gettin' in a couple of days of free beer?" Tebba asked.

"I might manage a pint or two," Lon allowed. Tebba knew the pub that his in-laws ran. "I forgot to have Sara ask her mother if there were any troops at Nassau Proving Range this week." If there were, the pub would be hectic over the weekend. Lon shook his head. "No, Sara would know to ask, and she would have said something."

"Well, enjoy yourself. Hard telling what the chow will be like this place we're going. The battle rations we take along might be the best food on the world."

It was unusual for Lon to leave before his men had been dismissed for the day, but he allowed himself the exception, starting toward the corner where Sara and the children were to meet him with a taxi ten minutes before noon. He spent thirty seconds regretting that he had not brought a change of clothes along. He would have to make the journey to East Bascombe in uniform. "No help for that," he muttered as he reached the corner and started looking for one of the lime-green taxicabs.

The cab came into view, around the corner from the road to the married officers' quarters, at two minutes past twelve. Lon, Junior, started waving through one of the side windows as soon as he saw his father.

"I stayed home from school today!" Junior announced when his father opened the door to get in.

"I know, sport," Lon said. "But that doesn't mean you get to skip your lessons. You can do them on the shuttle."

"Aw, that's no fun. I can't watch out the window if I'm doing schoolwork."

"Well, you won't want to do them while we're at your grandparents'," Lon said. "And it's one or the other."

"I can do 'em on the shuttle comin' back Sunday," Junior said, beaming as if he had just found a loophole in his father's reasoning.

"You'll be sleeping on the ride back. It'll be past your bedtime when we get on the shuttle in Donnelly," Lon said. He glanced across the backseat of the cab and saw that Sara was trying to hide her laughter.

"We went through this all at home," she said. "Twice." She tapped Junior on the shoulder and, when he turned to look at her, she said, "You'll do your lessons on the shuttle today, young man. That was the deal."

"You trying to pull a fast one on me?" Lon asked the boy.

"You're a captain. Mom's just a civilian," Junior said.

"You do what your mother tells you," Lon said.

Junior climbed up on his father's lap so he could see out the side window more easily. The boy wanted to see everything along the route from the base across Dirigent City to the civilian aerospace port. A half-dozen times he asked his father what something was, as if he had never seen any of these sights a hundred times before.

Lon answered each question patiently, idly watching the passing scenery himself. Usually, when he traveled this route, it was either going out on contract or coming back, and his thoughts on those occasions were more serious. Angie ignored everything. She had been asleep when Lon got into the floater, and she stayed that way until the taxi stopped near the entrance to the civilian terminal at the port. When she opened her eyes and saw her father, she wanted to climb across the seat to him immediately, calling "Daddy!" loudly until he reached over and took her, after Junior got off his lap.

"I'll get a porter for the bags," Sara said.

A journey in a civilian shuttle was much different from one in a military craft. This aircraft was quite a bit smaller than the landers that ferried the mercenaries of the DMC between ship and shore. The plane the Nolans rode from Dirigent City to Donnelly could hold a maximum of thirty passengers. Although it was capable of burning for orbit—to rendezvous with an interstellar liner, for instance—the plane's journey to Donnelly was far too short for that capability to be needed. Its flight path was almost a ballistic trajectory, topping out at less than twelve thousand feet, with minimal g-forces. The trip would take just under thirty minutes.

There were half a dozen empty seats on the flight to Donnelly. Sara sat on one side of the aisle, holding Angie. Lon and his son sat on the other side of the aisle, with Junior next to the window. At first Lon let his son gawk at the scenery, but once the shuttle was clear of Dirigent City, he handed the boy a portable complink. "Lessons," he reminded Junior.

"Aw, Dad," Junior complained, predictably.

"The sooner you get your lessons done, the sooner you'll be free to do something else. You don't have much work. Get right to it and you might be finished in time to watch the landing."

As soon as Junior opened the complink and started working through his schoolwork, Lon leaned back and closed his eyes. He didn't really expect to get much sleep—the flight was too short—but even a few minutes would help. There had been times when he had gone as long as forty-eight hours on no more than a couple of five-minute naps. An edge of hunger made napping more difficult than usual. Lon's stomach growled. He had eaten only a light breakfast that morning and had not taken time for lunch.

That's okay, he told himself. *Mildred will have something good and hot. I can eat as soon as we get there.*

Mildred was Sara's mother. *And I can always grab a snack at the terminal in Donnelly.*

He did sleep. Lon was certain of that because he woke suddenly when the shuttle banked to the right as it came in for its landing in Donnelly. Lon yawned and stretched, then glanced at Junior. The boy had shut his complink and was staring out the window again.

"You finish your lessons?" Lon asked.

"Yes, Dad," Junior said without looking away from the window.

Sara had chosen to rent a small floater—a ground-effect vehicle—for the drive to Bascombe East because it might be difficult to get a taxi to come out from Donnelly on Sunday evening for them to catch the shuttle back to Dirigent City. She also did the driving. She knew the route better, and Lon rarely drove. They did not have a family car. In Dirigent City, few people did.

It was just after one-thirty in the afternoon when Sara parked the floater in the narrow drive next to the Winking Eye, Bascombe East's only pub. Junior was out of the car and nearly to the pub's entrance before Lon got himself and Angie unbuckled. He didn't even have a chance to call for Junior to wait.

"I'll come back out to get the bags," Lon said. "We'd better get inside before Junior takes over the place."

He carried Angie and still opened the door for Sara. Early in the afternoon, the Winking Eye was not busy. There was only a single customer standing at the bar. Geoff Pine, Sara's father, was on his way out from behind the bar. Mildred was on her way out of the kitchen, with Junior at her side, almost tugging her by the apron.

The next few minutes were the usual chaotic welcoming scene. Even the lone customer was drawn into the ritual.

"Freddie, you recall my daughter Sara and her husband, Captain Lon Nolan. Look how my granddaughter has grown!" Geoff said. He had claimed Angie from her father and stood her on the bar, holding her so she wouldn't fall.

"Don't forget me, Grampa!" Junior insisted, moving around to the front of the bar. "I'm here, too."

"How could I forget you, Lonnie?" his grandfather said, chuckling. He passed Angie to his wife, then hoisted the seven-year-old boy with almost equal ease. Decades of lifting beer kegs had kept Geoff Pine in excellent physical condition. Almost every year at the village's harvest festival, he reached the finals of the arm-wrestling competition.

"Seems the last time I saw you, lad," Freddie Dowell said, "you weren't much bigger than your sister is now."

Junior wasn't certain, but he suspected there might be some kind of insult in that, so he just ignored the comment.

"We're gonna be here all weekend, Grampa," he said instead.

The specialty of the day was a country stew with three kinds of meat, large chunks of vegetables, and a gravy so thick that a spoon would stand upright in it, served with bread that Mrs. Pine had baked that morning. Lon ate two ample portions and washed them down with beer. Sara and Junior ate rather less. Angie had to be content mostly with her own food, though her mother gave her a little of the stew gravy.

Freddie Dowell left the Winking Eye. Sara's parents came out to sit at the table with the family.

"Should be a quiet weekend," Geoff said after bringing new beers for himself and Lon. "Nothing doing out at Nassau, that I know of. Haven't been many soldiers around all month. Now, *next* weekend should be livelier. That's when we have our harvest festival." He chuckled.

"Lively, indeed," Mildred said. "A royal excuse for everyone to eat too much and drink even more. By suppertime Saturday, you won't know which side of the bar you're on."

"Sounds inviting," Lon said, "but by this time next week, I'll be well on my way out-system." He had already told his in-laws what little he knew about the coming contract.

"You know, Lon, anytime you're ready to start pulling pints instead of triggers, you and Sara can come out here permanently and take over the pub. Mildred and I can retire and enjoy life a bit while we're still young enough to."

Lon's smile was hesitant. He still wasn't certain how serious Geoff was. Sara's father had started talking about retiring and turning the pub over to them some years back. "Not yet, Geoff," he said, shaking his head slowly. "I've still got to put in another nine years before I can draw even the minimum pension from the Corps."

"Besides, he's gonna be the General someday!" Junior claimed loudly.

"Don't count on it," Lon said, smiling at his son. "The Council of Regiments has never elected anyone General who wasn't born on Dirigent and been at least a second-generation member of the Corps. You might have a chance someday, but not me."

"Don't count yourself out, Lon," Geoff advised. "You've already been the exception to a number of rules. And there's no rule that says you have to be second-generation Corps to be elected General. The way things are going, you might become the youngest man ever to get his own regiment."

"Don't you start," Lon said. "I'm a long way from thinking about a regiment. I could still retire a captain if I stay in another twenty years."

Geoff barked a sharp laugh. "I'd make book against that, an' offer anyone ten-to-one odds. You know, I've still got a few connections in the Corps. I hear things. It wouldn't surprise me if you were a major the next time you come out this way."

"Maybe," Lon allowed, "but even that's still a long way from full colonel and a regiment."

•   •   •

After closing that evening, Lon helped his father-in-law with the clean-up. The children were asleep upstairs. Sara and her mother had finished in the kitchen and gone upstairs to talk.

"Something's bothering you, isn't it," Geoff asked after they had nearly finished with the necessary work. He refilled their beer mugs.

"What makes you say that?" Lon asked.

"You spend thirty or forty years behind a bar, you learn to read people. What is it?"

"I'm not entirely sure. That might be part of the problem." Lon took a long pull on his beer. "Maybe life's just starting to catch up with me."

"If you want to talk about it, I'm a good listener, Lon."

Lon remained silent for a minute or more, taking a couple of sips of beer to cover his hesitation. "It's not the ghosts, this time," he said then, so softly it was almost a thought.

"The court-martial?" Geoff asked.

"You know about that?"

"A murder is big news, especially in the Corps. And Sara told her mother you were on the court-martial. We followed the story pretty close."

"We had to send that kid to jail, and would have hung him if it hadn't been for the sister. But I can't convince myself that O'Banion didn't get exactly what he deserved. Sure, that Green kid made mistakes, bad choices, but part of me thinks he deserved some kind of medal for what he did. But we didn't have any choice. We had to convict him. There wasn't one vote for acquittal."

Geoff shrugged. "We have to have laws, and we have to enforce them. That's what civilization is about. All in all, we've done pretty well for ourselves here on Dirigent, even if the code is a little . . . draconian at times. Back when I was in the Corps, there was a man convicted of raping a girl. You know the punishment for that?" Lon nodded, but his father-in-law continued anyway. "They chopped off his balls and most of his pecker, left him just a tiny stub to pee with, and gave him ten years at hard labor on top of it.''

''This was different,'' Lon said. ''This was . . . well, what if it had been Junior protecting Angie? It could happen, fifteen, twenty years from now.''

''You teach 'em better than that Green kid's folks taught him. Make sure they know the right way to do things. That's what parents are supposed to do.''

Lon took another drink. His mug was nearly empty again. ''And Junior keeps saying he wants to be a soldier just like me.''

''What else?'' Geoff asked. ''This *is* Dirigent, and his daddy happens to be one of the best officers in the Corps.''

''I know. It's just that, lately, whenever he says that, it sends a shiver up my spine.''

8

By Sunday afternoon, Lon was feeling as relaxed and comfortable as he ever did. He enjoyed the company of his wife's parents, and even liked helping out in the pub, giving his father-in-law a little extra time to be with the children. His only contact with the Corps all weekend was when two of the MPs taking their month's tour of duty at Nassau Proving Range came in for dinner and drinks Saturday evening. He "bought" them a round of drinks, then sat and chatted with them for a few minutes. The MPs, one a corporal and the other a private, knew he was in the Corps, but not his rank.

"Maybe someday it *would* be nice to move out here and run the pub," Lon told Sara while they were driving to Donnelly Sunday evening. The children were sleeping. Junior had fallen asleep almost the instant the floater pulled away from the pub. Angie had needed only a couple of minutes longer.

"Someday when you get all the soldiering out of your system," Sara replied, speaking little above a whisper to avoid waking the children. The more they slept now, the better it would be. "Right now, it's okay for a day or two, but you'd be climbing the walls inside of a week, and you know it."

"I know," he agreed, nodding even though she was watching the road and not him. "But someday."

"Just don't let Daddy stampede you into doing it before you're ready."

"You think he's really serious about wanting to retire?" Lon asked.

Sara did not answer for nearly a minute before she said, "I'm not sure. He's always talked about retiring. When I was, I don't know, maybe ten or eleven, he started talking about just waiting for me to get old enough to take over. When I hit fourteen or so, it was when I got married and had a man to help me run the place. It's always been something of a joke, I think. But I do know they've managed to save enough to let them retire whenever they want to."

"He could always sell the pub and retire, anytime at all," Lon said.

"He'd never do that, not as long as he has any hope at all of passing it along to someone in the family. I don't think he can even conceive of the Winking Eye belonging to anyone else. He's the fourth generation of Pines to own it."

At least you have something to fall back on if some-thing happens to me, Lon thought. That was something they hadn't spoken of in five years, the constant chance that he might not return from a contract. Rank was no guarantee of survival. Over the centuries that the DMC had operated, even four colonels had died on contract.

Monday morning, Lon called for a staff car from regiment to pick him up. He had a duffel bag to take in with him, clothing and gear he needed for the contract. He took a few extra minutes at home, though, to say good-bye to his wife and children, taking care to assure Junior that this was not going to be a dangerous contract.

"We're just going to teach some colonists how to defend themselves," he told him. "No real fighting at all."

"I wish they were all like that," Sara whispered in Lon's ear at the door. "But I knew you were a soldier when I first saw you."

He laughed, avoiding the subtext, the worries she seldom confessed to, the possibility that one day he might not come home. Sara always seemed more secure about that than he was. "I hope so. I was in uniform."

Lon carried his own bag out to the staff car but the driver, a lance corporal, got out and stowed the duffel on the passenger side of the front seat, then held the rear door open for Lon.

I wish they were all training contracts, too, Lon thought as he waved good-bye to Sara and the children. Junior had come to the door, and Sara was holding Angie. *But if the time comes when all anyone wants from the Corps is training, we're out of business anyway.*

The drive was silent. Lon's driver did not speak until they had reached Lon's headquarters. "Good luck on contract, sir," the driver said as he lifted the duffel bag out of the floater. "Hope you have an easy one."

Lon grinned at him. "You and me both, Lance, you and me both."

"Want me to take this inside for you, sir?"

"No, thanks. Time for me to get used to doing things for myself again." He hoisted the duffel bag to his left shoulder and returned the driver's salute before heading inside.

Lon didn't get very far with the bag. As soon as he entered the orderly room, Weil Jorgen was up from behind his desk and took the bag.

"I'll get that, Captain. Set it right over here with the rest of our gear."

"No problems over the weekend, I trust?" Lon asked as he watched his lead sergeant set the duffel with his own and those of the men in headquarters squad.

"None that've come to my attention," Weil said. "That means nothing serious enough to warrant official notice. No missing bodies, no one in hospital or the guardhouse."

"Always good signs," Lon said, grinning. "The platoon leaders upstairs?"

"Yes, sir, for the last thirty minutes," Weil said.

"I'd better get up there before they drink enough coffee to slosh during the contract briefing."

● ● ●

Lon and his lieutenants walked across to battalion headquarters a few minutes before the briefing was scheduled to begin. Lon knocked on the executive officer's door and was called in.

"Glad you came early," Matt Orlis said. "Gives me time to make the introductions before the colonel gives his talk."

"Introductions?" Lon asked.

"You'll be taking three civilians from the munitions combine along, as well as giving Bancroft's negotiator a ride home," Orlis explained. "They're already waiting in the conference room."

That was just across the corridor. The four men inside all got to their feet when the officers entered.

"Mr. Isadore Stanley, envoy of the Bancroft government, Captain Lon Nolan. He commands the company that's going to help you out. His lieutenants, Tebba Girana and Harley Stossberg." Stanley shook hands with each of them, then Major Orlis introduced the three civilian Dirigenters to the officers. They were Homer Detweiler, Charles Chance, and Rob Menver.

"I'll go tell the colonel you're ready for the briefing," Orlis said after the handshaking was finished and everyone was getting seated again. He was gone for less than two minutes, and came back a step behind Lieutenant Colonel Hiram Black.

"This will be fairly short, Captain Nolan," Black said. "The contract is fairly uncomplicated, and you will have Mr. Stanley along on the trip to Bancroft to answer any questions that come to mind." He cleared his throat and glanced around the room before continuing.

"Your company will shuttle up to *Tyre* at sixteen hundred hours today." *Tyre* was one of the older small ships in the Corps fleet. It could carry one company of mercenaries or serve as a cargo transport as needed. "*Sidon* will accompany you, carrying munitions and equipment for Bancroft's own munitions industry, as well as additional supplies for your company. The three civilians who will be going along will inspect the factories Bancroft has now, suggest any worthwhile changes, and supervise the installation and testing of the machinery that *Sidon* will carry.

"Once on Bancroft, Alpha Company will establish a standard training regimen for the men of Bancroft's constabulary militia. The course, to last twelve weeks, will be for approximately one thousand trainees. In addition to basic military training for all personnel, the commissioned and noncommissioned officers of Bancroft's Constabulary Militia will be given training in light infantry tactics, with particular emphasis on counterinsurgency situations."

Nothing we haven't done a half-dozen times before, Lon thought as Black continued with the briefing. There was a brief glance at a map showing the primary population centers of Bancroft, but since no action against hostile forces was contemplated, that did not require much attention now. And it would all be available for Lon and his lieutenants to study at their leisure during the two weeks that the journey to Bancroft would require.

As promised, the briefing was short, only half an hour.

"I'll see you aboard ship, Captain Nolan," Stanley said, offering his hand. "The colonel has arranged for me to go up ahead of your lads, so I'm out of the way, I suspect."

"I'm sure it's not that, sir," Lon said. "A company of soldiers takes up every seat on two shuttles. You'd have to sit on somebody's lap, and that would be far from comfortable."

"We're going up early as well," Homer Detweiler said. "My colleagues and I will be riding *Sidon,* Captain Nolan, so we shan't be seeing you again until we reach Bancroft."

There was handshaking all around, until Major Orlis shepherded Lon and his lieutenants out of the conference room and across to his own office.

"This will only take a minute, Lon," Orlis promised, shutting the door after the officers were inside. "Two quick items. First, Bancroft is offering top rates for this contract, for the training program and the munitions factory replicators. Out of the blue, the way this came, there might be more going on than they've let on.''

Lon shrugged. ''Wouldn't be the first time. Nobody ever tells us everything.''

''No, they don't. But I want the three of you to keep your eyes open. If there *is* more doing, there might be the chance of more lucrative contracts later.'' Orlis waited for nods, then said, ''Second, we've made arrangements for conversion of funds to local currency. Since this is a training contract and you'll be stationed close to, ah, civilized services, you'll be able to give your men passes when they're off duty—at your discretion. Mr. Stanley has been given repeated assurances that our people know how to behave themselves in public, so see that they do.''

''I'll bring the lead sergeant up to speed,'' Lon told the lieutenants as they walked back toward A Company. ''You two brief your platoons.'' Lon paused for a second, then added, ''Just what Colonel Black had to say. We'll save the news about passes for now. It might be more effective later.''

''That's for sure,'' Tebba said. ''Tell them too soon and they won't be able to concentrate on getting ready for the job at hand. Major Orlis did say it was at your discretion. That means you don't have to let anybody out 'less they earn it.''

''And the first time anyone screws up, even a little bit, that'll be the end of it,'' Lon said. ''It won't be like Camo Town. The people of Bancroft don't have the experience to deal with a lot of raving-drunk soldiers, and I don't want them to learn from us.''

Eight hours later, Alpha Company was on its way out-system aboard the transport *Tyre,* accelerating toward its first jump through Q-space. That would not take place until *Tyre* and *Sidon* were five days out from Dirigent.

The two ships were among the smallest interstellar craft that the mercenaries employed. Each could carry a single company of men, with supplies to last three months in the field, or it could carry just supplies, enough to support a battalion for the same length of time.

Facilities were limited. Meals were eaten one platoon at a time in a galley that was crowded with fifty men in it at once. The gymnasium was little larger. It, too, was limited to a single platoon at a time, and everyone rotated to get in their exercise every day. In the troop bays, bunks were stacked three high, little more than shelves for sleeping. Platoon sergeants had cabins, two to a room. Only the lead sergeant and the three officers had private accommodations, and those were scarcely larger than closets. Isadore Stanley had a compartment in the crew's section of the ship, forward of the troop areas.

After Lon had eaten supper, he started forward. As senior line officer aboard, there were matters of protocol to observe. He went all of the way to the bridge, the command deck, some fifty yards short of the bow of *Tyre*. A naval rating at the hatch opened it and allowed Lon through.

"Ah, Captain Nolan, come on in," *Tyre*'s skipper, Commander Buck Tanner, said. He got up from his seat at the center console and moved toward Lon.

Lon saluted, casually. "Good to be riding with you again, Captain," he said. As commander of a naval vessel, Tanner automatically earned the higher title. *Tyre* was *his* vessel, his responsibility. Although the term "navy" had referred exclusively to spacegoing forces for nearly eight centuries, most navies still carried on the traditions of their seaborne ancestors.

Tanner was as casual with his return salute. "Your lads all settled in?" he asked.

"Pretty much. Still working through the supper rota."

Tyre's skipper grinned. "Our civilian passenger didn't make it to supper, I'm afraid. He came aboard spacesick. Couldn't handle the zero-g ride on the shuttle."

"Some folks are like that, Captain," Lon said. "My junior lieutenant gets spacesick almost every time we go off-planet, even aboard ship with artificial gravity. Says it's just knowing his feet aren't on the ground."

"I understand you've drawn a beer run," Tanner said.

"That's what we've been told," Lon said. "Teaching their militia the ropes."

"You sound as if you don't expect it to be that easy."

Lon shrugged. "Oh, it probably will be. But if I go in expecting the worst, anything better will look like picking a three-horse parlay at the Downs." The Downs was Dirigent City's lone racetrack. Horses ran there during two six-week meets each year, and dorries, a native quadruped that looked like a cross between a camel and an alligator, ran in two other meets.

"Never had any luck at the races myself," Tanner said.

"I got cured the hard way, not long after I won my pips. Lost half a month's pay in two hours," Lon said.

Both men laughed. "Anything I can do for you, let me know." Tanner extended his hand—the sign that the meeting was over. "I'm at your service."

Shipboard routine was limited. Meals and exercise were fit into each day. The officers and noncoms went over details of the training program they would administer for the Bancroft militia. Lon spent time studying the available maps for the planet, concentrating on areas around the towns but familiarizing himself with as much of the planet's land area as possible.

The only full stops that came to the routine were for each of the three transits of Q-space. The first warning of each transit was given thirty minutes ahead, even though the jump schedule had been made available at the beginning of the voyage. The first signal was the warning for the ship's passengers to return to their living quarters and strap themselves in their bunks. Another warning was provided thirty seconds before the start and finish of each jump. The full power of *Tyre*'s three Nilssen generators, which also provided artificial gravity, were needed to establish and manipulate the bubble of quantum space that permitted interstellar jumps. For the duration of each transit—rarely more than a couple of minutes—each ship was effectively in a universe of its own, theoretically tangent to every point in the universe of normal space. The bubble universe would be stressed at a carefully calculated point for the proper length of time, and then the Q-space field would be reversed, depositing the ship back in normal space. There were always three jumps to any interstellar journey—one from the system of origin to a standard "shipping lane" whose jump parameters were well known, the second along that lane, and the third in toward the destination system.

The jumps were spaced to minimize any distortion in the Q-space fields. The first jump did not take place until the ships were five days out from Dirigent. Three days always passed between jumps, and the third jump would leave the ships three to five days out from their destination, so any interstellar journey—whether between neighboring star systems or halfway across the local spiral arm of the galaxy—required fourteen to sixteen days.

Lieutenant Harley Stossberg's spacesickness ended three days out. Isadore Stanley got sick each time *Tyre* lost its artificial gravity for a Q-space transit.

"I hope I never have to go off-world again in my entire life," Stanley told Lon during a meeting the morning before the ship's final jump of the journey back to his home. "Next time they need a diplomat, they can damned well find somebody else."

"I know it can be rough," Lon said, nodding in commiseration. "But you'll be home in a few days."

Stanley groaned softly. "After one more jump through Q-space and another shuttle ride. I even asked the ship's medical officer if he could give me a patch to let me sleep through the zero gravity, but he wouldn't do it."

"Standard practice. My lads who get spacesick don't

get that either. The medics say it's dangerous.''

"You'd think by now they'd have come up with a pill or a patch to prevent it," Stanley said.

Tyre and *Sidon* emerged into normal space eighty hours out from Bancroft. After three jumps covering more than seventy light-years, the two ships appeared simultaneously, eighteen miles apart—and that by design rather than accident.

Lon spent the next three days and odd hours waiting to hear whether there was any change in conditions on Bancroft, to learn whether the mission would still be strictly training, or if he would have to renegotiate the contract to include more active duty for his company. That sort of thing happened all too frequently to the Corps. Governments thought they could negotiate a better deal "since you're already here."

But there was no request for any change from the government of Bancroft.

"The shuttles can set down right at the spaceport in Lincoln," Isadore Stanley assured Lon four hours before the mercenaries were scheduled to board the landers. Lincoln was the planetary capital. "We'll have ground transport on hand to take your people to their barracks at the new militia base. You'll have time to get settled in before supper, I believe." Shipboard time had been gradually adjusted during the voyage so the mercenaries would be on the same diurnal "clock" as the people at the destination—standard practice in the Corps.

"You're going down with the people on *Sidon*?" Lon asked, though he knew the answer.

"Yes." Stanley frowned briefly. "They're sending a shuttle over to collect me in about an hour. One extra bout of zero gravity I hadn't been counting on. But my government wants me to come in with the equipment, and—as you said before we left your world—the shuttles with your men will be fully packed without me."

Be glad you'll never have to ride a shuttle going in for a hot *landing in combat,* Lon thought, suppressing a smile. *Accelerating toward the ground until the last possible second, then reversing thrust. You'd really get sick then.* "But it will be over soon enough," he said. "You'll be home, both feet on the ground."

"And ready to keep things like that," Stanley said firmly.

The rifles of Alpha Company held neither magazine nor cartridge when the men boarded their shuttles for the ride to the surface of Bancroft, but the ammunition pouches on each man's belt were full. The DMC took nothing for granted. Its men would not set foot on any planet but Dirigent without the means to defend themselves. The shuttles themselves were armed with rapid-fire cannon and rockets, ready to cover a retreat or a defensive deployment. If necessary.

"We don't go in looking like we're expecting trouble," Lon had reminded his sergeants, "but keep your eyes open."

It was a gentle ride to the surface, not a combat landing. The two shuttles from *Tyre* went in together, in formation, and landed near the spaceport's lone terminal building. The cargo shuttles from *Sidon,* with the first loads of equipment and the four civilian passengers, did not leave orbit until the mercenaries were on the ground and the senior pilot had radioed back that there was no sign of trouble on the ground.

There was even a band waiting to greet the Dirigenters with festive music.

9

The men of Lon's company emerged from the two shuttles with rifles slung over left shoulders and the face-plates on their helmets raised—both measures designed to appear friendly, nonthreatening. There was no mad dash to establish a defensive perimeter either, the way they would have on a combat landing. Instead they fell in by platoon, between the shuttles and the terminal, just as they would have returning to Dirigent from a contract. Platoon sergeants went through the routine of dressing ranks, then stood the men at parade rest.

The band had started playing as soon as the doors on the two shuttles opened, some rousing air that Lon thought he had never heard before. A handful of local dignitaries was also present, standing a little apart from the musicians. Two camera operators were videoing the reception. Farther off, behind a series of low barricades decorated with brightly colored pennants, several dozen civilians watched—without much show of emotion, one way or the other.

Lon and Tebba walked directly to the welcoming committee after handing their rifles to Lead Sergeant Jorgen. The man at the center of the committee wore a black top hat, an anachronism that could only be a badge of office. Lon saluted him.

"I am Captain Lon Nolan, A Company, 2nd Battalion, 7th Regiment, Dirigent Mercenary Corps, at your service, sir," he said, taking his helmet off and holding it under his left arm. "This is my executive officer, Lieutenant Tebba Girana."

"Pleased to meet you both. I am Roger Sosa, governor of Bancroft. Welcome. I trust you had a pleasant journey?" The governor spoke softly, in friendly tones.

"We stayed dry, sir," Lon said, which appeared to baffle the governor. Lon worked to keep from smiling at the look on Sosa's face. The remark might not have made sense to anyone but a soldier.

"My people have provided barracks for you in our militia compound," Sosa said after an instant's hesitation in which he decided to ignore Lon's remark. "The entire facility is new, so you should have no problems."

"That's good to know, sir," Lon said.

"We'll get you and your people settled in this afternoon, give you a chance to look over what we have, and so forth. Tomorrow morning you can meet with Colonel Henks, the commander of our new constabulary militia, and his officers, and get the training regimen planned out. This evening I would be pleased if you and your officers would join us for dinner at Government House. Colonel Henks and his staff will be present. It will give you all a chance to meet informally before the work begins."

"We would be honored to accept, sir," Lon said, nodding slightly. Some series of rituals was almost inescapable on a contract such as this. It was, Lon reflected, better than rushing immediately into combat with too little time to size up the situation. *Maybe they were telling the truth up front,* Lon thought. It would be a refreshing change of pace. *Maybe they* don't *have any real threat facing them.*

"I'll have a staff car pick you up at, say, six-thirty?" Sosa suggested.

"At your convenience, sir," Lon said. It was then slightly past two in the afternoon, local time.

"And now, Captain, there are a few of our leading citizens I would like to introduce you to," Sosa said, gesturing to the other civilians with him.

• • •

Lincoln was a fairly large town for a thinly settled colony world. The population figures in the DMC database had indicated that the capital of Bancroft held about sixty thousand people, with the planet's total near three hundred thousand. There were three other towns with populations between fifteen and thirty thousand, with the rest of the Bancrofters scattered among scores of villages and mining outposts. As with many other colony worlds, Bancroft's lifeblood was its natural resource—minerals and rare metals. Only compact and valuable cargoes—primarily raw elements, items too exotic to be easily synthesized in factory replicators, and intellectual achievement—made economical exports across interstellar distances.

For Lon, the most immediate novelty about Bancroft was that the settlers had concentrated in the northern temperate zone rather than in the tropics or subtropics. It was early spring when A Company arrived in Lincoln. The temperature was in the upper fifties, Fahrenheit, under a warming sun in a clear sky. Deciduous trees along the edge of the spaceport were just sprouting their new crop of leaves. It reminded Lon, a little, of his childhood home in the western portion of North Carolina—especially since he could see a line of low mountain peaks just off to the west. Lincoln itself was in the foothills of a considerable mountain range.

"At least we shouldn't bake or freeze on this one," Tebba said during the ride to the militia compound. He and Harley were with Lon in a staff car leading the convoy.

"Not like some of the places we've been," Lon agreed. "But it might get warm enough when summer gets here, near the end of the contract." He had his battle helmet on his lap and was watching one of the displays on the inner surface of the faceplate, scanning for monitoring electronics. Routine caution. There was no indication that the passenger compartment of the floater was bugged.

"We've seen more than our share of tropical *para-*

dises," Tebba said. The stress he put on the final word altered its meaning completely. Lon just grinned.

"When we get to the barracks, scan everything, just to be certain," Lon said, whispering, scarcely moving his lips. Their driver was in a separate compartment, glassed off from the mercenaries, and showed no indication that he had any interest in what they might talk about.

"Of course," Tebba said, nodding.

The floater turned a corner then, and the Dirigenters could see the militia compound ahead of them and off to the right.

"I'll be damned," Tebba said under his breath. "Look at that."

Lon was looking. "Like something from Earth, a thousand years ago," he said. "A frontier stockade. I've never seen one this big, though."

"What are you talking about?" Harley asked.

"When Europeans first settled North America, they built wooden forts like that as protection against the indigenous population they were displacing," Lon said. "Chop down trees and build walls with them, logs stuck in the ground in a tight palisade. It was a place of refuge for families in the area whenever there was trouble with the natives."

The near wall of the fort appeared to extend for at least two hundred yards. The side wall that Lon and the others could see seemed to be somewhat shorter, but still considerable. The logs that formed the palisade rose forty feet and were around two feet in diameter. It was a formidable structure, but it looked totally out of place with modern buildings of plascrete and metal just across a paved boulevard.

"You could burn through that thing in thirty seconds," Tebba said, shaking his head. "Or blow it into toothpicks with a handful of rockets and grenades."

"The design wasn't foolproof even when all it had to block were arrows and spears," Lon said.

"We're gonna have to take holos back with us or no

one will believe something like this actually exists," Tebba said.

"So get a camera and make like a tourist," Lon said, laughing gently. The design was authentic to Lon's eye, even inside. The buildings were of log construction as well, lining the inside of the defensive wall, one- and two-story structures.

"I've seen reconstructions of early forts like this on Earth," Lon said just before the car pulled to a stop in front of one of a dozen identical buildings inside. "The biggest would have fit easily in this parade ground." There was an open area, two hundred by three hundred feet, in the center of the fort.

"That must be the headquarters building, over there," Harley said, pointing at the largest structure inside the walls, centered against the far wall, directly opposite the gate the convoy had entered through. There were two flagpoles just in front of the building, and it had a covered veranda in front.

"And this apparently is our home for the next three months." Lon pointed to the nearest building, the one they were parked in front of. Their driver got out and opened the rear right-hand door, where Lon was seated. He was the first of the Dirigenters out of the vehicle.

"It's considerably more modern on the inside, sir," the driver said. The name tag sewn on the chest of his uniform read BLAZE. "The government just wanted the historical look on the outside. We're not that far past the frontier stage, sir. My dad's parents were both born in log cabins."

Lon sent his lieutenants off to see to their platoons, then followed the driver inside the building.

"Each of these barracks is designed to house a hundred men, Captain," the driver said. "Open troop bays on the ground floor and half of the upper floor, plus half a dozen private rooms that can be used for senior personnel or for office space, as needed. And storage rooms along the side of the upstairs against the stockade wall. The next building over is equipped for recreation purposes. There are three of those in the compound.''

"I'm sure we'll make out just fine," Lon said. "Tell me, are you part of the militia we're here to train?"

"Yes, sir. I'm an acting corporal.'' He grinned rather sheepishly. "Whether that rank becomes permanent depends on how I do in training. The colonel told us all that when we moved into the barracks last week.''

"Have you had any training at all?" Lon asked.

There seemed to be embarrassment in Corporal Blaze's grin. "Not very much, sir. Just marching and stuff like that. Some of the men have been in the police business longer, but most of us are new.''

Lon took a quick walk through the one building. There was indeed no sign in the interior of the primitive exterior. The troop bays and smaller rooms might almost have been part of the DMC's main base. After Lon's people started hauling gear in, Corporal Blaze excused himself, said he had to return to his unit. He gave Lon a link code to call if he needed anything.

"Tebba, we'll put first and second platoons in this building, the others next door. Tell Harley to find himself a room above his men. We've got space for platoon sergeants and above to have private quarters.''

"Glad you decided that way, Lon. We've already started moving them in on that basis.''

Lon nodded.

"Weil has started doing what you wanted,'' Tebba said, alluding to the electronic scan. "He said he'd let us know as soon as he's finished.''

"We'll use this room as orderly room. Give Weil the room next to it for his quarters, and I'll take the next. Find one you like, then turn the others over to the platoon sergeants. Put Phip down on the end, as far away as possible. In case he starts snoring again.'' That had started only after Phip Steesen was promoted to corporal. The snoring came and went, without any discernible pattern—except that it never happened during a combat contract, when there was danger within reach.

"See to the men, then we'll hold a quick meeting up

here. Platoon sergeants and up,'' Lon said.

''There's one thing that puzzles me about this,'' Tebba said. ''How come we don't get to meet the militia big shots until this evening? Why weren't they at the port to meet us, or here? You'd have thought that would be laid on without much thought.''

''Don't ask me. There wasn't room in my duffel for the old crystal ball. Maybe Colonel Henks just thinks it's below him to greet a mere captain. Or maybe he doesn't want our heads to get too big for our helmets.'' Lon shrugged. The absence of any militia officers had seemed strange to him as well. ''Maybe we'll find out at dinner.''

''Maybe the colonel didn't get his brass polished in time,'' Tebba said, laughing off his concern . . . for the moment.

The recreation buildings also held the mess halls, on the second story. There were civilian cooks and staff. Lon walked through the mess hall that would serve his people. ''Looks like we eat in shifts here, too,'' Lon observed to Lead Sergeant Jorgen as they looked over the facility. ''This might serve eighty at a time.''

Weil nodded. ''I make it eighty-four seats, sir. I'll check with the head cook and set up the schedule. The men won't be too happy about shifts, or waiting in line.''

''It's better than it might have been, Weil. Let's go with lines and waiting for breakfast and try to set schedules for the other meals. The men get to grumbling, tell them that if they're good we'll have passes for some of them to get out, evenings and weekends, and that will cut down on the crowding.''

''Passes?'' Weil said.

''At my discretion. Sorry, I forgot to tell you about that. There'll be arrangements for the men to draw their pay in local currency. That's one of the things we need to set up with Colonel Henks and his staff. It won't be the first few nights anyway, Weil. We've got to get the training program started before anyone gets a chance to lark off—and it's strictly a matter of 'on good behavior.' I don't want *any* incidents with the locals.''

"Right, sir. On the eating situation, I'll check and see if there are tables and chairs so we can use part of the rec hall for meals as well. That will speed things up a little.''

By the time they got back to the barracks, A Company was well settled in. Bunks had been made and clothing stored.

"All the comforts of home, almost," Phip Steesen said when Lon and Weil entered the bay that held second platoon. "Do you know if there's a canteen that serves beer and things?''

"Not that I've seen, Phip. Maybe over in the rec hall. I wasn't looking for taps. I don't have your thirst.''

When the car arrived for Lon and his lieutenants, it was near sunset. There were high, thin clouds in the west, diffusing the fading sunlight, spreading a reddish glow over the horizon. Bancroft's Government House was nearly a mile from the militia post, at the far end of a broad avenue flanked by businesses. There were only a few people visible on the street, but most of those turned to look at the passing car. Lon wondered if it was because they knew who was in it . . . or simply because vehicle traffic was rare in Lincoln. He suspected it might be the latter. He saw no other cars or trucks moving during the ride.

The seat of government was only moderately imposing. It was not the largest building in town, even excluding the palisaded militia base at the other side. Two stories tall and only eighty feet wide, it looked more like a substantial private residence than the center of planetary government—and the residence of the colony's chief executive. The building was plain in style and painted white. A circular drive had its apex near the two sets of double doors that served as main entrance.

A man in what appeared to be red and purple livery came out and opened the car door for Lon and his companions. Lon stretched, as unobtrusively as he could, and looked around while Tebba and Harley got out of the car behind him.

Although it was not quite sunset, the temperature had dropped noticeably. There was an edge of chill to the air, the breeze from the northwest a reminder that though winter might be gone, it was too soon to forget it completely. Lon breathed deeply, welcoming the coolness. The car had seemed stuffy.

The doorman opened the door to the mansion and held it while the three officers entered. They were met by another man in the same uniform. "Good evening, gentlemen. May I take your hats?"

That ritual completed, the butler led them down a corridor to the right. They were shown into a large parlor, where the governor, his wife, and a half-dozen other people were waiting—some of them individuals who had been at the spaceport to greet the mercenaries. No one wore military or police uniforms. There were more introductions and handshakes all around. Before those were finished, the three munitions experts from Dirigent were brought in, with Isadore Stanley, and there were more introductions.

"A drink, gentlemen?" Governor Sosa offered. "We can take refreshment while we wait for Colonel Henks and his staff."

A servant arrived on cue with a tray of drinks. Lon took one and sampled it—some sort of dry white wine, tart, almost sour. Wine was not Lon's favorite beverage, but he tried not to show any distaste. He knew he did not have to consume much. He nodded to the governor, as if to compliment the wine. The governor smiled broadly.

"So, Captain," he said, "what do you think of our militia compound?"

"Impressive, Governor," Lon said. "The exteriors appear true to their Terran antecedents, but on a much grander scale, larger than any of the reconstructions I saw on Earth. And the interiors lack nothing of modern convenience.''

Lon noted the point at which Sosa lifted an eyebrow. He was expecting the governor's next question.

''You've been to Earth?''

''I was born there, Governor, eastern North America.''

''Most interesting, Captain. I don't believe we've had any settlers come to Bancroft from Earth in at least fifty years. We've been left pretty much to our own resources, as far as growing our population base. Our contacts with the mother world have fallen dramatically since Union and Buckingham became better-paying, and more congenial, markets for our raw materials. Earth wants everything at prices that amount to thievery.''

''I've heard that elsewhere, Governor,'' Lon said, nodding. He had, on virtually every world he visited that had any communication at all with Earth. ''They want everything they can get but can't—or won't—pay full value.''

''They tell us it is our *duty* to subsidize the billions of people on Earth, that it is a debt that time, distance, and generations cannot lessen,'' Sosa said, warming to the topic. ''They think we should impoverish ourselves for their benefit.'' He shook his head. ''We will not live as slaves for anyone here. It's not as if Earth has done anything for *us* since our ancestors arrived on Bancroft.'' The governor shrugged, then used a continuation of the gesture to reach for a fresh drink from a passing tray.

''I do understand Earth's problems,'' Sosa said after sampling the new drink. ''With eight billion people on the world and so few natural resources left, they have to look for anything they can find, anywhere. But they need to trade value for value.''

Governor Sosa turned his attention to the two lieutenants then, and Mrs. Sosa led Lon over to some of the local notables.

•   •   •

Forty-five minutes later there was still no sign of Colonel Henks and his senior officers. A couple of times a servant had come in and whispered something to the governor. Sosa had looked moderately annoyed each time and had whispered instructions back. But he did not offer explanations to his guests.

"I've got the distinct feeling that there's something going on that doesn't sit well with the governor," Tebba said softly during one of the rare occasions when he and Lon managed to be alone, away from any of the Bancrofters. "Where the hell are the militia people?"

"Your guess is as good as mine, Tebba," Lon whispered back. "They must have a damn good reason for being late to a formal dinner with the governor."

"Something tells me the reason is going to be a pain in the ass for us."

"Yeah," Lon said. "Supper might be absolutely ruined by the time we get to eat."

Tebba snorted and moved off to find a drink. Lon was still nursing the first glass of wine he had taken. The glass was more than half full. A couple of minutes later, Harley came over to Lon.

"If I had known supper was going to be so late, I'd have had a snack before we left," he said, glancing around nervously to make certain that no one could overhear.

Lon smiled. "I doubt it will be much longer. If the rest of the guests don't show up soon, I imagine the governor will decide to go ahead and start the meal without them."

He did not find out if that was the case. He had scarcely finished speaking when four men in dress uniforms, not overly gaudy but . . . distinctive, were shown into the parlor.

Governor Sosa broke away from the conversation he was holding and moved toward the newcomers. Lon and his lieutenants did likewise, with less dispatch.

"Captain Lon Nolan, this is Colonel Daniel Henks, the commander of our constabulary militia."

The two men shook hands. "Captain Nolan, my executive officer, Lieutenant Colonel Digby Rose, and my battalion commanders, Major Wes Crampton and Major Ace Alon." Each man nodded smartly as he was introduced.

Lon introduced his two platoon leaders. Before the conversation could get any farther, a servant entered the parlor and announced, "Dinner is served."

Everyone migrated toward the dining room. Colonel Henks moved ahead quickly and took the governor aside. There was a hurried conversation between them, conducted in whispers, punctuated by frowns.

Lon was seated directly across the banquet table from Colonel Henks, just a couple of seats from Governor Sosa's place at the head of the table. As soon as everyone was seated, three servants came in bearing trays and set the appetizer course in front of the guests. It wasn't until after they had finished that Lon had a chance to speak to Henks again.

"I trust there's no serious difficulty, Colonel?"

"A minor problem, Captain," Henks said over a brief frown. "As head of security services, there was a crime scene I had to inspect in Long Glen, a village about forty miles from here. That merely took longer than I expected."

The colonel's tone was easy to read. He did not want to discuss the matter. Lon did not press.

10

Colonel Henks did not wish to waste an entire day to sort out the details of the training program. He and Lon talked for a few minutes after the governor's dinner ended, long enough to decide that the physical conditioning would start first thing in the morning—calisthenics and a two-mile run.

"My men have been getting some conditioning the past two weeks," Henks said, "but they're certainly not to the peak I expect of them, and your people will want to run their own evaluations, in any case."

"Fair enough, Colonel," Lon replied. "My men need a good workout as well after the trip here from Dirigent. I had planned already to have them out working in the morning."

"Then we can go over your training requirements, Captain, the facilities you think we need, schedules, that sort of thing. I'm anxious to bring my people up to speed as quickly as possible."

"We'll bring them along just as fast as they're capable of, Colonel, I promise you that. Three months gives us plenty of time to get your thousand men through a solid training course and help you pick out a cadre to train others when you need them. Once we get things moving, Lieutenant Girana and I will focus on the tactical training for your officers and noncoms, and Lieutenant Stossberg will do the direct day-to-day running of the other training. We've done this before, Colonel," Lon added, sensing that Henks needed some reassurance. "And the Corps has had time to develop a very efficient curriculum."

Back at the militia barracks that night, Lon found Weil Jorgen waiting. He was sitting on the low porch in front of the barracks, smoking a cigar.

"Thought I'd best find out what the schedule's going to be for tomorrow," Weil said.

"We start at reveille," Lon told him. He gave him his instructions, in line with the earlier conversation with Colonel Henks. "Find out what our trainees are made of. Tebba, Harley, and I will be out as well. The three of us, you, and the platoon sergeants will space ourselves around to get a good look at the conditioning of the militiamen. The squad leaders can look after our people."

"We all need to get a little more exercise than we did aboard ship," Weil said.

"Yes, we do," Lon agreed. "We'll work it in, one way or another. After breakfast, figure on starting training on close-order drill and inspection of the local weapons. We're going to have to get a few of those so we can evaluate them before we get to heavy gunnery training."

They talked for a few minutes longer, then Lon went inside, and up to his room. He was tired, ready for bed, but he had work left to do before he could sleep. He opened his complink and linked into the Bancroft news net. He wanted to find out just what had happened at Long Glen, and what else was happening that might affect the contract.

What he learned did not ease his sleep.

"I read about your trouble in Long Glen," Lon told Colonel Henks the next morning. They were in the colonel's office and Lon had just finished sketching out the general format of the training curriculum. It was time for a break.

"A few people have decided that it's easier to let

others do the work of mining and then just take the minerals,'' Henks said, frowning. ''They've gotten bolder of late.''

''Six people killed, another twenty wounded, and half a village shot to pieces sounds more serious than that, Colonel,'' Lon said. ''I know you haven't asked for help on this, and it's not part of our contract, but do you mind if I offer a few thoughts on the matter?''

Henks hesitated before he said, ''I'd greatly appreciate it if you can offer some help, Captain. It's largely because of these bandits that our government has gone to the expense of establishing this constabulary militia to augment the law enforcement we had before.''

''Well, I think you *are* moving in the right direction with that, Colonel. Attacks of this sort are not within the scope of most traditional police forces. The first thing that came to mind when I read the reports of these bandit raids was, What do they do with the ores and so forth they steal? Unless they have a way to funnel it back into the legitimate trade flow, they must have their own ways of getting the goods off-world. Either way, if you cut them off from their pipeline, you take the profit out of it for them, force them out of business.''

Henks started pacing, talking while he walked. ''We have been investigating that end of it for nearly a year, Captain. It wasn't difficult to see that they had to have some way to realize a profit from the raids. Basically, we can account for the origin of every ounce that we ship to market legitimately, right back to which hole in the ground it came out of. There is a chance that we might miss small amounts, or that a few producers might be in league with the raiders, but that couldn't possibly account for all of the thefts.''

''Other ways to get it off-world?'' Lon prompted.

''We run into certain practical difficulties there, Captain. We're simply not equipped to police space around Bancroft. We don't have a single spacecraft of our own, only a small fleet of relatively old shuttles to ferry things to and from interstellar transports in low orbit. And we don't have enough satellites in orbit to give us reliable, continuous coverage of even the settled portions of the world. Someone could park a transport so it would be occulted by our moon and slip long-range shuttles in past the little surveillance we do have without trouble. Hell, they could run a hundred flights a year in and never have to worry much about detection."

"I can offer one bit of concrete help on that, Colonel, at least while we're here. Our two transports maintain continuous surveillance of space around them as it is. I'll alert the skippers about the possibility and have them relay any sightings to us here. Maybe just the presence of two armed transports will be enough to stop any landings for the duration of the contract. And if a ship does come in, we might at least be able to identify where it comes from."

"Thank you, Captain. We would be most grateful," Henks said.

"Glad to help." That was the truth. Lon was happy to have a way to assist the locals without additional cost to the Corps. The goodwill that could build might be most valuable in the future—and not just on Bancroft. "Now, we'll dig right in to our primary job, getting your people ready to solve the problem on the ground."

Bancroft's constabulary militia was organized in ten companies of a hundred men and officers. Not all of the men were raw recruits. Nearly a fifth had served in the BCM's predecessor, known as security rangers. They had provided the cadre around which the BCM was built—officers and senior noncoms—and formed one entire company of the new force. That company had gone to Long Glen with Colonel Henks the day of the Dirigenters' arrival on Bancroft. Lon found out only later that they had pursued the raiders for several hours, which was why the colonel had been late to dinner at Government House.

"We'll accelerate the training of your veteran company, Colonel," Lon told Henks shortly after he learned about it. "Work with them on pursuit tactics. You can use them as a strike force, a rapid response team, especially if you can earmark one of your shuttles for their use. You could have them on the ground at the site of a raid quickly then."

"That's how I've been using them," Henks said. "And, most times, having a shuttle standing by won't be a problem. It's only when we have a transport overhead for loading that we need all of them at once, and the way the schedule breaks down, we're not likely to have a ship in until very nearly the end of your stay here."

In less than a week, the training was running as smoothly as if this were just one more class passing through a boot camp that had been in operation for years. Obstacle courses, firing ranges, sand-filled pits for hand-to-hand combat instruction, and the other essential training sites were quickly outfitted by civilian and militia labor under the direction of the Dirigenters. The BCM received new equipment, helmets with built-in night-vision systems and radios, and camouflage uniforms suitable for the terrain where they would be used.

After four weeks, the men of Bancroft's constabulary militia were starting to look and act like real soldiers. Some of the stress lines on Colonel Henks' face started to fade.

"I never thought I'd see this much progress so fast, Captain," he told Lon during one of their daily conferences on the state of training.

"It's early days yet, Colonel, but they are doing well," Lon said. "I've seen boot camp classes on Dirigent that didn't look this good so soon. You can be proud of your men, Colonel, and my hat is off to whoever devised the process that selected them."

Henks smiled, a rarity in Lon's experience. "We had our choice of men, Captain. We put out a call for volunteers and had more than four thousand responses. A lot of men who had worked in the mines, or who were looking forward to a lifetime working in them, were anxious for any alternative. We want to build a professional force, not just a ragtag group of volunteers who'll just come forward—maybe—when they're needed.''

Two days later, Lon had a chance to see how some of the trainees could function in a real situation.

The alarm came in just after dawn, while instructors and trainees were at their daily calisthenics. The mining camp known as Three Peaks had been raided during the night. Casualties were heavy, but the totals were unknown yet. It had taken the survivors nearly three hours to repair their communications antenna to get news of the raid out. Colonel Henks sent his rapid response team running for weapons and field gear.

"We've got the shuttle alerted," he told Lon. "By the time we get to the spaceport, the pilots will be aboard and have it ready for takeoff."

"You have room for a couple of observers, Colonel?" Lon asked.

"Glad to have a couple of your lads aboard, Captain."

"I had myself in mind, along with one of my platoon sergeants," Lon said.

Henks nodded. "The trucks will be here to take us to the port in six minutes," he said after looking at his watch.

"We'll be ready." Lon turned and started looking for Phip Steesen. When he spotted Phip, Lon whistled and gestured to draw his attention, then made a pumping motion with his right arm to indicate that Phip should double-time to him.

"You've got four minutes to get in battledress and grab your rifle and ammo," Lon said. "We've got a little observation to do. I'll meet you at the trucks when they come in."

"How many of us?" Phip asked.

"Just you and me and Colonel Henks's rapid response company. Let's get moving."

Both men trotted toward their barracks, almost turning it into a race. Lon was the first up the stairs and to his room. The time he had given Phip was scarcely enough for Lon, even though everything was laid out, ready to grab. He did get back out of his room and started down the stairs before Phip started running along the corridor above him.

"What the hell's going on?" Phip asked when they got back outside. The trucks were just coming through the entrance to the compound, moving slowly. There was no need to run now.

"Raiders hit a mining camp called Three Peaks. The colonel is taking his strike team to try to pick up the trail. We're going along to see how they handle themselves."

"How much lead time do the bad guys have?" Phip asked.

"Three hours now. I don't know how far we are from the scene. Figure another half hour by the time we get on the ground at Three Peaks."

"Something tells me the best we can hope for is that they won't find anything they can follow and come back without contact," Phip said. "It could get dicey if the raiders stick around to ambush the cops rushing to the scene. How many of them are we talking about, anyway?"

"No idea at all," Lon said. "I doubt even Colonel Henks could make a good estimate yet. But my own guess would be fewer than twenty. Anything above that could be hard to support in the wild."

"Not if they've got contacts to get their loot off-world," Phip said. "They could have an army out there."

"Then the sooner we find out, the better. I'll alert *Tyre* to have a shuttle ready to come down and bail us out if necessary. That make you feel better?"

"Poco," Phip said. The musical direction for "a little" had entered the slang of the Corps only in the past couple of years. Lon wasn't certain how that had happened, or why.

The company that formed Colonel Henks's strike force was double-timing toward their buses, rifles at port arms. Henks and Major Crampton were already in place, apparently ready to go along with their militiamen.

Lon saluted when he reached the militia commander. "Colonel, Major. I believe you both know Platoon Sergeant Phip Steesen." Both officers nodded.

"We're starting to get a few more details about the raid," Henks said, speaking softly to the Dirigenters while his troops started to file aboard the four buses that had pulled up. The report is that we have fifteen confirmed dead and another dozen wounded. That's virtually everyone who was at the camp, as far as I can make out."

"You have medical response on the way as well, Colonel?" Lon asked.

"They'll take off thirty seconds after we do, a full trauma team, and every portable trauma tube in Lincoln," Henks said. He gestured toward the nearest bus. "It's time to get aboard."

The convoy of buses raced across Lincoln to the spaceport, driving right out onto the field and next to the first of two shuttles waiting with engines already warming up. The militia company moved through the two entrances to its shuttle at a jog. Lon, Phip, and the two militia leaders followed at a brisk walk. As soon as they were aboard, the hatches were sealed.

"Our seats are there, at the front," Henks said, pointing.

The accommodations were not the equal of those in a DMC shuttle, but this craft was designed more for hauling inert cargo than people. The militiamen sat in web seats that folded down from the bulkheads. They were certainly not sturdy enough to keep passengers safe during the high-speed maneuvers that DMC shuttles routinely used during combat contracts, and just rendezvousing with a ship in low orbit would be uncomfortable—if not dangerous—for passengers. The shuttle was built low and wide, using the expansive underside of the fuselage for lift.

"How far is Three Peaks, Colonel?" Lon asked as the shuttle started racing toward takeoff speed. He had the faceplate of his helmet up so he could talk to the militia commander. The new helmets the Bancrofters used were nowhere near as sophisticated as DMC gear— that would take longer to achieve—and they did not share any radio channels yet.

"One hundred thirty miles, to the southwest," Henks said. He had to raise his voice to be heard over the thunderous noise of the shuttle's twin jets. "We'll need twenty minutes to get there. One of the more isolated of our mining operations. Just offhand, I think there are only two farther away from the main towns, and one of those is on a large island in the tropics, more than a thousand miles away."

Lon took out his mapboard, a specialized complink that all DMC officers and sergeants carried, and unfolded it. He keyed in a few commands. "Can you point Three Peaks out to me, Colonel?" he asked, moving the mapboard so the other could see it.

Henks took the unit and looked at it for a moment. It was the first time he had seen one in use. He had to locate Lincoln first, then moved his finger along the screen. "There," he said finally, tapping the screen.

Lon took it back and adjusted the scale, centering the display on the mining camp. At maximum magnification the buildings of Three Peaks, and three separate mine openings, were visible.

"How do you manage that, Captain?" Henks asked.

"Direct observation from our ships, Colonel. Anything in line of sight can be updated continuously, day or night."

"Can you find the raiders with that?"

"Not likely, Colonel, unless they're awfully damned careless. If they're under cover of trees we wouldn't have a chance, and that area seems to be pretty well forested. Other than that, we could only track them if they were actively using electronics."

"We've tried spotting them with electronic emission detectors from the air and on the ground, without luck," Henks said. "Either they don't use them or we've just never been close enough to catch them using them. I'm not sure what the range on our gear is, but it couldn't match this, I'm sure."

"To get full use from this, you'd need a few satellites to give you coverage and feed it to a ground station. The equipment is available from Dirigent, Colonel. It's something you might want to consider for the future." Years before, Lon had gotten over any embarrassment at touting Dirigent's exports. It was part of the job.

"How do you plan to deploy, Colonel?" Lon asked when they were halfway through the flight.

"The landing strip is right next to the camp. Only level space around that will hold shuttles, and we had to blast quite a bit of rock out of the way for that. The men will exit the shuttle and move out to secure the perimeter of the strip and the camp. Then we'll see to the survivors . . . and find out what we can do, if anything."

The shuttle's approach was steep, the glide fast. Lon was glad that there were no monitors to show him the exterior view. He was nervous enough, thinking that certainly the pilot would botch this landing, come in too heavy to stop in the small landing zone without badly shaking his passengers. Lon held his breath through the last thirty seconds.

There was a jolt as the shuttle's wheels touched the ground and the pilot reversed thrust on the jets to brake the vehicle quickly, but the landing was not nearly as hairy as Lon had feared it would be. *The other shuttle will have even less room to come in,* he thought.

By that time the two doors were open and the militiamen were filing out of the shuttle. They did not move as smartly as Lon's men would have, and there was a moment's hesitation outside as they formed up into squads and platoons. But getting organized did not take as long as it might have with amateurs, and in just over a minute they were trotting off toward their initial assignments.

"That's something you might want to spend some training time on later, Colonel," Lon said. "Getting the men out and into operation faster. It may not be something you'll do often, but the day might come when cutting thirty seconds off at the start could be important."

Henks nodded, but it was clear that he was not paying much attention. He had more immediate concerns. His first glance outside was to see that the second shuttle, the one carrying the medical team, was on the ground. Its hatches had not been opened yet, but Lon decided that was prudent—waiting to make certain that the area was secured before exposing noncombatants.

Lon scanned the entire area quickly, lowering the faceplate on his helmet so he could make use of its magnification and camera. The exteriors of all the buildings showed bullet holes, but what Lon was interested in was seeing that there was no evidence of ordnance larger than rifles or pistols. There were no blasts that could have been caused by rockets or explosives, and he did not see the characteristic scorch marks an energy weapon, a beamer, would have left.

One man showed himself in the doorway of one of the buildings—cautiously at first, just looking past the side of the open door. Then he came out. He was dressed in dirty work clothes, and there was blood on his left arm. The man came a few feet away from the building and stood there, waiting for someone to come to him.

"Did you bring doctors?" he asked, his voice weak, as Colonel Henks and the two Dirigenters moved toward him. "Two more men have died." Almost as an afterthought, he added, "My brother Jim was one of them." Then he collapsed, crumbling to the dirt before anyone could reach him.

Lon got to the man first and felt the side of his neck. He was relieved to feel a pulse, weak and thready but still there. The second shuttle had opened up and several people were running toward the buildings. One of them came to the aid of the injured man.

"We'll have a look around on our own, Colonel, if you don't mind," Lon said, gesturing to include Phip. "Keep out of the way while your medics work."

Henks nodded absently. He stayed near the fallen man just long enough to see the medics start to treat him, then headed toward the doorway the man had come through. Major Crampton had already moved off with one of the platoons, toward a trail that led downhill, into the forest.

Lon gestured for Phip and they went off in the direction in which Crampton had gone.

"They got hit hard here, Lon," Phip whispered. "Automatic rifle fire, large-caliber stuff, like the rifles the militia uses." The Bancroft weapons used 8.5mm ammunition, a full millimeter larger than Dirigenter rifles.

"We'll try to recover a slug," Lon said. "The lab boys back home might be able to tell where it was made." He shook his head. "Elephant guns." He did not have to explain the reference. Phip had heard it before.

"We going into the woods after them?" Phip asked.

Lon shook his head again. "If you mean you and me, no. Let's walk the perimeter up here. Crampton headed off this way, as if he thought it were the only possible route raiders could have taken. I want to see for myself."

The camp was situated on a broad shelf along the side of a moderately steep hill. Lon's mapboard told him they were only fourteen hundred feet above Bancroft's sea level, so it could not be called a mountain. The three peaks that gave the camp its name were obvious, three broken heights along the ridge at the southwestern side of the camp. The cleared level area was some two thousand feet long but nowhere more than a hundred wide.

"Doesn't look like it's too steep for armed men to climb anywhere along the edge," Phip said as they walked toward the side of the camp area. "Plenty of trees to help out, and all. We could sneak the whole battalion straight up the side and get out the same way."

"Maybe, but if there weren't guards posted, the raiders wouldn't need to sneak up the hard way. They could walk straight up that road."

"Must have had to haul equipment up that way originally to clear this," Phip said. "If everything comes in and goes out by air now, they wouldn't have any use for a ground route."

"There's nothing below, no town or village," Lon said. "Henks told me the mining crews spend a month up here, then rotate home for a month. It's just workers, no families."

"I guess that's good, under the circumstances," Phip said, turning to look back toward the buildings. "No women and kids getting massacred."

"Just widows and orphans," Lon said under his breath. He wasn't certain that Phip had heard.

They continued to walk the perimeter. Squads of militiamen had been there before them, setting up observation posts and looking for evidence that the raiders might have come or gone by a route other than the cleared roadway along the side of the hill. Men with powered binoculars scanned the valley and the opposite slope slowly, looking for any trace of the raiders.

On the other side of the clearing, Lon and Phip climbed up to a point between two of the peaks. There was a well-used path, and a militia squad had preceded them. Five men and their sergeant were standing together. Several of them were pointing at something on the reverse slope.

"Here, Captain Nolan," the sergeant—his name tag read GERMAN—said. "It looks like they came up over the top on this side. See." He pointed down the other side.

Lon moved closer to the edge and looked. The path leading down that slope seemed almost as easy as the one he had just come up, and it went farther. It finally disappeared into the forest a hundred feet below. Up close, though, Lon could see evidence that a lot of feet had walked it.

"Unless there's something down there that the miners visit regularly," Lon suggested. "You'd better tell your CO, though. It's something that needs to be checked out. Good job spotting it, Sergeant."

"I already radioed the news to my captain, Captain," Sergeant German said. "We've still got another fifty yards of the ridge to check, but I don't like to leave this until someone else gets here."

"Tell you what, Sergeant. The two of us will walk the rest of your area. Give us one man to radio anything we find. You and the rest of your lads can stay here until reinforcements arrive."

"Right, sir. Thank you." Sergeant German turned and shouted, "Murphy, you go with the captain."

Murphy came over quickly, looking between his sergeant and Lon. "Yes, sir," he said.

"We need you along in case there's anything to radio back," Lon explained. "We're going to walk the rest of the section your squad is responsible for."

While they walked, looking down the southwestern slope for any other trace of men passing, Lon radioed *Tyre* and spoke directly with the skipper.

"You have our two blips onscreen, Captain?" Lon asked. He had talked to *Tyre* before, to make sure that a shuttle would be ready, and to let the skipper know what was in the works.

"Clear as a bell, Captain."

"We're looking for any sign of armed men on either side of this hill, and we found indications of men either coming up or going down the southwestern slope. There's a road of sorts to the northeast, and there may be other passable routes as well. Do as close a scan of the area around this hill as you can, out to about twenty miles."

"Will do. I'm linked to *Sidon* right now. We've got enough angle to do a decent three-dimensional observation, but that still won't show us much under the trees unless they're using electronics.''

''I know. We've just got to see what we can rule in or out. Let me know as soon as you can.''

''We've got the scan running now, Captain. Nothing's jumping off the screen. That means no radios transmitting, no energy sources above the background noise, no active electronics. And the computers aren't picking out any motion that could be human. We'll keep watching, though.''

''Thanks, Captain,'' Lon said. ''I know it's a long shot, but I want to cover all bases.''

After he had signed off his link with *Tyre,* Lon switched to a channel that connected him just to Phip. ''I don't really expect anything to come of the scan, but wilder coincidences have happened before.''

''Sounds like you want us to tangle with these raiders,'' Phip said.

''No, but I would like to see just what the locals are up against. That intelligence might come in handy.''

11

"I hate to say this, Colonel, but as long as all you can do is react to these attacks, you might never be able to get on top of the problem,'' Lon said. He and Colonel Henks were alone in the colonel's office. It was ten days after the raid on Three Peaks, and another raid had taken place—two hundred miles from Three Peaks—just the day before.

''Right now, my options are unfortunately limited,'' Henks said. He appeared listless, tired, sitting slumped in his chair, without any of the military ''starch'' he normally displayed.

''From what I've been able to see, Colonel, you need to do one of two things. Either you have to infiltrate the raiders to learn about their numbers, sources of supply, and details of raids in advance, or station men at each possible target. Even then, your goal, at first, has to be obtaining prisoners so you can learn more about the gang or gangs you're up against.''

''I know that very well, Captain Nolan,'' Henks said with a slight edge. ''I've had agents investigating undercover, trying to find a route to the raiders that way, but with an absolute lack of luck. We don't know anything about them, and we haven't even been able to uncover reliable rumors. We don't know where or how they recruit people. We haven't been able to determine satisfactorily that the raiders are even recruited on Bancroft. Our databanks might not be one hundred percent accurate, but we haven't been able to discover enough people dropping out of the system to account for the minimum number of raiders we believe are operating. That leads to the strong possibility that they come from somewhere else, and receive their supplies the same way.''

''Which makes infiltration effectively impossible,'' Lon said. Slowly, Henks had provided Lon with more information about the raids that had taken place on Bancroft for more than a year.

Henks nodded. ''As for the other, well, I do plan to station platoons at each of the most likely targets, but not before they're fully trained. Until then, I might just be providing additional casualties. I don't want to waste men. The last several months, most of the miners have been armed. After the first few raids, the men started taking their rifles and shotguns along to the mines, establishing sentry posts and everything else, and it hasn't done a bit of good. The raiders strike fast and hard. So far, the miners haven't managed to capture or kill a single raider.'' He paused, his face molding itself into a pout. ''In fact, letting the miners arm themselves has been counterproductive. From the first time the raiders encountered armed opposition, they've been far more ruthless, as concerned with killing as stealing.'' He shrugged. ''But until I can provide a better alternative, I can't disarm the miners. They'd quit working. This way, at least they believe they have a chance.''

Lon walked over to the single window in the office and stood looking out for a minute. Then he turned back toward Henks.

''The problem may be bigger than you realize yet, Colonel,'' he said, speaking softly. ''I've had the combat intelligence center aboard *Tyre* analyzing the data we've been given or picked up from the local news net. The raids come too frequently, and at locations too widely separated for all of them to be the work of one gang. We haven't been able to spot any shuttles or trucks operating away from the towns and settlements, which limits the distance your raiders can travel per day and what they can carry, especially since some of the raids have netted more than a ton of metals or minerals. You haven't detected any local recruitment of men, any local source of food and other supplies for them. The raiders may well have off-world conduits for those as well as to ship out the stuff they've stolen.''

"You think we're being systematically raided by some other world," Henks said.

"It's almost a statistical certainty, Colonel. I had several of the bullets from the Three Peaks raid analyzed. They were all eight-point-five-five-millimeter rounds, and from that and the trace elements in the alloy, we believe that the planet of origin for the ammunition was Mars.''

"Mars? The Mars next out from Earth?"

"Yes. The colony on Mars is even larger than your population here, Colonel, and munitions is a major item of export for the Martians. Ninety percent of that trade is closely regulated by the old Confederation of Human Worlds on Earth—not the breakaway confederation on Union—but roughly ten percent of the weapons and ammunition manages to fall through the cracks, unaccounted for officially. Even accounting for operations we know that the Confederation winks at, perhaps seven or eight percent of the munitions is going places we don't know about.''

"So we're being raided either by Mars or by someone who is buying weapons and ammunition from there?''

"It's a damn good guess, Colonel, but you're going to need confirmation by capturing one or more of the raiders to question under drugs. Unless you get lucky and shoot down one of the transports that comes in to bring supplies and haul off booty.''

"There are nearly a hundred different targets here the raiders can hit, Captain. Some large, some small. We haven't found a pattern to the raids. The targets aren't always the most lucrative at any given moment. Two places have been hit twice. Others have been spared while villages and camps all around them have been hit. Even when we get these entire thousand men trained, I won't be able to garrison every possible target. And if the raiders scout their objectives before hitting, they can just avoid the ones with garrisons.''

"Bancroft is vulnerable, Colonel," Lon said. "That is going to remain true regardless of how this current problem is resolved. Until you have enough observation satellites in orbit to tell you whenever a ship enters the system, and you have the means to intercept any unauthorized ships, you're going to be easy pickings. That's the blunt truth. Your population base is relatively small, and you have opened a considerable number of areas for mineral exploitation. You don't belong to either branch of the Confederation of Human Worlds or to the Second Commonwealth, which means you can't count on outside protection.''

"Which is why we hired your people, and the munitions equipment that arrived with you, Captain Nolan," Henks observed. He straightened out, his depression partially offset by growing annoyance at having his world's vulnerabilities spelled out at such great length.

"Which is why you hired us," Lon agreed with an easy nod.

"I do know the problems, Captain," Henks said, his voice not quite as tense as it had been.

"I just want to be clear, Colonel. I didn't mean to imply criticism. Your problems aren't unique, and there are several ways you could tackle them. None can be guaranteed to be easy, or inexpensive. I can lay out the alternatives for you, but only your government can decide which—if any—of them to select.''

Henks grunted. "There is no political desire here to join either Commonwealth or Confederation. The empire-makers on Union are too heavy-handed. They're not looking for allies but subjects, slaves, just like the people on Earth. Alliance with the Second Commonwealth would be less onerous, but they do exact a small tax on trade goods, and our people are loath to surrender any measure of sovereignty. And we are simply not wealthy enough to buy or build even a single warship to patrol our system. That is unlikely to change any time in the next century. Observation satellites and perhaps half a dozen aircraft to intercept unauthorized landings are possible—perhaps in a decade, with considerable luck. Spending the money to hire enough ground troops, a warship, and a fighter squadron long enough to bring an end to this predation is out of the question. The possibility was discussed, and almost led to the dissolution of the government and a call for new elections. We were left with the only choice that remained politically and economically feasible, hiring mercenaries to train our own people. Which, I hasten to add, you have been doing most admirably, Captain. They're coming along much more rapidly than I dared to hope.''

''I agree,'' Lon said. ''In fact, with the accelerated training we've been giving your rapid response company, they'll be ready to begin operating independently within two weeks. And most of the other companies are ahead of schedule. If you have more recruits and the gear to outfit them, we can double up on some of the present units and start training perhaps another two hundred men. That fits within the scope of our contract, Colonel.''

''It would help,'' Henks said.

''I know you plan to increase the size of the BCM, run your own training courses after we leave, but we can give you a little push. It depends on how quickly you can assimilate recruits.''

''I would appreciate the boost, Captain. I'll see what the situation is.''

''If we start making preparations now, we could be ready to start training the new men in two weeks, when we graduate your rapid response unit.''

''Let's plan on it then, Captain,'' Henks said. ''I'm almost certain we can get authorization to recruit another two hundred men and have them ready to start training in two weeks. That'll be the midpoint of your contract, correct?''

"Correct, Colonel."

"You know, there's one thing that might do my people more good than anything else, Captain. To see one band of these raiders caught and hurt, by our own militia or by your men, to see that it is really possible."

"I understand that, but my discretionary powers are limited by our contract. I can't put any of my people into a combat situation without a rider to the contract and additional compensation. I do have the authority to negotiate that, if your government desires it . . . and we can find any of the raiders to hit."

"Just expressing a wish, Captain," Henks said. He did not *quite* sigh.

The people of Lincoln welcomed the Dirigenters warmly, and never gave the impression that they were only interested in getting back some of the money they were paying to have the mercenaries on their world. Even Camo Town never felt that comfortable. Lon was not extravagant with the number of passes he allowed his men. On average, it worked out to one night a week, and one weekend day every two weeks, that each man was allowed to go into town. The one rule Lon enforced was that his men should always travel at least in pairs, with each man responsible for the behavior of the others with him.

"We don't want anybody drunk and disorderly," Lon told them. "And even the best of intentions aren't always enough."

Lon even held himself to that rule, on the rare occasions when he left the militia base for an hour or two in town. One of the lieutenants or sergeants would go with him as escort.

"You know, even though this is the largest town on Bancroft, it feels more like Bascombe East than Dirigent City," Lon told Phip one evening near the middle of their three-month contract. Lincoln had gone from early to late spring. Temperatures were routinely warmer, hinting at summer's heat. Trees had reached their full plumage. There were always flowers in bloom.

It was Friday. The new class of recruits would begin training on Monday. Lon, Phip, and Dean were walking from the militia base to the nearest pub in Lincoln. Lon could not recall the last time the three of them had gone on pass together, on Dirigent or anywhere else. It gave him a comfortable feeling of well-being.

''They're just not used to fleecing soldiers efficiently,'' Phip said, chuckling. ''They give honest measure in their drinks, and more than honest measure with a meal.''

''Oh, you've bothered to waste time eating on pass?'' Lon asked, elbowing his friend.

Phip sighed expansively. ''Ah, the good old days aren't what they used to be. Not since you made me responsible for other men. I told you that you were ruining me.''

''You were ruined before he first landed on Dirigent,'' Dean said. ''You were born ruined.''

They were in uniform, so there were limits to the banter. None of the three could completely forget their professional relationship, the way they could—occasionally— in civilian clothes on Dirigent. And they were not totally off duty. Although they wore garrison uniforms and did not have battle helmets with them, each man had a pocket radio. They could be reached instantly at need.

A couple of times, local citizens called out greetings and waved in passing. When they entered the first pub, the bartender came out from behind his bar to lead them to the best available table in the public room, and offered the first round on the house.

''A man could get to enjoy this,'' Phip said after the bartender went for their drinks. ''Kinda makes me wish we could do more to help them than teach their lads how to fight.''

''Don't go spoiling for a fight, Phip,'' Lon said. ''Getting rid of their raiders could be a long and nasty job, and that's not what they're paying us for. Let's not talk about work this evening. We'll have a couple of drinks, a meal, and maybe stroll about a bit before we go back to the barracks and turn in.''

"You were a lot more fun before you got married."

"He's right," Dean said. He looked around. "You know, this world has a lot to offer. A lot of good people, and opportunity to have a good life. Be a nice place to settle down and raise a family."

"Don't tell me *you're* getting the itch now," Phip said.

Dean shook his head, then shrugged. "I don't know. Just an idle thought, I guess. But it seems they might welcome a few immigrants, men who could contribute to their constabulary militia." He took a long drink, then shook his head again. "I don't figure anything will come of it, but it's something to think about in the quiet hours."

Lon did not drink enough to get drunk, but when he started his second beer, he slipped a killjoy patch on his arm anyway. A killjoy would take a man from dead drunk to stone cold sober in minutes, neutralizing the alcohol in the bloodstream. The meal was good, the evening comfortable. Lon and his friends were on their way back toward the militia camp when Lon received a call from Colonel Henks.

"Captain, the governor would like to see you as soon as possible, preferably this evening."

"Very well. I'm in town now, about five minutes from the camp."

"Give me the location and I'll pick you up. Governor Sosa said it was urgent."

12

No one questioned the presence of Phip and Dean. The three Dirigenters were picked up within minutes and sped toward Government House with Colonel Henks. They were met at the door and led into the north wing of the building, to the left, and shown into the governor's office.

Roger Sosa was sitting behind a large desk of highly polished wood, leaning back, staring toward the upper panes of one of several large windows that covered most of one wall of the office. He was dressed casually. For a few seconds he did not seem to notice that anyone had come into his office.

"Come over and sit down," Sosa invited. He got up from his desk and met the military men at the more informal conversation area near the windows. Two leather sofas and several easy chairs surrounded a coffee table. Lon introduced his companions. The governor shook hands with everyone, then they sat.

Lon found himself directly across the table from the governor. Colonel Henks sat to the governor's left. Phip and Dean were at Lon's right.

"I apologize for interrupting your evening off, gentlemen," Sosa said once everyone was settled. "Captain Nolan, Colonel Henks described your recent assessment of our situation with me. Unfortunately, it agrees far too well with my own estimate. The colonel and I spent some time discussing the possibilities, and I then consulted with the legislative council. The losses we have suffered do limit our options, since the government's revenues are derived from the off-world sale of our metals and minerals, but as of this evening, I have legislative approval for amending our contract with your company, if you agree, Captain.''

''We're certainly open to negotiating additional assistance, Governor. Exactly what do you have in mind?'' Lon asked.

''A punitive strike against the raiders, providing a suitable target can be located. Since there might be several groups operating more or less independently, I hesitate to ask for the complete elimination of the, ah, problem. As you told Colonel Henks, that could be a far more ambitious project, beyond the capacity of the force you have here, and bringing in more mercenaries and the air and space strike capacity to back them up is, regrettably, far beyond what the council is prepared to fund.'' Sosa paused, glanced at Henks, then continued.

''These raids are killing our citizens, Captain. Since they started, we have had nearly a hundred killed and perhaps twice that many wounded. The personal suffering weighs more heavily than the financial losses we have endured in the same time, and those have been . . . considerable. The estimate is that the raiders have taken nearly three million pounds, to use the Commonwealth monetary standard, or about seven million Confederation dollars.''

Lon did a rough conversion to Dirigentan currency in his head. The figure he arrived at would be enough to hire a full regiment with supporting warships and Shrike fighters for two months. ''A considerable amount,'' he said, nodding.

''The political reality is that my government has to show that it can move effectively to protect our people and stop the raiding. Bluntly speaking, Captain, we need a victory, any kind of victory, against these raiders. A large segment of the public is beginning to lose confidence in us.''

I'll bet, Lon thought, but he did not let that reaction show on his face. Political reality drove many contracts.

"I do have the authority to negotiate a rider to our contract, within certain limits, Governor. I have to answer to the Council of Regiments back home, and be able to justify the terms and mission I agree to commit my men to. We would have to agree on a clearly definable mission, one that is possible and does not pose an inordinate threat to my men. The Corps does not like to waste men. That's not just a statement of pious theory. If our men can't feel confident that they have a damn good chance of coming back from any assignment, they're less likely to join the Corps, less likely to stay in."

Three hours later, Lon and the governor of Bancroft signed the rider to their contract.

"I'll give you a ride back to the barracks," Colonel Henks offered when the last formality was finished and the men had shared a drink.

"Thanks, Colonel," Lon said, "but I believe we'll walk. The cool air will help me clear my head and I can start thinking about how we're going to implement the new mission." Lon heard Phip's subdued groan but ignored it.

"You're in the wrong racket, Lon," Phip said once they were outside starting the long walk across Lincoln to the barracks.

"What do you mean?" Lon asked.

"You should be in business. The way you took the governor to the cleaners, you could be a millionaire in a year."

Lon chuckled.

"Look, I've never seen that side of you before," Phip said. "The way you were in there, whew."

"It's not the first time I was contract officer, and I've sat in on some that make this look as simple as ordering a round of drinks at the Dragon Lady. This was nothing, really. You should hear the dickering when they're talking about a full regiment, two or three warships, and a squadron or two of fighters."

"Yeah, well, I don't remember hearing of any contracts where we were promised a piece of the action. Ten percent of any of the stolen goods we recover?"

Lon let out a full-bodied laugh this time. "I did wing that. The governor was so concerned about the financial losses they're suffering, I let him think he was getting a break on the base price and snuck that in to cover it. Besides, it's ten percent of what we recover over and above the price of the additional services rendered."

"You think we've really got a shot at finding these raiders and hitting them?" Dean asked after the group had walked another block. "The ships haven't had any luck spotting them so far, have they?" There were few secrets within a unit on contract.

"Nothing certain," Lon admitted.

"Don't shine us, Lon. What's that supposed to mean?" Phip asked—just a breath before Dean could.

"Just what I said, nothing certain. But there have been a couple of blips that need closer checking. Now that we have the rider to our contract, I can authorize using *Sidon*'s shuttles for survey work in closer. We just might find something that way."

"You've been stonewalling the colonel the whole time we've been here?" Phip asked.

"Not at all. Before, it wasn't within my discretion to use the shuttles for offensive survey work unless I could justify it because of a clear threat to our people. I couldn't. Those things cost money to operate. We did everything we could for the Bancrofters before, and a couple of times I came close to crossing the line. This extra contract makes up for that."

"Especially if we recover a couple of tons of refined gold and platinum," Phip observed.

As soon as he got to his room in the barracks, Lon opened his complink and composed a message to send back to Dirigent with a copy of the rider to the contract and his latest report on the training mission. He spent thirty minutes writing about the new contract, taking considerable pains with the wording. His efforts would be reviewed by the Corps contract office and might well come up for debate in the Council of Regiments.

When he was satisfied, he linked through to the watch officer on the bridge of *Tyre*. "I'll need to speak with Commander Tanner and the skipper of *Sidon* first thing in the morning," Lon said after relaying the gist of the new contract.

"I can wake the captain now if it's necessary," the duty officer on *Tyre* said, though it was clear from his tone that he hoped it would not be.

"No, morning's soon enough for the conference. But I do need to get an MR on its way to Dirigent as quickly as possible," Lon said. A message rocket was the fastest way to send information between systems. An MR had its own Nilssen generator to jump through Q-space. That meant two weeks each way, but radio traffic required years to cross interstellar space—one year for each light-year of separation.

"I need the skipper's approval to send an MR."

"Well, then, I guess you'd better wake him. This does need to go out right away, the files I've just transmitted, and the mail that's accumulated since the last one," Lon said. "I'll be up for a bit yet, if Commander Tanner has any questions."

"Very well, Captain. I'll send the yeoman to his cabin now."

Lon called the duty officer aboard *Sidon* next, leaving an open link in case there was any comeback from *Tyre*. This time he simply told the duty officer that he would need to confer with Commander Freng in the morning, and mentioned the amended contract.

"The skipper just left the bridge, Captain Nolan," *Sidon*'s watch officer said. "I'm sure he's still awake, if you'd like to talk with him now."

"Very well." It was a matter of courtesy more than urgency, but courtesy did count. Although the skippers of the two ships technically outranked Lon, the fleet was only an ancillary arm of the Corps, and Lon *was* the contract officer for the operation. He had the authority to require support services from the ships.

Before Commander Freng came on the link, Commander Tanner was on the open link from *Tyre*.

"I just want to confirm what I was just told, Captain," Tanner said. "About the MR and about the new contract requirements."

"Sorry to disturb your sleep, Captain," Lon said. "Commander Freng will be joining us momentarily, since his watch officer said he was still awake. I had thought to confer with both of you in the morning. It was just the MR I thought should go out immediately."

"I sleep lightly away from Dirigent," Tanner said. "We might as well get this hashed out now."

As soon as Commander Freng joined the conference, Lon spent five minutes outlining the new mission he had negotiated with the Bancrofters. He also transmitted copies of the agreement to each skipper. Freng was the first to notice the clause about recovery of stolen material.

"A percentage?" he asked, breaking in on what Lon was saying. "You managed to get a percentage of what you find?" He laughed. "I swear I've never heard of that before."

Tanner was equally amused. It took the edge off being disturbed in the middle of the night.

"I'll get the first shuttle out running your survey right away," Freng said a minute later. "I'll have CIC calculate the search pattern based on what we've seen and the locations of the various raids."

"I appreciate it," Lon said. "We can wait for morning before we bring *Tyre*'s shuttles down to carry the men when we find a target. Unless we get something hot in the next couple of hours, I won't bother anyone before reveille. I'll just make sure our Charge of Quarters knows to alert me if you find anything."

The noise of two DMC shuttles coming in for a landing next to the militia camp was an extra in the morning, bringing even the slowest riser to instant alertness in the barracks Alpha Company inhabited. It was a sound that every man in the Corps was familiar with, and the surprise of having them land so close—instead of on the far side of town, at the spaceport—brought a rush of adrenaline to most of the men.

At reveille, Lon gave the entire company the basics of the amended contract. "We'll use three platoons for any operation, leave the schooling for the remaining platoon to handle while we're gone," he said. "First platoon will take the training mission, and Lieutenant Stossberg will remain with it." Lon paused and looked around. There was not much light yet. Reveille in Lincoln was scheduled for six o'clock, and sunrise that day was ten minutes later.

"I don't know when we'll be going out. That depends on how long it takes to find a target. But except for first platoon, we go on alert as of now. When *Sidon* finds us a target, we could go out on less than five minutes' notice. That means no passes until we get back."

The men were too disciplined for Lon to hear any moans. But he could imagine them.

"After breakfast, draw your weapons and give them a good cleaning. Make sure your helmet electronics are functional and the rest of your gear fit for the field. I do have one piece of good news," he added. "*Tyre* is retrieving an MR from home. That means we should have a mail call sometime this afternoon."

Lon watched for reactions after he dismissed the men, and sent them to breakfast. Only three men in the company had known anything about the change of plans before reveille—Phip, Dean, and the corporal from fourth platoon who had drawn the Charge of Quarters duty overnight.

"When did this all come about?" Tebba asked. He and Harley had both gone straight to Lon.

"We negotiated the new contract last night at Government House," Lon said. "I didn't expect to confer with *Tyre* and *Sidon* until this morning, but the way things worked out, we did that about oh-two-hundred. *Sidon*'s shuttles are running search patterns, looking for the raiders. *Tyre*'s boats, as you might have noticed, are here waiting for us.''

"This is going to be strictly a Corps operation?" Tebba asked. "Just *our* people?"

"It's going to be our operation," Lon said, nodding. "I'll offer to let Colonel Henks send observers along, maybe a squad from their rapid response company. They know the flora and fauna we might encounter, if nothing else. Local knowledge can't hurt. Besides, that one company is almost up to our standards."

"What about the training schedule here?" Harley asked. "With the new class reporting in Monday, and the way we've speeded up training for everyone else, asking one platoon to do the work of four is slightly on the ridiculous side."

"We make do, Harley. Co-opt Bancrofters from the rapid response company to proctor the field exercises. I'll make arrangements with Colonel Henks. This is the big one as far as the locals are concerned. They need something to show the voting public."

"Oh, it's like that," Harley said.

"Yes, it's like that," Lon agreed. "Now let's get something to eat."

"I can't give you a detailed plan of operations now," Lon told the men of the three platoons that had been selected for the attack on the raiders. Breakfast was over and Lon had gathered the men in front of their barracks. They were, mostly, sitting on the worn grass.

"We're flying blind for the present," Lon continued. "We don't know where we will be going in or when, or how stiff the opposing force will be. Until we locate a target, we can't even begin to devise the operation. When we do locate the enemy, we may have to do our planning in the shuttle on our way in. I know you don't care for that kind of improvisation. Neither do I. But it's all we have this time. On the plus side, the opposition is almost certainly amateur, as far as military operations go. They're pirates, out for booty. Individually, there may be a lot of mean SOBs, but they probably won't have a lot of unit cohesion. We hit them hard, they'll probably fall apart. They haven't faced hard-core professionals before. Of course, we can't count on them running for home.'' Lon smiled briefly.

"I have every confidence in you. You're experts, professionals in all the best senses of the word, and you've spent the last month and a half teaching others your skills. Whether you realize it or not, that's a damn good way to improve your own ability. You have to *think* about what you're teaching. Some of you have been on operations similar to the one we expect. Most of you have seen combat. The few who have never been on a combat contract have at least had your full training and you're surrounded by veterans. We'll see you through this.''

It was a comfortable day to be outside and inactive. There were scattered clouds in the sky and a refreshing breeze. The temperature would likely hit eighty by mid-afternoon, but it was just seventy as Lon paced back and forth in front of his men.

"I can't even tell you how long the wait might be. *Sidon*'s shuttles might locate a target for us within the next ten minutes. On the other hand, it might be ten days, two weeks, or more. I know. That's a real bitch. I hate waiting as much as any of you. It's still better than dropping out in the middle of nowhere with no idea where the opposition might be and stumbling around looking for them on the ground for ten days or a month, with no guarantee that we would ever get within a hundred miles of them.''

Waiting. At times, Lon thought that was worse than combat. Until memory reasserted itself. The most vivid memories came in sleep—the chaos, the horror, the smell of death, and the cries of dying men. The terror. The questions: *Why would a sane man ever do this vol-*

untarily? How can anyone choose this for a career? Lon had first asked himself those questions a lifetime before, during his first exposure to combat, on a colony world called Norbank. He still had no satisfactory answers, no explanation. He was not a native Dirigenter, raised from earliest childhood to accept that war was the world's business, that being part of the Corps—one way or another—was as much patriotic duty as practical necessity. And his old mantra, "All I ever wanted to be was a soldier," no longer seemed sufficient—especially since his son had started to echo it. For Lon, that desire had been born years before he had any experience of battle, before he knew what being a soldier really meant. And the rationalization that combat, deadly peril, filled only a small fraction of his days seemed an evasion.

Lon spent the rest of Saturday morning alone in his office, his complink hooked through CIC aboard *Tyre* to the shuttles running their search patterns. For the present, only one shuttle was flying at a time. They spelled each other, taking three-hour shifts. If—*when*—one of them found something interesting, the other shuttle might be brought in to permit better three-dimensional probing, with each craft standing off to the side, flying circular routes to give them the best penetration available.

It was lunchtime when Tebba Girana knocked and entered Lon's office without waiting for an invitation. He shut the door behind him and went over to Lon's desk.

"You should know that Harley thinks you saddled him with the stay-behind job because you don't think he's good enough for the operation," Tebba said softly. "He's still young and insecure enough that he needs reassurance."

Lon leaned back and sighed. "I should have thought of that myself, Tebba. Thanks for reminding me."

"You get to be fifty years old, you pick up on some things a little easier," Tebba said.

"Don't give me that crap," Lon said. He looked at

Tebba and grinned. Girana was indeed fifty, and his hair was beginning to show just a little gray. But that was the only visible sign of age, and it was almost by choice, Tebba refusing to maintain the cosmetic appearance of youth. The molecular health implant systems—the crowning achievement of nanotechnology, according to some—that everyone on all but the most primitive of colony worlds received at birth held the aging process at bay. Old age did not truly begin until after a person reached the century mark. Tebba Girana was as fit, mentally and physically, as he had been at twenty. And experience made him better.

"I'll talk to Harley after lunch," Lon said. "We all go eat, then you find something to do while we talk."

Lon did not mince words. "You wouldn't be here if you weren't fully qualified, Harley. There are reasons why I picked Tebba over you to go along on this punitive raid, but you not being good enough isn't one of them. Forget that crap. Don't go feeling sorry for yourself. Sure, experience is part of it. Tebba has been at this work longer than either you or me. And he knows how I work and think, doesn't have to stop and ask questions in the middle of trouble. Hell, he's been close by to keep me out of trouble since I joined the Corps. But you're not being left back here to twiddle your thumbs and teach recruits which left foot to step off with. If we manage to get our butts in a sling, it's going to be up to you and first platoon to bail us out. You and the Bancrofters we've been training. And no matter how good they've shown themselves to be, I trust you and first platoon more than their rapid response company."

Harley shrugged. "I didn't question the arrangement, Captain. I do know how to obey orders. But yes, I was wondering why I was being left behind. It's hard to get that experience you talk about from the sidelines. Tebba is second in command. It seemed natural that he should be the one to stay back, more in line with the manual."

"Most times you'd be right, Harley," Lon said. "About

not risking the CO and XO at the same time. Hell, going by the book, I could make a damn good case for staying behind myself and sending the two of you off.'' The thought *Then why the hell don't you?* flickered through his head and was banished automatically, almost without notice.

''But we're here to help the Bancrofters. They're paying dearly. If I don't go, they might suspect that we're not giving them full value. I'm taking Tebba instead of you because he does have all that experience. He's been in the Corps since long before you were born. You'll have your chances, Harley, probably more than you want.'' Lon paused, then added, ''Trust me on that.''

''Waiting is a pain in the butt, Captain,'' Harley said.

Lon grinned. ''Tell me something I don't know.'' He hesitated a second, then said, ''You might pass along the word that we've got all the mail downloaded from the MR. It should be ready for distribution shortly.''

A little later, Lon called Tebba, Weil Jorgen, and the three platoon sergeants who would be going along into his office.

''There's no word yet from the shuttles,'' Lon started, to get the unasked but unavoidable question out of the way. ''There are a couple of things I want to cover now. When we go out, I'll double as platoon leader for second platoon and keep Weil with me unless circumstances dictate otherwise. If it becomes necessary to split third and fourth platoons, I might use Weil as acting platoon leader for one of them. The rest of headquarters squad will stay behind, but we'll take the medics for all four platoons.

''That's about all we can deal with in regard to the operation. We'll carry all the ammo and food we can, since we don't know what we'll need. If this goes on very long, we should be able to bring in supplies by shuttle since we're not facing an organized military force.

''The men are going to get antsy very fast with this

waiting, especially since they can't go anywhere. Do your best to keep on top of that. Don't let tempers flare. Run inspections, put them to recleaning weapons, whatever you have to do. But unless things get . . . testy, let them rest and get extra meals in, just as if we were on ship waiting for a combat landing.''

"Sir?" Platoon Sergeant Wil Nace of fourth platoon raised a hand halfway. "No idea at *all* how long this waiting will go on?"

Phip and Dav Grott, third platoon's sergeant, nodded. The question interested them as well.

"Not a clue, Wil. The shuttles are looking for the proverbial needle in a haystack, and they don't even know where the farm is. If this goes on more than three or four days, I'll have to start rotating one platoon out at a time, play musical chairs with the arrangements, and I don't want to do that. Too much chance for confusion." All of the men in the room had been with Lon since his cadet days. He had fought beside each of them, and he trusted them implicitly. And they trusted him equally.

"If we're not facing pros, we might pick up an extra advantage if we go in at night," Phip said. "That could be like making them fight with one eye tied behind their backs."

"Don't get overconfident, Phip. Our reliable intelligence about the opposition is effectively zero. We don't know anything more than the caliber of rifle they use."

"I've read all the reports by the survivors, Captain, same as you," Phip said. "There hasn't been one mention of anyone seeing night-vision gear, even when the raiders struck at night."

"Not conclusive. They might just not want the Bancrofters to know they have that capability," Tebba said before Lon could say essentially the same thing. "Don't let the opposition know any more than you have to."

"I've got a different question, Captain," Weil Jorgen said. "Since we're not going against regular military units—so far as we know—and most likely won't face tanks or aircraft, do we take the usual complement of rockets and launchers along?''

Lon hesitated. It was a question he had not considered. ''You may be right, Weil, but I don't want to go in without any protection against air or armor. Let's say one launcher and rocket load per platoon. Anything comes up that takes more, we'll have to rely on the shuttles. Any other questions?''

''Not a question, exactly,'' Weil said. ''But the mail is ready for distribution.'' The system was not as complicated as it seemed. Individuals, on either end, wrote their letters on message chips. Those were collected and transcribed to the larger message chips that could be included in an MR's minimal payload, to be transcribed back to individual chips on the other end, suitable for playback on complink or portable reader. ''I've got the bundles for each platoon on my desk next door. Captain, I've transferred your stuff right to your complink—personal mail and a couple of official messages you might want to look at while you've still got us all here.''

Lon nodded, then opened his portable complink and keyed up a directory. He scanned the list, noting two personal letters—a very long file from Sara and a shorter one from Junior. There were also a number of official documents from Corps headquarters. Lon stopped as one of the files caught his attention. He called that file up and quickly scanned the screen.

''I'll be damned,'' he whispered.

''What is it?'' Tebba asked.

''Take a look for yourself,'' Lon said, turning the complink so Tebba could read the screen.

Tebba read, then looked at the others in the room. ''Gentlemen, may I introduce Major Nolan to you?'' he said, chuckling. ''As soon as we return to Dirigent, he will be relieved as commanding officer of Alpha Company and assigned to staff duties at battalion. But the promotion was effective fifteen days ago.''

''Tell them the rest of it,'' Lon said when Girana stopped.

"There's plenty of time for that later," Tebba said.

Lon snorted. "When we return to Dirigent, Tebba will relieve me as commanding officer. His promotion to captain will be effective the same day."

The meeting dissolved in dual rounds of congratulations.

Lon sat on the edge of his bed and held his complink on his lap. It had been seventeen days since the last message rocket had arrived from Dirigent, seventeen days since he had read the last letter from Sara. He was anxious to turn directly to the new letter from her, and the letter from his son, but Lon forced himself to read through all of the official dispatches first. There might be something important in those—more important than the two promotions.

The time lag of interstellar communications meant that conversations were extremely disjointed. Some of the official documents referred to reports Lon had sent to Dirigent nearly six weeks earlier, and they could not take into account anything he had sent less than a month before. And it would be at least two weeks before Dirigent could receive any response from him—*if* he ordered another MR dispatched at once. Unless it was vital, he would not, since he had just sent one out early that morning.

He needed a half hour to read through or listen to all of the files from Corps. There was nothing requiring immediate action, nothing critical to the mission. Satisfied, Lon turned to his personal letters then, starting with the letter from Sara.

Sara's letters were almost journals. She tended to speak at least a few lines every day while Lon was on contract, telling him what the children had done, how her day had gone, news and gossip around the Corps. If she recorded her narrative while the children were home and awake, they would be sure to appear onscreen at least briefly. Angie might sit on her mother's lap throughout the session. Some days an entry might go on at great length if there was a lot to tell—or if Sara simply wanted to ''talk'' to him at length. It was a way for Lon to feel as if he were not missing so much. But it wasn't *quite* the same as being home. Occasionally Lon found himself talking back to his wife's image on the screen . . . until he realized what he was doing. Then he might sigh and shake his head, or chuckle at the lapse.

Three days before the end of the letter, Sara managed to surprise Lon. ''There is something going on that might interest you,'' she said at the beginning of that day's entry. ''Kalko Green has become something of a cause here. I don't know *exactly* how it got started, but there is a growing movement here intending to free him, or at least get his sentence reduced. A petition drive directed at the General, people all over the nets arguing for a pardon, or commutation of his sentence to time already served—even though it has only been a few months. There is a measure of . . . outrage, I guess I have to say, at the way Sergeant O'Banion had behaved. Folks are saying that it is more of an injustice that Green was imprisoned than it was that O'Banion was killed. Two members of the court-martial have already added their names to the petition. It would help the cause if more members of the court-martial supported this movement. What do you think?''

When Sara passed on to the next topic, Lon paused the playback and stared at her now motionless figure on the screen. *Pardon? Commutation?* he asked himself. Either one would be, so far as he knew, virtually unheard of in the Corps, though it was within the scope of the General's executive authority.

I'll have to think about that, Lon decided. *I wish she had told me which members have already signed the petition.* He recalled wishing that there had been some way to avoid convicting Green. But to try overturning the verdict? Lon couldn't get it out of his mind. A couple of times after he resumed the playback of Sara's letter, he found his thoughts drifting, found himself missing what she had to say.

Junior's letter was much shorter, recorded in two bursts of energy. The boy talked too fast and had difficulty staying still enough to avoid popping out of frame over and over. He went on at some length about his excitement over his father's promotion to major. Sara had mentioned that, too; three days before the order was issued, she spoke of it as an accomplished fact. In the second of Junior's sessions, he had something else to be excited about.

"We just got back from looking at our new home," Junior said, bouncing around so constantly that he was partially out of frame far more than he was completely within it. As a major, Lon would be entitled to larger, somewhat more comfortable, housing. "It's *huge*," Junior said, spreading his hands as far apart as he could get them. "Angie and I can each have our own rooms, and they're all so *big*. The house is two blocks from here, right down by the bus stop. I want to move right away, but Mama says we have to wait until you get home. Please hurry home, Daddy."

Sara. Kalko Green. Junior. Lon set his complink aside after he had finished watching his son's letter for the second time. The boy was always so excited about everything. Lon' smile was short-lived, though. Junior had also reiterated his desire to be a soldier just like his father. "I'm going to be the General someday," he had boasted, puffing out his chest by taking in a deep breath and holding. it. "Then I can live right there in the Headquarters building."

I think I'd rather see you living above the Winking Eye and working in the pub, Lon thought. *A safer life, and saner.* But it wouldn't do any good to say that to the boy, not now. Lon could almost hear the inevitable rejoinder, "Then why don't you quit and work in Grampa's pub?" Lon knew he would have no intelligent answer to that.

If I thought it would be enough to squelch his desire to be a soldier, it might almost be worthwhile leaving the Corps and taking over the pub, Lon thought. He shook his head. It wouldn't work. On Dirigent, the Corps would always be there to attract any growing boy.

Kalko Green. When the name came back into his head, Lon squeezed his eyes shut for a moment. *I can't get away from him, even now.* There always seemed to be something to remind him of the hapless young man. There had been times, standing in formation looking at the men of his company, when Lon had found himself wondering if there were any Kalko Greens among the faces or—more troubling yet—any Holfield O'Banions. He had belabored the possibilities in the days after the court-martial, even onto *Tyre* during the trip to Bancroft. Make sure the men know what they *should* do if they ever come up against a man like O'Banion. Make sure there is no one like the dead sergeant hiding in the company. Look for the signs. Don't ever let a man get as far as O'Banion had.

Lon paced around his room for twenty minutes or longer. The mail from home had not been as pleasantly distracting as usual. There was too much time just now for thinking. Brooding.

The waiting continued.

13

An hour before sunrise, Monday morning, the waiting ended.

Lon was wakened by the incoming message alert on his complink. He had taken to turning the volume up to maximum before he went to bed, to make certain he would not miss an important call by sleeping through it.

The caller was the duty officer in CIC aboard *Tyre*.

"We've just heard from *Sidon*'s shuttle, Major Nolan. The raiders are attacking a mining village right now. The fighting is in progress. It started less than five minutes ago. I'm downloading everything now."

Lon had already hit a buzzer to rouse Lead Sergeant Jorgen. The buzzer was set up for only this purpose. Jorgen would rouse the men.

"Thank you, Lieutenant," Lon said. "We'll head in as quickly as we can get to the shuttles." He was already moving, sitting up on the edge of his bunk, reaching for socks and boots. He had slept in battledress. He cut off the link to CIC and called up a map centered on the location of the raider strike.

"Identify location and describe terrain," he said once the map was onscreen. While the complink complied, Lon completed dressing.

"The mining village of Tuplace is located seventy-three miles southeast of Lincoln," the artificial voice of the complink said. "The most current population figures list two hundred and seventeen residents, almost equally divided among men, women, and children. Tuplace is one of the older mining villages on Bancroft, having been founded within five years of colonization. There are four working mines around the village, producing gold, a variety of trace elements, and a unique variety of quartz that has several applications, most notably in newer-model Nilssen generators and in communications equipment. There are also two abandoned shafts.''

''Pause,'' Lon instructed. ''Transfer feed to my helmet. Hold.'' He put his helmet on, slid his mapboard into the leg pocket of his battledress uniform, and picked up his rifle. He was ready to go. Only two minutes and fifteen seconds had passed since he hit the alarm to rouse his men.

The sounds of men rushing to get dressed and out of the barracks had been an audible backdrop to the computer's report. The sounds were starting to die down. By the time Lon got outside, the three platoons that were going on the mission were in formation. Platoon sergeants were checking the muster.

Beyond the log palisade wall, the engines of the two DMC shuttles were being started, run up to power. The shuttle crews had been sleeping in their craft.

''The raiders are hitting a village about seventy-five miles from here,'' Lon announced as soon as the order to fall in had been given. ''The attack is going on now. We'll work out our plan of attack en route. Let's get moving.''

He turned the formation over to Tebba Girana, who started the men double-timing to the gate. While he followed, Lon listened to the continuation of the computer report.

''CIC reports that communications with Tuplace has just been interrupted. Before that, reports from the ground were that the raiding force had come in from the southeast, along the valley, and had hit that side of the village. Tuplace had put out trip wires along the land routes in, and had approximately three minutes' warning of the attack, long enough to get some weapons to bear on the attackers. The estimate on the ground was that there had to be at least thirty weapons firing into the village. *Sidon*'s shuttle pilot estimates a minimum of twenty-five.''

Tuplace was in a valley, on high ground next to a small stream. The mines were on either side, with horizontal shafts into both of the enclosing hills. As was the case with most of the mining sites on Bancroft, the ores were refined within yards of the mines.

Lon brought Tebba and the sergeants into a conference and added Lieutenant Colonel Digby Rose, who was observing for the Bancrofters.

''Colonel Rose, do you know anything about this area we're going into?'' Lon asked.

There was a slight hesitation before Rose said, ''I've been there. Nothing in particular stands out in memory. A forested valley, maybe ten miles long. Neither slope is particularly steep, as I recall. I don't know about clearings for your shuttles, though, other than right at the edge of the village, and that seems to be where the fighting is.''

''My first impulse is to land one shuttle out away from the village on either end, try to box the raiders in between us, if we can find LZs,'' Lon said. He had CIC and the shuttle from *Sidon* looking for landing zones already. Lon's company was not equipped with the means to jump in; they had neither parachutes nor jet packs.

''If there's nothing close, the attack could be over before you can get anyone in position,'' Rose said, protest clear in his voice. ''That's a heavily forested region. I know there's a clearing right next to the village, but it could be miles to the next one. The people of Tuplace could all be dead before you get there.''

''They might all be dead now, Colonel,'' Lon said. ''If we can't find an LZ close enough to let us get to Tuplace quickly, we'll go to plan B.''

''What's that?'' Rose asked.

''Use the weapons these shuttles carry to blast our way in right there at the village.'' *And hope the raiders don't have rockets to shoot us down,* Lon thought. Even without that, landing in the middle of a firefight was not something he looked forward to. It could be costly in the only accounting that mattered—the lives of his men.

Thirty seconds later, Lon knew there was no alternative. The nearest clearings large enough to take a shuttle were more than a dozen miles from the village. There was only the rough strip right at the edge, where the transport shuttles came in to pick up the produce of Tuplace's mines.

He got out his mapboard and had Tebba and the sergeants slave their mapboards to it. In thirty seconds Lon roughed out the plan of attack. They would come in from the northwest, over the village of Tuplace, hit the suspected raider positions with rockets and rapid-fire cannons, and land in the clearing on the southeastern end of the village—most likely under direct fire from the raiders.

"We can't be certain that the fight will still be clearly defined," Lon warned the others. "Communications hasn't been reestablished with the village, but *Sidon*'s shuttle reports that there is still shooting and that—as far as they can tell—the raiders are still outside the village."

"No communications—that means we can't tell the villagers who we are, or that we're coming in," Dav Grott of third platoon observed.

"So tell the men to watch their butts as well as their heads," Tebba said. "The locals should be able to figure out fairly quickly which side we're on."

"Two minutes," Lon said. "Get the men ready. Lock and load." He switched channels to tell the two shuttle pilots what they were going to do. "Give us as much fire support as you can," he told them. "These raiders shouldn't have antiair rockets."

"You guarantee that, Major?" one of the pilots asked.

"I wish I could."

• • •

Lon slipped a magazine into his rifle and ran the bolt to put the first round in the firing chamber, then flipped the selector switch from safety to auto. He took his pistol out long enough to jack a round into the chamber, then reholstered the sidearm, leaving its safety on. He closed his eyes long enough to take three slow, deep breaths, part of a routine to keep himself calm. Two of his radio channels were open, one giving him information from the cockpits of the shuttles as the pilots moved down toward their attack and landing. The other let him monitor the passenger compartment through the open noncoms' channel. By concentrating, he could keep the multiple sources from blending into meaningless babble, and that concentration helped him to focus on what he had to do, keeping extraneous worries from claiming his attention.

As the shuttle opened up with its weapons, Lon spared himself time for a quick prayer—*Please don't let me fail my men*—that he repeated each time he led his men into danger.

The landing was hard, throwing Lon against his safety harness with enough force to be momentarily painful. "Up and out!" he shouted on his all-hands channel. "Arc perimeter, short. Watch yourselves."

Arc perimeter, short. Those instructions called for a specific deployment, one that the men had practiced over and over on Dirigent. Instead of forming a complete circular perimeter, they would form into a line over 120 degrees of arc, 15 yards out from the shuttles, facing the known enemy. Once the men were in position and had the enemy under fire, Lon could order any modifications necessary.

The shuttles continued to fire their Gatling guns after they touched down and the ramps were dropped to let the soldiers disembark. That was done as rapidly as humanly possible, the men going through the two exits in each shuttle by twos and spreading out to the left and the right, running forward and diving to the ground, answering fire and seeking targets.

There was very little incoming fire during the first seconds. The shock of the shuttles' assault had temporarily silenced the raiders. It was only after half of Lon's men were out and on the ground in their initial perimeter that a few rounds started coming toward them, out of the forest.

Dawn was not far away. Overhead there was already some light, but it had not penetrated into the trees. But the darkness inside the forest could not hide the raiders from the night-vision lenses of Dirigent battle helmets. Heat signatures and movement. Dropping to the ground behind the wedge of his men, Lon scanned the woods, quickly spotting close to two dozen individuals in several clusters. They had taken cover from the rockets and cannons, but the raiders had started to show a little of themselves. They had to, in order to fire.

"Second platoon, echelon left, fire and maneuver. Try to get across the creek and flank them. Fourth platoon, echelon right, fire and maneuver. Third platoon, maximum covering fire. Shuttles, same thing, maximum covering fire. Go." Lon gave his orders and added his own rifle to the task of keeping the enemy down while two-thirds of his men moved to envelop them.

Once the doors had opened on the shuttle, Lon had no time to think about anything but the needs of the instant. This was the ultimate proving ground, where a soldier earned his pay, justified the years of training, and discovered—or rediscovered—his own abilities and limitations. Training, drills, and experience took over. You did what you had to do, often so quickly that there literally was no time to think out each action, each decision. It had to come automatically . . . or you could die.

It was not that any of the soldiers—enlisted men or officers—could be mindless automatons like the cannon fodder of a thousand years and more before. "A dumb soldier is a dead soldier," more than one drill instructor had barked at his charges over the years. It took intelligence and education to be a mercenary on Dirigent. The equipment required that, if nothing else. But the hard thinking had to be done in advance, as much as possible, not in the middle of a firefight.

Lon had grown over the years. He no longer felt a need to micromanage his men in combat. He decided on the tactics, gave the orders, and trusted his subordinates to carry them out. He did not try to watch every move. That ability to focus was hard-won, in arenas as deadly as—and often larger than—the mining village of Tuplace, Bancroft.

For the time being, the most effective contribution Lon could make to the effort was with his rifle, seeking out targets in the forest and shooting at them. He did not keep conscious score. Hits just meant fewer of the enemy to endanger his men.

Two minutes. Three. The enveloping movements on either flank had not had time to get very far yet. But the amount of incoming fire was slackening rapidly.

"They're pulling back," Lon said on his channel to Tebba and the platoon sergeants. "We clear the immediate area, set up a secure perimeter, and account for any raiders still inside, alive or dead. We need prisoners, not bodies." *Now* he could make that distinction. Coming out of the shuttle and setting up the initial perimeter, Lon had avoided saying that. In the first minutes, it had been much more important to do what he could to minimize the danger to his own men and establish a secure toehold on the area.

"Major Nolan!" He needed a second to recognize the voice as the pilot of *Sidon*'s patrolling shuttle.

"What is it?" Lon asked.

"Two small shuttles moving toward you from the southeast, clipping treetops. I don't recognize the type."

"Can you intercept?"

"Not before they reach you. We didn't spot them, Major. We weren't looking for shuttles and they came in along the valley floor, low and fast. They're running less than a hundred feet above the ground."

"How long do we have?"

"None, Major. They're damn near on you now."

The pilots of the two shuttles on the ground had been listening in. They moved the aim of their cannon up and waited. Sitting on the ground, the shuttles could not fire rockets at aircraft. The fixed launchers were on either side of the fuselage, below the wings, and the aimable pod lowered from the belly of the shuttle.

Lon broadcast a warning on his all-hands channel and barely got that out before the two shuttles came racing over, machine guns or cannons firing through the landing strip in the middle of the valley floor.

The mercenaries and their two shuttles were exposed to that fire for only three seconds—the incoming aircraft were simply flying too fast for more time on target—but in that time more than a thousand rounds marched up the valley. Lon heard rounds striking the skin of the shuttle directly behind him and saw the moving trails of dust kicked up on the ground as they crossed third platoon.

It seemed miraculous that only three men on the ground were wounded—and one killed.

"Get the rockets ready for when they come back," Lon ordered. He had no doubt that the hostile aircraft would return. He did not waste time congratulating himself for ordering that his men not go into this operation without any of their shoulder-fired rocket launchers.

"Where the hell did those come from?" Tebba asked, anger and indignation raising his voice half an octave. "Where do backwoods bandits get fighters?"

"Not fighters, armed shuttles," Lon said. "And I don't know where they came from any more than you do." Lon had thought that only Dirigent armed its shuttles. Most worlds used shuttles merely to transport troops or supplies, protecting them with aerospace fighters if necessary.

Lon moved third platoon away from their own shuttles, into better cover toward the ridge on the right. While they moved, he called the pilots of the two landers to check on damage.

"Still checking," the first pilot said. "We've got

holes in the fuselage, but the diagnostics say we can get off the ground. We just can't get too high without patches.''

"Zag is hit in here," the second pilot said. Zag was his copilot. "One pane of the cockpit canopy was shattered. My crew chief is bandaging Zag's arm now." There was a slight pause before he added, "I guess it's not too bad."

"Can you get off the ground?" Lon asked.

There was another pause before that pilot said, "Not for at least an hour. We had some control circuitry damaged as well, and it's going to take time for the system to repair itself."

"Then get out of the box and get to cover. Those unidentified shuttles might have rockets as well." Lon told the other shuttle to take off and get up where it could operate. "If you get a good shot at the bogies, be my guest," he added.

By that time, Lon was fifty feet above the floor of the valley, on the slope of the hill, under cover of the straggly trees that grew on that rocky flank of the valley. He sucked in a deep breath. Climbing the slope and talking at the same time had about depleted him. That was when the pilot of *Sidon*'s shuttle called again.

"Those two shuttles dropped at least forty men on rocket packs," he said. "Four miles northwest of your position. You're up against more than a few bandits, Major."

"Tell me about it," Lon said. He had no trouble at all sounding sarcastic.

"Those shuttles haven't turned back toward you," the pilot said next. "They're still running hot and low, following the valley northwest."

"Can you get in position to fire on them?"

"Closing in," the pilot advised.

"Dump them."

"Four hot ones away," the pilot reported less than five seconds later. "Enemy separating, beginning evasive action. They don't have much room for that. Four more hot ones away.''

On the ground, Lon heard the first explosion just after the pilot started cackling about ''one down.''

There was a decidedly different sound to the blasts of rockets exploding against rock and dirt rather than an enemy shuttle. The second enemy craft pulled clear, moving east now.

''He's faster than I am,'' *Sidon*'s shuttle pilot said. ''I can't catch him up. Two more hot ones away, but the range is extreme, and growing.''

''If those miss, detonate them in the air,'' Lon said. ''There's a town somewhere over in that direction. We can't drop munitions on the people we're supposed to protect.''

The self-destruct explosions, when they came, were much too far off for Lon to even hope to hear them.

14

Forty minutes had passed since Lon's men landed at Tuplace. The sun was well up. The top half of the hill along the southwestern side of the valley was lit by bright sunlight. The valley floor and the side of the other hill were still in shadow. Lon's men had secured the village. Medics were treating the few wounded mercenaries and the greater number of wounded villagers. Two villagers had been killed in the initial assault by the raiders. One more had died during the second fight, of injuries suffered earlier.

Six dead raiders were found. No wounded. The Dirigenters had not managed to take a single prisoner.

"If there were any wounded, they were carted off by their mates," Phip Steesen said when he came to report on the results of the search. Because he had a few items taken from the dead raiders to show Lon, he had not simply linked through from his position on the new perimeter the platoons had formed around the mining village.

"You find anything on the dead to tell us where they came from?" Lon asked. He had set up a command post in the entrance to one of the mines, on high ground above the village.

Phip shook his head. "No ID of any kind, damn little of anything, not even a snapshot with a background we might be able to place. The camouflage pattern is new to me. The weapons are what we expected, but there are no serial numbers or manufacturer's marks on them. I field-stripped two of them myself. Whoever is behind this wanted to make damn sure they stayed anonymous.''

"CIC couldn't identify the enemy shuttles from the video *Sidon*'s shuttle took either," Lon said. "Nothing in the database that even comes close. And men operating with rocket packs."

"You thinking what I am?" Phip asked.

"We're up against professional soldiers," Lon said, and Phip nodded. "Someone is paying good money to have pros raid Bancroft."

"But where from?" Phip asked. "I thought we had top-notch intelligence on the other major mercenary worlds, and those shuttles didn't come from some start-up outfit."

"The Corps might not even know the names of all the worlds renting out soldiers. The way new colonies are being settled, and old ones growing, intelligence can't keep up with everything. And it might not be a mercenary world at all," Lon said. "The banker might be recruiting personnel from one world—or a half dozen—and buying equipment somewhere else. Or supplying it from wherever the operation was set up."

"We didn't find any grenades or rocket launchers," Phip said. "That doesn't mean they don't have 'em, but it might mean that the men on the ground don't have anything but rifles."

"Get back to your men, Phip. This isn't over yet. They didn't drop forty or more extra men just to impress us with their jet packs."

As Lon was walking the path down to the buildings, Digby Rose was on his way up. He had been talking with people in the village, trying to reassure them that they were being protected now as much as trying to learn exactly how the attack had started.

"I've spoken with Colonel Henks on the radio," Rose said when he joined Lon in the mouth of the mine shaft. "The news about the raider aircraft disturbs him greatly."

"It disturbs me as well, Colonel," Lon said. "Not so

much that they're here, but the fact that we didn't spot them until they were so close."

"Do you plan to attempt to find the wreckage of the one that was shot down?" Rose asked.

"I hope we have that chance," Lon said. "But that wreckage is a long way from here, and the raiders have at least forty men on the ground between us and it. And raiders on the other side as well. I don't expect they've moved too far off."

"The repairs to your damaged shuttle?"

"Should be complete within the next thirty minutes or so, for the one on the ground. Plugging the holes in the other one will have to wait until we get back to Lincoln."

"How do you plan to proceed?" Rose asked. Without coming right out and saying it, he was clearly informing Lon that Bancroft did not consider the downing of one raider shuttle as the victory the mercenaries had contracted to provide.

"Right this minute, I plan to consolidate our position here. The forty men those shuttles dropped to the northwest could be almost on top of us by now, and we don't know for sure how many were already on the ground in the other group. If, by some odd chance, they don't come to us, we'll go after them once it gets dark tonight. The dead we found weren't wearing night-vision gear, so we should have a distinct advantage in the dark."

"You have no way to know that the raiders will attack. They must know they're outgunned. Instead of attacking, they're probably making tracks just as fast as they can away from here."

"They'll attack. That was certain from the minute they dropped reinforcements. But very shortly, we'll know where they're at. I've got scouts out."

There was a long hesitation before Rose finally nodded, once, curtly. "I am glad to see that you have both options covered, Major."

"This is what we do for a living, Colonel," Lon said, smiling to take any sense of rebuke from his remarks.

"We have to know our job. Mistakes are too costly. I've already had one man killed. I don't like to lose men, and I'm damned sure not going to lose any by making careless errors."

Wil Nace of fourth platoon was leading one of the scouting parties. He had taken his men up over the ridge and started northwest, looking for the raiders who had jumped from the shuttles with jet packs. The equipment was as much his target as the men. If the raiders had abandoned the propulsive units—likely, since they were heavy and would be a distinct drag moving through the forest—Wil hoped to retrieve one. That might give a clue to its planet of origin. If A Company couldn't determine where the jet packs had come from, taking all of the captured material back to Dirigent would let the laboratories there have a crack. Eventually some clue would be found, if only from analysis of the metals.

Lon had radio channels open to both of the squads that were out, but the men observed tight sound discipline. Even though they could use subvocalizations and be heard only through the radio links, they were careful. Lon heard only a few brief orders being relayed as the squads worked their way toward the targets.

After Lieutenant Colonel Rose wandered away, Lon took out his mapboard and opened it. He could track his men on that. Their helmet electronics allowed the shuttles overhead to keep tabs on them, and the locations showed up as green blips on the mapboard, updated continuously. Had the enemy been using active electronics, the shuttles would have been able to spot them as well, and they would have showed as red dots. But there was no red on the mapboard.

"Major." Wil Nace's whisper was almost inaudible, even though Lon had the volume on his earphones set almost to maximum.

"Yes, Wil," Lon replied, almost as softly. The sound insulation in Dirigenter helmets was excellent.

"We have the enemy force in sight. We're about a

mile and a half from your position. They're moving your way, very slowly. They know what they're doing. They're as quiet as we would be.''

"How many?" Lon asked.

"I counted forty-six," Wil replied. "Do we follow them back, or go on and try to get one of the jet packs?"

Lon hesitated. He wanted a jet pack to look over, but he also wanted as many of his men as possible for the firefight that seemed certain to follow. "Send three men after a jet pack and anything else they can find." Nace had a full squad, twelve men, with him. "The rest of you tag along with the rocket men, but stay high on the slope, out of the line of fire. I don't want them to know you're there."

"My sentiments exactly," Wil said.

"If we can hit them from both sides, we might force them to surrender," Lon said. "I want live ones to question, Wil. It could be vital."

"We'll do our best. If they weren't moving in such good order, I'd suggest cutting tail-end Charley out of the pack, but we'd never do it without being spotted."

Lon signed off and waited for some report from the other scouts. Second platoon's fourth squad had split into its two fire teams and was moving along the slopes on either side of the valley. Their assignment was, Lon thought, more dangerous than Wil Nace's. The raiders who had retreated from the village might have stopped to set up an ambush almost anywhere. And they might be good enough to remain undetected until the Dirigenters were well into their kill zone.

We've got more than two-to-one odds in our favor, Lon reminded himself. *We should be able to handle both groups of raiders, even if they coordinate and attack simultaneously.* But that could not keep him from worrying. It was his men who might have to pay the price.

The worrying stopped only when the next call came in.

"Major, we've spotted raiders," Corporal Taw Reillor, who led second platoon's fourth squad, said. "We're nearly two miles from the LZ, as close to the ridgeline as we could get without broadcasting our positions.''

"I've got you on my mapboard," Lon said. "What's the situation?"

"I've counted thirty-five of them, including four men being carried or helped along—wounded. There was one more, but he must have died. They left him behind, took his rifle and ammo."

"You get a chance to search him?"

"Negative, Major. He's only about eighty yards from where the rest of the raiders stopped, and I think he's supposed to be bait for an ambush. The raiders put one man high on either slope with what look to be clear fields of fire. The rest are setting up defensive positions. Wait. . . ."

Lon waited.

"Major, they just started moving their wounded farther back, but the rest are staying in place. They're not digging in. I don't know if they expect us to follow them or if they're supposed to be the anvil the other bunch drives us against."

"You alert your other fire team?" Lon asked.

"They're holding position, out of the way like we are. Major, we could take out half this bunch in the first volley."

"Negative!" Lon said quickly. "That would still leave enough of them to return the favor. Stay out of sight. Pull back if you have to, to make sure."

"They won't see us," Reillor promised. Stealth was second nature to the mercenaries because they worked hard at it in training. "Between the trees and the rocks, we could move the whole company past them."

Lon smiled. There was probably more than a kernel of truth to what Reillor said.

"Don't get cute, Taw," Lon said.

"Not me, Major. I had my butt half shot off once. I'm not about to tempt Fate again."

• • •

Lon left the mine entrance and went down to the village's buildings, just to take a quick look around. The residents had barricaded themselves inside as best they could, moving furniture against the walls and windows, giving themselves what extra cover they could. The women and children had been moved into another of the mine shafts, back to the first cross shaft, out of the line of any gunfire outside.

Next, Lon inspected his men's positions. The men, too, were ready for a fight, shallow trenches dug and bolstered by piling dirt and stone around the edges. Positions had been dug for the squads that were out as well, so they would have a place to flop if they came back in one step ahead of hostile bullets.

Then he headed back toward the mine opening he was using as a command post. He had one fire team from second platoon deployed around the entrance, a last line of defense in case the raiders got through. Then he linked through to Tebba, who had taken up a position on the other side of the valley.

"This stinks, Tebba," Lon said. "One batch setting up positions too far away from us to be part of a fight here, the other group moving in against heavy odds. They have to know we outnumber them. They must have seen our shuttles on the ground before they jumped."

"But they might not know who *we* are," Tebba said. "Maybe they think we're just more miners, or Henks's old police force—someone they can run over or off. If they are from off-world, with no local contacts, that could be the answer."

"Or maybe they've got more surprises for us. More men coming in we haven't spotted yet, or a shuttle coming back for another go at us."

"You've got two shuttles and the long eyes aboard our ships looking," Tebba reminded Lon. "Now they know what to look for, they won't sneak shuttles in again without more warning. That last shuttle ready to take off yet?"

"They finished the repairs," Lon said. "I told them

to be ready to get out of here on short notice.''

"You don't think we need the extra electronics above watching?''

"Probably not. I'm going to get them up out of the way before the shooting starts, though. Maybe another ten minutes, the way the rocket men are moving toward us.''

"Don't knock it, Lon. If we had jet packs, we could have done a lot better this morning instead of just dropping our shuttles in their laps. We could have snuck in and creamed them before they knew we were here.''

"Maybe. I'd just as soon ride down on my butt as one of those things. When we trained with them last year, I felt like I had a big red bull's-eye painted on my ass, just begging for a bullet. They're not that much faster than 'chutes, and a hell of a lot less safe.''

Tebba laughed softly, but Lon didn't hear all of it. He switched channels to take a call from Wil Nace.

"They're about to hit you,'' Wil whispered. "I don't think they're expecting major opposition. They're not digging in, just taking cover behind trees and rocks, sliding as close as they can. They move like professionals, but the attitude—''

Wil did not get to finish his comment. The shooting started then, a barrage of automatic rifle fire. Even though Lon was well out of the line of fire, he pulled back a step farther into the mine shaft. Reflex. There was no need for Lon to issue orders to the men on the perimeter to return fire. He had given instructions before.

There were only forty Dirigenters directly facing the raiders who had starting firing into the village. A few more of Lon's men could bring their weapons to bear from the flanks. At first, most of the incoming fire went high, over the men on the valley floor, seemingly directed more at the village's few buildings, where the miners had barricaded themselves.

"I told them they should get underground with the women and children,'' Lon muttered under his breath. But that had been refused, vehemently. The men of Tuplace wanted another crack at the raiders who had struck in the night.

The raiders quickly redirected their fire when they started taking rounds from the Dirigenters. The response was coordinated, disciplined, another piece of evidence that these raiders were no ragtag assemblage of ruffians.

"Okay, Nace, hit them from behind," Lon instructed after the firefight had been in progress for two minutes. "Hit and run. Circle back around them."

The urge to move to the shaft entrance and peek out to watch the action was strong, but Lon resisted it. He could not needlessly expose himself. The area around the mouth of the shaft was open. He would be clearly visible to the enemy, an inviting target. He listened, both directly and through his radio links, and watched what the camera on Tebba's helmet showed. There was a change in the raiders' pattern of fire after they found themselves with enemies on two sides. The sounds were easy to read, since Lon knew what was causing the change.

"Taw, any change with the raiders on your end?" Lon asked, switching channels briefly.

"They seemed to perk up when the shooting started," Corporal Reillor replied, "but they don't show any sign of getting ready to run to the rescue."

"If they do, hit them, then get out of range. Take out the snipers and anyone else you can reach. Don't get bogged down in a firefight, and don't start anything unless they head this way."

"Right, Major."

Lon lifted his faceplate and rubbed at his right eye. It had started to twitch annoyingly. "None of this crap makes sense!" he said loudly, even though he was alone. He had clicked off his transmitter first.

The raiders Reillor's men were watching should not have been sitting where they were. Either they should have been coming back to help in the fight, or they should have been moving as fast as they could in the other direction.

"One or the other," Lon muttered. "They can't still

be expecting the other team to drive us into their kill zone.''

He linked into the channel that the shuttle pilots used among themselves. ''You're sure there's no sign of more of those shuttles heading our way?'' he asked. ''The situation we've got here, the raiders must be expecting help from somewhere.''

''Major, there's not a thing in the air within eighty miles of you but us, and we're not showing anything on the ground like trucks or armor moving your way. We'd see heat signatures if there were. If the raiders have more resources, they must already be in your area, on the ground. You want us to take a run at the positions of the raiders firing at you?''

''No. Save your munitions. We might need them more later,'' Lon said. ''We're doing okay here—for now, at least.''

''We'll keep watching. Anything shows up, you'll know as fast as we do,'' the pilot promised.

The explosion on the slope above the mine entrance knocked Lon to the ground. Dirt and rock fell from the roof and walls of the shaft. Several timber beams cracked loudly.

15

Tuplace was a *mining* village. The workers had stored explosives in a bunker half dug into the side of one of the hills they worked, above and southeast of the village. Much of the load detonated at once. The hill shook. A crater was formed in the area right around the cache—a man-made volcano spewing rock and ash, dirt and fragments of trees. The force of the explosion felled trees out to a distance of three hundred yards, in the valley and on both slopes facing it. Every building in the village was damaged. Two were totally destroyed. Shattered trees flew like primitive rockets. Shards of wood scattered with the force of bullets. In the mine shaft behind Lon, there was a cave-in, first one section directly under the explosion, then in the tunnels near that, sections of roof collapsing like dominoes.

At the sound of the blast, most of the men exposed in the valley and on the slopes went flat, some covering their heads. The actions were not always in time. And some of the detritus of the blast went far enough to fall in among the party of raiders that had jumped into the valley on jet packs.

The gunfire stopped.

"Major?" Wil Nace said into his transmitter. "Major Nolan?" There was no answer. Wil switched to the frequency his patrol was on. "Disengage. We've got to get back there and find out what happened."

Nace and his men had been in the firefight for no more than four minutes. They had started taking return fire, but no casualties. Now Nace led them away from the enemy, moving over the ridge as soon as he thought it safe. The squad moved quickly toward the village and the cloud of smoke and dust that had not yet settled.

On another radio channel, Taw Reillor was also trying to contact Lon, with an equal lack of success. For a few seconds the fury of the explosion had numbed Reillor. The ground shook under him—the shock wave was massive, even at such a distance. Debris rained down from the blast. But the shock passed, and the corporal started calling to find out what had happened. When Lon did not reply, Taw switched channels to call his platoon sergeant, Phip Steesen. Phip did not respond immediately—for a good reason. The blast had temporarily deafened him, as it had many others.

"I can't get any response from the major," Reillor said when Phip finally did answer his calls. "What the hell happened?"

Phip's ears were still ringing, making it difficult to understand the corporal. "The mountain blew," he said, shouting. "That's all I know. We're belly-button deep in shit."

"Hey! Wait a minute," Taw shouted back. "The raiders here are starting to pull back. They're leaving!"

"Stay put until I find out what to do," Phip said. "You try the lieutenant?"

"No. Should I?"

"I'll do it. Get ready to move in a hurry, though. We may need you back here."

Smoke and dust were still rolling through the valley, obscuring vision. Phip could feel small debris continuing to flutter down. It was almost like snow, or maybe sleet, except that there was nothing cold about this precipitation. Something in the mix started Phip coughing, so violently that it was nearly a minute before he could control it and call Lieutenant Girana.

"We can't contact the major," Phip reported. "I'm gonna take a couple of men up there and see what's up." He did not ask permission. No matter what Girana said,

Phip was going. He had already made that decision. "The raiders Taw was watching are beating it. I haven't heard from Nace."

"His men are on their way in," Tebba said. "Go ahead. See what you can find out about the major. The bunker where the locals stored their explosives blew, up near the top of the other hill. Must have been booby-trapped by the raiders."

Phip was already moving. He took the two nearest privates—Shen Flowers and Hobart "Hobo" Jennings from his platoon's first squad—and started running toward the hill and the mine shaft where he had last seen Lon. There was almost no gunfire coming in now, just a few stray shots on the side where the raiders who had jumped into the valley were.

The slope had become a major obstacle course as a result of the explosion. Broken trees, rocks, and pieces of the village's buildings were scattered everywhere, especially near the bottom of the slope. Higher up, rubble was still tumbling down, the tail end of the landslide that had nearly cleared the upper slopes in a fan shape out from the point of the blast.

Dust was still boiling out of the mine entrance where Lon had established his command post, a sulfurous yellow, thick enough to make it impossible to see anything through it, even with the infrared assistance of a helmet's night-vision system. It worked its way up under the faceplates of the Dirigenters' masks, almost threatening to choke them.

Phip did not slacken his pace. He went straight into the churning maelstrom. Only after he was inside the entrance did he slow down. He had to. Visibility was less than a yard. Phip did not so much *find* Lon as trip over him. Phip nearly fell flat on his face. He used his rifle to catch himself, and turned, going down on one knee to see what had tripped him.

Holding his breath to keep from inhaling more of the dust, Phip felt the side of Lon's neck for a pulse. It was long seconds before he felt the first beat, faint. But he adjusted his fingers and the beat was stronger, but slow, too slow. Phip slung his rifle over his shoulder and started dragging Lon toward the entrance—a slightly brighter area in the dust cloud.

At the entrance, Shen and Hobart spotted them and helped Phip carry Lon off to the side and farther up the slope, looking for clear air. Lon started coughing hard, nearly convulsing with the effort of breathing.

Phip tried to talk but couldn't. He lifted his faceplate, then grabbed his canteen and took a mouthful of water—swirling it around, then spitting it out, just trying to get rid of some of the dust. He had to do it a second time before his voice was ready to work.

"Hobo, you and Shen look around for the guys who were here, Zeffo's fire team. They were outside, deployed around the entrance, the last time I saw them," Phip said while he pulled off Lon's helmet. He leaned closer, listening and looking for movement in Lon's chest, a sign that he was breathing regularly.

Breathing, coughing. When Lon started to choke again, Phip lifted him to a sitting position. When the spasms eased, he held his canteen to Lon's lips.

"You've got to wash out some of the dirt," Phip said when Lon groaned, a deep, rumbling sound somewhere low in his throat.

"Take a sip, roll it around, then spit it out," Phip instructed when Lon finally managed to open his eyes just a little. The eyelids were caked with dirt, making it difficult for Lon to get his eyes open. He leaned forward a little. Phip tipped the canteen toward Lon's lips and watched to make sure that his friend did not take too much water right away.

Coming back was a slow and painful process. Lon felt as if someone were sitting on his chest. Each breath took a herculean effort. He was not truly aware of Phip for several minutes, even after he had rinsed out his mouth twice, then taken a small sip of water to swallow. The muddy taste didn't matter. The sensation of drinking was restorative. The water might have been some magic elixir. But it also brought the dawn of pain. Lon had been too numb to feel much of anything before, but now . . . He groaned again. His head throbbed madly. There was a maddening ringing in his ears that pulsed and faded. The other aches took a bit longer to assert themselves—back and shoulders, one hip, both knees, left hand and wrist.

The touch of water on Lon's face was an almost electrical shock as Phip tried to wash away the dirt caked around his friend's eyes.

"What hap—" was all that Lon could rasp out before he started coughing again.

"The explosives bunker blew," Phip said. "We're still trying to sort things out."

The mountain did *fall on me,* Lon thought. "Water," he whispered.

"Take it easy yet, Lon," Phip said. "Just a little for now. We've got to have one of the medics check you out. There might be internal injuries."

While he helped Lon drink, Phip clicked over to the radio channel that connected him with Tebba Girana and reported that Lon was alive but hurt.

"Stay with him," Tebba said, needlessly. "We're still trying to find people."

"He needs a medic, when one can get here," Phip said. "The sooner the better."

The dust settled. The smoke dissipated. In the valley, everything was covered with a thick layer of yellow dirt and gray ash. Men walked or limped through the apocalyptic landscape. Time seemed to pass in slow motion, even an hour after the explosion.

During that hour, responsibility for treating the wounded and accounting for the dead had fallen to Tebba Girana. He had also sent scouts to trail the two groups of raiders, to make certain that they did not double back undetected to attack Tuplace and its defenders.

The Bancrofters had suffered most. In the buildings,

there were twenty dead and another dozen badly wounded men. Lieutenant Colonel Rose, the observer, was one of the dead. He had been with the villagers. Among the women and children, who had been hidden in one of the other mine shafts, casualties were lighter—one dead and a dozen injured, and most of the injuries were minor. The mine they had been secreted in had been less affected than the one Lon had been in.

Ninety minutes after the explosion, the casualty count among the mercenaries stood at five dead and sixty injured, with three men still unaccounted for. Only a third of the wounded men were hurt seriously. The rest were treated and returned to duty. As quickly as the seriously injured men could be stabilized, they were moved to a shuttle that landed to pick them up. Dirigenters and Bancrofters. The first shuttle loaded as many of the wounded as possible, to hurry them to Lincoln and better medical care. A second shuttle was on its way from Lincoln with a half-dozen extra trauma tubes. It landed just after the first took off.

Colonel Henks was on the incoming shuttle. He was the first man out of it, hurrying. But he stopped as soon as he saw the extent of the destruction. Mercenaries had to push around him to get to the trauma tubes and other medical supplies on the shuttle. Some of the wounded could not be moved to the shuttle. The tubes had to be taken to them.

One passing medic was the only person to hear Henks's comment on seeing the results of the blast: "My dear God!"

Slowly, Henks became aware that he was in the way and moved farther from the shuttle and the open door. He stood with his mouth hanging open, transfixed by the hellish vista. Several minutes passed before one of the mercenaries came up to him.

"Colonel Henks? Major Nolan asked me to bring you straight to him."

Henks blinked and looked at the man who had raised his helmet faceplate. He needed an instant to recognize

Tebba Girana. "Thank you, Lieutenant," Henks said. He gestured weakly. "I've never seen destruction like this."

"It doesn't come much worse," Tebba said without looking in the direction Henks had gestured. "Not and have anyone live through it. If you'll come with me, sir?"

Tebba led the way up the slope. Lon had not moved far from the mine entrance, but he had declined to go back inside, even though the dust had stopped rolling out of it. At the moment, he was sitting propped up against a rock. His helmet was lying on the ground next to him, and he held his head in his hands, still not fully recovered from his relatively minor injuries. He remained moderately dizzy. The tinnitus was still an annoying buzz. His hearing was muted, as if his ears had water in them. People speaking to him seemed to be at a great distance. A medic had confirmed his suspicions that he had suffered a concussion.

"Lon, here's Colonel Henks," Tebba said when Lon did not look up at their approach.

Even now, Lon lifted his head only slowly, and not as far as he would have in other circumstances.

"Colonel. We've made rather a botch of things so far," Lon said. "We think the raiders booby-trapped the village's explosives bunker and set it off remotely." He shrugged, infinitesimally because any movement increased his aches, even after a med-patch. "We may never know for certain, because we're not equipped to do the sort of investigation it would take to find proof one way or the other."

Henks was slow to answer. He was still looking around at the destruction. From the side of the hill, above the valley and closer to the site of the explosion, the devastation seemed infinitely worse. He marveled that anyone had survived at all.

"There's no defense against an attack like that, Major," he said finally. "Except to be somewhere else when it happens."

"We should have checked that bunker, Colonel," Lon said. "It's something we should have thought of."

"They would have set if off sooner then, caught whoever you had sent to inspect it," Henks suggested.

"Maybe, maybe not," Lon said. "My guess is that it was on a timer. The raiders who had been hitting the village when we arrived were gone by then, too far away to see what was going on here."

"The other group was close. They could have triggered it," Tebba said, talking more to Lon than to Henks.

"Where are the raiders now? Do you know?" Henks asked.

Tebba replied, "Both groups disengaged, took off in opposite directions. We've got men following them. The last report I had, it appears that they're moving toward a rendezvous east of here. They're not going to get a chance to have their remaining shuttle pick them up. We're maintaining an air patrol. That other shuttle shows up again, we're going to dump it the way we did the first one."

"I've got people heading to that site now," Henks said. "One of our shuttles and half my rapid response company."

Lon looked up more now. "I want to see that shuttle, Colonel. I want comprehensive, detailed video and samples of the materials. It may take some time, but we're going to find out where that shuttle came from. We're going to find out who's behind this." Anger surged in Lon, suppressing the discomfort of such a long speech. When he had finished, he coughed, then took a drink of water to lubricate his throat again.

"You will have all the support we can give you, Major," Henks said. "When you are ready to resume your pursuit of the raiders, my rapid response company will be at your disposal, and any of the other companies you feel are up to the job."

"Thank you, Colonel," Lon said. "We'll give you the victory you want over these raiders yet."

Tebba took over. "We are keeping an eye on them on the ground, Colonel. The scouts will stay on the trail as long as necessary, until they follow the raiders to their camp or until we're ready to hit them again."

"Your men are equipped to stay out for several days, perhaps a week or more, without support?" Henks asked.

"They're carrying rations for three days and can supplement them off the land if they have to," Tebba said. "I don't expect it will take us a week to get ready to hit the raiders again, but even if it took twice that long, I'd feel confident that our men are up to the job."

It was a long day in Tuplace. The wounded, villagers and Dirigenters, were treated on-site or evacuated to Lincoln. The dead villagers were buried. The dead mercenaries were flown to Lincoln, then up to *Sidon*. Their bodies would be returned to Dirigent. A transport shuttle came in to remove the gold and minerals that the raiders had been after. Then the remaining villagers were evacuated. Their homes were too badly damaged for quick repairs to make them habitable again. Colonel Henks promised that the homes, the village, would be rebuilt.

Finally, after everyone else had been moved from Tuplace, the rest of the mercenaries left. The last missing soldier's body had been found in the rubble. Every man was accounted for.

"You're going to keep people near that raider shuttle?" Lon asked Henks before they boarded the last flight out of Tuplace.

"As long as necessary," Henks said.

"I'm going to want to see it for myself in the morning," Lon said. "I need to see it."

Before the shuttle's crew chief closed the door, Lon looked out at the hill and the new crater at its top. *This isn't over yet,* he thought. *We'll have our day.*

16

Of the sixty Dirigenters who had been injured by the explosion in Tuplace, fourteen were going to need extended periods for regeneration and recuperation. Most had lost limbs, or portions of limbs. One man had broken his back and neck, severing the spinal cord in two places. The remaining injured men were fit for duty before sunset, the day of the blast. Four hours in a trauma tube could repair just about anything short of amputation or major neurological damage.

"We can't give the men time to brood over this," Lon told Tebba and Weil on the flight back to Lincoln. "As soon as we get back to barracks, put them to cleaning and repairing weapons and equipment. Get replacements down from the ships for anything lost or too badly damaged to repair." He paused. "The electronics in my helmet were wiped out by the blast. We might have a lot of that kind of damage. And my rifle . . ." He shook his head. "I poured about three pounds of dust from the barrel. I dread to think what it's going to take to get the mechanics of it functioning again."

"The rifles shouldn't be that big a problem," Lead Sergeant Weil Jorgen said. "Unless barrels are bent or parts in the receiver broken, it's just elbow grease and such. We've got canned air to blow out dirt. It's the helmets that worry me. At least a third of the men lost some or all of their electronics. We're going to have to bring down a lot of replacements, parts if not entire helmets, and it's going to take six to eight hours to make sure every man has a fully functional helmet. It's a good thing we carry a lot of spares on the ships, or we'd be out of luck.''

"Can we bring the armorer's mate down from *Tyre* to check the rifles?" Tebba asked. "Give him enough of our men to help out, but get the expert to certify the weapons?"

"Good thinking," Lon said, nodding. "Make the arrangements. I want the company battle-ready before anyone beds down tonight. We get a good night's sleep then, and get ready to head back out tomorrow morning. We've got men out there. I don't want to leave them hanging a minute longer than we have to.''

"I thought you were going to wait, and let the raiders get back to their camp first," Tebba said.

Lon was slow to reply. "We may yet. It depends on a lot of things—how long it takes them to get there, whether our people remain safe, and what kind of reception we get in Lincoln. I want to finish this business as quickly as we can, safely. Get back to the training routine.''

The mild analgesic Lon had been given was wearing off. The stronger patches might have been dangerous with his concussion, and in any case, he wanted to keep his mind clear. Now he ached—all over, not just his head. He felt as if he had just gone through a twelve-round boxing match . . . after running a marathon. He hurt, and he was exhausted. Concentration was difficult. All Lon really wanted to do was curl up in the least painful position he could find and sleep for ten or twelve hours. But he had to see to his men, and get the company back up to a battle-ready condition first.

"We lost nine men today," he said softly. "Fourteen more might not return to duty before the end of the contract. That's not good, and it wouldn't have been even if we had managed to put down every last one of those raiders.''

"I know what you're thinking, Major," Weil said. "But that explosion, that's outside the normal run of things. We're actually damned lucky. Our losses could have been a hell of a lot worse. There might have been ten tons of explosives in that bunker instead of two or three. We could easily have ninety dead instead of nine. It's a miracle we don't.''

"I agree with Weil, Lon," Tebba said. "We could have lost everyone but the men in the two fire teams we had out away from the village. The bunker those charges were in was solid. Most of the explosive force was directed out and up, away from us.''

Lon squeezed his eyes shut. He knew how much worse it *could* have been, but that did not make him feel any better about the men he *had* lost.

A light rain was falling when Lon's shuttle landed next to the militia compound in Lincoln. When Lon stepped out of the lander, he looked up into the rain, thinking how appropriate it was. *No time for sunshine now,* he thought. *Thunder and lightning might be even better.* But this was not a storm, just a gentle spring shower. He walked slowly toward the gate and through to the barracks. Most of his men had returned ahead of him. Squad leaders and platoon sergeants had already started their men at the necessary chores of cleaning and repairing.

"Get chow call as quickly as possible," Lon told Weil. "Whatever the cooks can come up with. And anything they can think of in the way of special treats."

"Yes, sir," Weil said. He was having difficulty walking as slowly as Lon was. "I know this is out of the ordinary, and not covered by regs, but how about serving beer with supper? That'll pick their spirits up quick as anything, and there won't be time enough for anyone to get drunk."

"Go ahead," Lon said. "Just don't log it on the menu."

Five hours later, Lon had moved past exhaustion to a state of numbness that left him feeling as groggy as he had been after regaining consciousness from the blast that morning. He had spoken with nearly every survivor of the fight in Tuplace, inspected dozens of rifles and helmets, commiserated with those who had lost friends and squadmates. He had spoken by radio with the men who were still trailing the raiders. The two groups had rendezvoused and kept moving. The raiders had made camp just before sunset. They had marched hard until then, though, averaging better than four miles an hour, overland, through rough country. "They're in damn good shape, Major," Taw Reillor had reported. "Kept us moving lively to keep up with them."

"Just don't let them spot you," Lon said. "We'll get to you as quickly as we can. With any luck, they'll lead you straight to their main camp."

"They won't see us," Taw said. "I can give you a firm head count on them, though. There are seventy-eight of 'em."

"We're set, Lon," Tebba reported near ten o'clock that night. "Every man has a serviceable rifle and helmet. We've replaced all of the mapboards and portable complinks. Both of *Tyre*'s shuttles have been fully repaired and restocked with ammunition and rockets."

"Okay, tell the men to hit their racks and get some sleep."

"I've already released the platoons," Tebba said. "First platoon will handle the duty assignments tonight."

Lon nodded. "No reveille in the morning, not for the men who were out today. Breakfast at eight, work formation at nine."

"We going straight back out?" Tebba asked.

"I'm not going to make that decision tonight," Lon said. "My brain is still scrambled. We'll talk it out in the morning, us and Colonel Henks."

"You do look like you need your sleep, Lon," Tebba said. "You should have sacked out an hour ago."

"No, not before the men," Lon said.

•   •   •

The men who had been lost. Different ways in which the situation in Tuplace could have been handled. The explosion. The pain. What to do next. Sara and the children. Home. *Don't let your son grow up to be a soldier.* Reports he needed to write. There was so much competing for Lon's attention that he could concentrate on none of it. The clutter started his head buzzing again. He sat on his bunk, elbows resting on his thighs, trying to quiet the mental cacophony without success.

"I should at least record a note to Sara," Lon told himself, but the effort was more than he could summon energy for. *No, I guess not,* he thought. *The way I feel now, she'd see it in whatever I said or wrote. She'd worry too much.*

Slowly, he tumbled over into bed. He had taken his boots off earlier. That was as far as the undressing went. Before he could remind himself to get out of his clothes, he was asleep, dropping into peaceful oblivion.

At least he would remember nothing of what passed during the hours he slept, but he tossed and turned almost the whole night. There were times when he groaned in virtual pain or cried out in sleeping fear. But the nightmares were not sufficient to wake him, or to imprint themselves on his mind when he woke, just before dawn, as he would have wakened on any normal morning.

Lon's clothing was soaked with sweat. He still felt physically exhausted. But he laid that off against the rigors of the day before. He sat up, yawning and stretching, trying to pump his mind up to something like normal alertness. After a few minutes he got up and stripped off his clothes before walking down the corridor to shower. Cold water at full blast, then hot water, then cold again at the end.

It helped.

When he finally shut off the shower, the sound of water dripping from his body was all Lon could hear. Lon was far enough from the bays where his men slept that he couldn't even hear snoring. He dried off, then wrapped a towel around his middle for the walk back to his room.

In the room, he turned on only the small reading lamp over the headboard of his bed. The splash of the narrow-beam lamp on the bedding provided enough illumination for Lon to find fresh clothes and dress. He did not think of going back to bed, even though it was only a few minutes after five in the morning. He used a quiet power shaver while sitting on his bed, not bothering with a mirror. He checked the results by feel.

Once he was "fit" for the public, Lon went to the company's orderly room. Platoon Sergeant Ernst Grawley of first platoon was sitting there, feet up on the desk, acting as Charge of Quarters. He brought his feet down and stood when Lon entered.

Lon waved him back down. "Have you heard anything from the men trailing the raiders?" he asked.

"Not since . . . about twenty-one hundred last night, Major," Grawley said. "The raiders were bedded down. Our guys were ready to do the same, one man on watch. Corporal Reillor said they wouldn't call until the raiders started to move this morning, unless something happened. I guess nothing has. You want me to give them a call, see what's going on?"

Lon shook his head. "Let them be."

"You gonna let first platoon go out next time, Major?" Grawley asked after a moment. "We need our turn."

"It's not a game, Ernst," Lon said. "You've been in the Corps long enough to know that." Grawley was the only one of Alpha's platoon sergeants who had not been in third platoon when Lon was a cadet. Grawley had been first platoon sergeant almost as long as Lon had been on Dirigent. Grawley was due for promotion to company lead sergeant—and would have had that promotion already if he had not declined to leave A Company.

"It's what we do, Major. Our job. And right now, first is in better shape than any of the other platoons."

Grawley was shaking his head. "I never think of it as a game."

"Sorry, Ernst. I shouldn't have said that." Lon took in a deep breath, then let it out slowly. "I haven't decided what we're going to do next. I need to sit down with the lieutenants and sergeants and talk it through. And before that, I've got to find someplace quiet to sit and think about it myself."

"I could take a walk, get a cup of coffee, if you want to do your thinking here, Major. Time to get my platoon up anyway."

"Thank you, Ernst. I relieve you as CQ."

"Thank you, sir." Grawley stood, saluted, and left the office, closing the door behind him.

I should have gone back to bed for another hour, Lon thought as he looked at the door. *I've got the feeling this is going to be another long day.*

He sat at the desk, keyed the complink to show a map of Bancroft, and zeroed it in on the position of the men who were following the raiders. The answer was somewhere in that area.

It has to be, Lon told himself. Either the main camp of the raiders or a landing zone for their shuttles, a place where they could be picked up and moved.

"This time we pick the time and the place," he said. "And this time we finish it off."

17

It was 0930 when Lon convened his meeting. Tebba, Harley, Weil, and the four platoon sergeants were in the office with him. Extra chairs had been brought in so everyone could sit.

"I've got some ideas," Lon started. "I'm going to lay them out for you, and I want feedback. You see a way to improve the plan, speak up. Shoot down any flaws. I want to get this all hashed out and smooth before I present it to Colonel Henks.

"The first thing is I don't want to leave a single squad of men out in the field too long trailing the raiders. It's not that I have any reservations about the ability of our men to operate like that for as long as necessary. They simply shouldn't have to.

"On the other hand, if it's at all possible, I want to hit these raiders after they get to their main camp. The two batches we faced at Tuplace may not be all of them. One problem is that these raiders might not go all the way to their main base on foot. They could be heading to a rendezvous point for air pickup. If that's the case, we'll try to dump the shuttles that come in for them."

"After yesterday, I don't think they're likely to try that," Tebba said. "They know we've got birds with teeth, and we already dropped one of their shuttles. They can't have unlimited resources or they'd have been more open about their operations. I think those raiders we're tracking are going to go all the way to their camp—or their next target—on foot."

"I agree, sir," Weil Jorgen said. "They'll save their

air transport for when they really need it.''

"I was simply presenting the options," Lon said. "I also think that it's going to be walking for them. Either to their base or their next target. If they aim for another mining village or camp, we might simply repeat what happened at Tuplace—get there after the raiders hit, find ourselves in the middle of the shit again. I don't want that. So . . .'' Lon let that hang for twenty seconds.

"Late this afternoon, I propose to take the same three platoons out. We'll find an LZ far enough from the raiders that they won't see or hear us. We rendezvous with our patrol and move in parallel to the raiders until they get to their base or move into position for another raid.'' Lon held a hand out. "Hold on, Ernst. Don't start bitching yet. Let me finish." Grawley had obviously been ready to protest his platoon being excluded again.

"If they go to a base, we'll set up, ready to go in, and wait. I'll call in first platoon and Colonel Henks's rapid response company. We'll hit the raiders on every side, make damned sure they can't slip away from us. If they attempt to strike another mining target instead, we'll be in position to keep them away from the civilians and call in the backup just the same. We're going to finish this batch of raiders." Lon paused to look at the faces of the others.

"The reason for going in part now and part later is simple: We don't know that this is the only group there is. If another band hits a target while we're hiking through the woods following these, there have to be people here to go after them. After what happened in Tuplace, I want a platoon of our people included. We did badly enough yesterday. None of Henks's people are up to facing that by themselves.

"Satisfied, Ernst?" Lon asked.

Grawley grinned. "Yes, sir. I guess that'll do."

"Harley?" Lon turned to his younger lieutenant.

Harley nodded. "Something comes up, we'll handle it.''

"Now, ideas, gentlemen. I want to polish this until you can shave in it before I go see Colonel Henks."

It was lunchtime before Lon went to the militia commander's office. Henks had meals brought in and listened while Lon laid out his proposal.

"I must admit," Henks said, "I was worried about the responsibility you laid on a single squad of men. If they were spotted, I don't think any of them would have made it out alive."

"That wasn't my primary concern, Colonel. I do have faith in my men. I know how good they are. But I don't want to take a chance of losing track of these raiders. We want to end their activities, and we want prisoners so we can learn where they came from and who's footing the bill."

"Quite," Henks said, nodding. "Are you sure my people will be up to their end of the operation you've outlined?"

"Obviously, we won't know that for certain until the time comes," Lon said. "But they've done well in training, better than we could have demanded. They're as ready as we can make them. And since you'll have my people along as well, the odds will never be better for them."

"I shall be along when the time comes," Henks said.

Lon smiled. "I expected that, Colonel."

"Since you are the veterans, the professionals, I shall willingly accept your leadership in the operation."

"I appreciate that, Colonel," Lon said. He was relieved as well. The question of authority had to be resolved in advance. It was spelled out in the rider to the contract that Lon had negotiated, but he was glad that Henks had brought it up.

"Do you still want to fly out to look at the raider aircraft that crashed?" Henks asked next. "We can go out and get back in little more than an hour."

"Your people are still guarding the site?"

Henks nodded. "I'd like to bring them back as

quickly as possible. They've been collecting what they could, and recording everything on video. Perhaps some of the debris will tell us who we're dealing with.''

The flight was uneventful. Lon and Henks rode in the cockpit with the Bancrofter pilots, so they had a clear view from the air of the scene. The raider craft had gone in hard, snapping trees and losing bits of itself for three hundred yards before it came to rest. The ground immediately around the remains of the fuselage was fire-blackened, and the nearest standing trees showed where they, too, had burned.

''Good thing it's been wet,'' Henks said. ''Could have started one hell of a wildfire in the dry season.''

''We'll have to land three-quarters of a mile farther on,'' one of the pilots said. ''There's no place to set down closer.''

Henks nodded. ''We can manage from there.''

The clearing where the shuttle landed was scarcely large enough, even without the other Bancrofter shuttle already parked at the edge. The pilot banked and braked, getting his craft level no more than three seconds before the wheels touched down. Lon held on as tightly as he could, and gritted his teeth. The landing was, perhaps, less dangerous than a combat landing in a Dirigenter shuttle, but Lon had never experienced one of those from the cockpit, where he could see everything the pilots could.

Several militiamen were waiting to escort them to the wreckage. Colonel Henks set a brisk pace, surprising Lon and—apparently—his own men. The militiamen who had been on the scene since the day before had worn a bit of a path through the forest, but it was still not a simple route.

''There wasn't any identification on the two pilots,'' one of the militiamen explained as they neared the site of the crash. ''We had to bury the bodies, the pieces we could find.''

"No problem," Henks said. "If we need to examine the bodies later, we can dig them up."

Lon stopped short as soon as he could see the wreckage clearly. Much of the fuselage of the crashed shuttle was still intact, but it had been bent twenty degrees to the right. The wings had been ripped off, along with the weapons pods, antennas, and every other protruding feature. The nose was squashed. The canopies fronting the cockpit had popped out, and the openings now looked like squinting eyes. There was still the smell of fire and burned lubricants.

"Did you find any cargo?" Lon asked. "Weapons, ammunition, field rations, anything like that?"

"Bits and pieces, Major," the sergeant in charge of the recovery efforts said. "We've been collecting it all, the way we were told. What we got is back on our shuttle, ready to go to Lincoln. There isn't a lot recognizable, though."

"A good lab can bring out quite a lot," Lon said. "Just by analyzing all of the metal and composites we might be able to tell where the items came from."

Lon walked slowly around the wreckage, scanning the hull of the shuttle closely. If there had been any identification markings, the fire and crash had obliterated them completely. *UV and IR scanning might pick something up,* Lon thought. *We get through this next operation and still have questions, we can do it then.*

For the present, he was not concerned with that. They still had the chance to take prisoners, and that would certainly yield answers. No one could resist the truth drugs that were available to Lon. All he needed was someone to administer them to.

The tail of the shuttle had snapped off and lay separated from the rest of the fuselage by forty yards. That left an opening into the passenger compartment of the shuttle. Lon stepped up into it, switching on the night-vision system of his helmet. The rows of plastic seats on either side of the compartment had been heavily damaged by the crash and the rocket that had caused it. Lon estimated that there might have been sixty seats altogether, and room for eighty cubic feet of cargo.

"Pretty basic," Colonel Henks said. He had been slow to follow Lon into the fuselage, and he did not bother to make as close an examination of the remains.

"It was sure as hell functional when it hit us at Tuplace," Lon said. "I'm going to look into the cockpit."

"I'll go talk to my men, see if anyone noticed anything useful," Henks said. "We don't want to waste more time than we have to if you want to get the other operation started today."

Lon nodded. Henks's distaste for this job did not startle him. Lon walked back to the front of the passenger compartment. The Bancrofters had pried open the hatch between that and the cockpit. It had been bent, and wedged shut. Getting it open had been difficult.

Not much was left of the cockpit. It had been small to start with, and the crushing effect of the crash had reduced it considerably. The seats for the two pilots had popped free of their anchors. The control panel had buckled in several places. The instrumentation had been removed by the Bancrofters. There was not a monitor or gauge left in place.

Lon looked under the seats and through the holes in the instrument panel but saw nothing that might be of use. After stretching over the panel to look out one of the openings, Lon retreated through the shuttle and climbed down.

"Your men did good work," he told Henks. "I assume they collected samples of the fuselage metal as well?"

"Several pieces, fuselage, wings, and tail assembly. Used a torch to cut pieces free," Henks said. "Do you see any need to leave men to guard the wreckage now that we have everything you wanted?"

"No. Nothing here is of any possible use to the raiders. I can't see them mounting an operation to recover this junk."

Junk. Lon had decided as soon as he first saw the

wreckage that the raider craft had not been nearly as well constructed as Dirigentan shuttles were. In a crash such as this, everyone aboard one of the Corps' landers would have died, but the shuttle itself would be in better condition. *Not allowing for the effects of the rocket that hit it,* Lon conceded.

The two Bancrofter shuttles returned to Lincoln together. Lon ascertained that there were laboratory facilities in the capital that could do the sort of analysis required, and he arranged for the results to be linked to CIC aboard *Tyre.*

"We can run the results against our databanks," Lon told Colonel Henks. "If we get enough matches, we ought to be able to tell what world the ship and its fittings came from, and that could lead to finding out where the raiders came from."

"You think they might not be the same?" Henks asked.

Lon shrugged. "It's possible, but far from certain. It's possible that the shuttle came from one world, the weapons and ammunition from another, and maybe the raiders themselves from a third, or several others. And the people behind it might be from still somewhere else. When we get the analysis done, we should be able to narrow it down, at least a little."

"If we don't take any prisoners in the next operation?"

"Prisoners are still important," Lon said. "But having hard evidence to go along with what prisoners tell us is better."

18

All three platoons were shorthanded because of the deaths and injuries requiring extended regeneration and recuperation. There were too many empty seats in the two shuttles that Lon and his men rode, even allowing for the fact that one platoon was staying behind. There was no banter among the men as they filed aboard and strapped in. Most of the men hid behind the faceplates of their helmets, concealing their faces—and their thoughts. Lon checked with platoon sergeants and squad leaders individually, then conferred with Tebba and Weil. There was no hard-and-fast plan of attack. The company would rendezvous with the men who had been trailing the raiders since they left Tuplace. The three platoons would separate then, one flanking the raiders on either side, the third following.

Until . . . whatever.

"How long are you prepared to keep this up?" Tebba asked his boss. "And don't give me that 'as long as it takes' line of crap. You have to have some limit in mind."

There was a long pause before Lon answered. The two were in separate shuttles, so they could not look at each other and read expressions or gestures.

"We're carrying provisions for five days," Lon said eventually. "If necessary, we'll go at least that long. Then . . . it depends on the situation, whether we can get a drop of rations without spooking the raiders we're following. But I really don't see this taking more than five days. The raiders covered thirteen miles yesterday after the explosion. And the last report we had said they had already covered that much today and were still moving. In five days they could cover a hundred miles. On the course they're following, that will take them to within a hundred miles of the coast.''

''Nothing says they have to be heading for their base,'' Tebba reminded Lon. ''They might be aiming for another target, or just drawing us away from everything. No matter how cautious we are, there is a chance they know we've been watching them.''

''If they're heading for another target, we should know within forty-eight hours,'' Lon said. ''They'll have to change course to hit any of the mining sites. I had Colonel Henks locate all of them. They're marked on our mapboards.''

''You still haven't answered my initial question,'' Tebba said. ''Just how long are you prepared to follow these raiders?''

''I don't know, Tebba,'' Lon said after another long pause. ''We can't keep it up forever, but I haven't decided yet where to draw the line.''

The DMC shuttles stayed low, no more than fifty feet above the highest treetops, and the pilots kept their speed relatively low. There had been considerable discussion about where the landers would set down. Clearings large enough to take them were few and far between in the untouched forests of Bancroft. They needed a place that was close enough to the raiders and their shadows for Lon's platoons to rendezvous with their scouts, but not so close that the raiders might hear the shuttles coming in.

''We're going to have a hard march coming up,'' Lon told Tebba and the sergeants. ''It's not going to be possible to land within five miles of the men we've got following the raiders. We'll be almost due south of the bad guys when we land, and our course will be northeast, aiming for rendezvous with our people before dawn tomorrow.''

"That's going to put an awful strain on the men," Tebba said on a private channel to Lon. "Tonight and all day tomorrow without sleep?"

"Maybe three hours for sleep," Lon said. "We push as hard as possible during the early stages this evening, check to make sure we're close enough for a final push in the hours before sunrise, then bed down for a bit. We can do it. I want us in close as quickly as possible, just in case they're getting near to where they're going."

"It's not a race, Lon," Tebba said softly. "If they reach their base, they'll probably stick around a day or two, minimum. It's no good running a race and then fighting as soon as you cross the finish line."

"I know, Tebba," Lon said, weariness showing in his voice. "But the rendezvous will be a lot safer if we can do it in the dark, then get the platoons positioned around the raiders before they start out tomorrow morning."

The landing zone was a narrow floodplain on the northern side of a fast-moving stream. At present, the creek was narrow, not quite to the flood, four to five feet deep. The ground was covered with tall grass that hid any obstacles that might be there. The LZ was so restricted that the shuttles could not land together. Lon's lander went in first, unloaded, and took off again to make room for the second shuttle. Even coming in slow it made noise, enough for Lon to worry that the raiders might hear it even five miles or more away.

Lon moved with his men to set up a quick perimeter, just beyond the limits of the grass, where the forest resumed. The grass had proven to be five to seven feet high, and very thick, which made movement through it like wading through chest-deep water. But where the trees began, the grass quickly ended.

The trees bordering the LZ were coniferous, quite similar to trees Lon had known on Earth as a child—*Christmas trees,* he thought with a brief and private smile. These trees were tall, straight, and narrow, with the lowest branches often no more than three or four feet off the ground. They provided decent shelter for his men, as they formed a defensive perimeter while the men waited for the second shuttle to come in and unload its troops.

After the second shuttle had taken off, Lon called Corporal Taw Reillor, the senior man in the group that had been tailing the raiders. "We're down," Lon said. "Could you hear or see any trace of us coming in?"

"Not a breath, Major," Reillor said. "And I'm sure the raiders didn't either. We're between them and your LZ."

"Stay back far enough that they can't spot you, even by accident," Lon said. "We're going to try to rendezvous with you before sunrise tomorrow."

"We're being careful," Reillor said. "And I know I'll be glad for the company. I get to feeling like the mouse trying to bell a cat."

"Just remember where the mouse can end up," Lon said.

While Lon was on the radio, Tebba Girana organized the company for the march. Scouts and flankers were sent out. The rest of the men in the three platoons were in their squads, ready to follow.

"Two minutes and the point squad should be far enough out," Tebba told Lon when they met.

"Who has the point?" Lon asked.

"Dean Ericks. Your old squad," Tebba said.

"*Your* old squad, you mean," Lon replied. As a cadet, waiting for his chance to earn lieutenant's pips, Lon had been assigned to the second squad of third platoon. Tebba had been the squad leader. And Lon's closest friends had been Dean, Phip, and Janno Belzer. Janno had resigned from the Corps after getting married, nearly ten years back. Lon still saw Janno and his wife, Mary, but infrequently.

"Our old squad," Tebba allowed. Both men had their helmet visors down, so they could not see each other's grins. The interlude served its purpose, though. Lon felt slightly more relaxed, less on edge. This early in the operation, that was good. It would not do to get too tight so soon.

The line of march spread out over nearly five hundred yards. The paths they found—animal paths reinforced by generations of use—were narrow. The mercenaries generally had to move in single file, and keeping decent intervals between men and platoons did the rest. Lon took his position halfway back in the lead platoon. Tebba moved in the middle of the rear platoon. Lead Sergeant Jorgen was in the center. The three leaders maintained their relative positions even when the platoons flip-flopped their order so that each had a turn at each place—point, center, and rear. The squads on the flanks and ahead were also rotated. Theoretically, those changes of assignment would help keep men from getting careless through boredom.

Every hour, the company stopped for five minutes, just long enough for men to take a drink of water and get off their feet for a short break. Lon checked his mapboard to make certain they were still on the proper heading and that the raiders had not changed course.

"At least the weather's cooperating," Phip Steesen commented during one of the breaks. "The temperature's decent and it's not raining. What more could a foot soldier ask?"

Lon grunted. "I've heard you ask for a lot more. Like trees that run beer instead of sap."

Phip laughed softly. "The way I figure it, there's got to be at least *one* world in this galaxy where the tree sap is something like beer. That's not too much to hope for, is it?"

"And maybe that sap would only run for a week or two each year. That'd fix you fine."

"Hey, don't churn my dreams. They're all I have," Phip protested weakly.

Lon calculated that they had three hours of daylight from the time the march started. As planned, he pushed the company hard during those first hours, more so when the topography forced a detour that was certain to add a mile to the distance they had to cover to make rendezvous with Taw's scouts.

Clouds started to form overhead. Between the increasing cloud cover and the trees, dusk came early. Lon pushed himself and his men. Instead of stopping long enough for a meal right after sunset, he held off until it was almost night dark and the men had been forced to switch on their night-vision systems.

But he would not press them beyond rational limits. He ordered a meal stop—thirty minutes. After four hours of hiking over rough terrain, the men needed more than five minutes to rest. Sitting on the ground, leaning back against the trunk of a tree, felt like luxury even to Lon. The calves of his legs had started to tighten up from the strain. Like his men, Lon was carrying more than his own weight. Full field kit, including weapons and ammunition, added fifty pounds.

"We're making good time," Tebba commented on his private channel to Lon. The two officers were nowhere near each other—a standard safety precaution in territory where the company might be attacked without warning. No one grenade, shell, or burst of rifle fire could take out both of them. "You still think we need to push all the way to make rendezvous tonight?"

"As long as it's possible, yes," Lon said. "The raiders aren't lollygagging, so we can't either." Then, to forestall the arguments he suspected might come from Tebba, Lon added, "We'll push on for another three hours, then take stock. I hope that puts us close enough to close the gap in an hour. That'll give us three and a half, maybe four hours for sleep."

Tebba did not speak, which spoke loudly to Lon.

"Once we catch up, we won't have to go any faster than the raiders," Lon said. "But until we get close, we can't do a damned thing for the people we've got on their tail. We'll just have to make do, sore feet and all."

"I know, Lon," Tebba said.

"I never ignore your advice, Tebba," Lon said.

"Even when I don't take it, I take it into consideration. It's just that, this time, we need to do it fast."

Before the company stopped to sleep, they moved away from the route they had been following, off to the side more than two hundred yards, on the remote chance that someone was following *them*. Sentries were posted. Each fire team would always have one man on watch within the encampment. And one sergeant would always be awake, ready to respond instantly to any threat.

Lon stood near the center of the bivouac, waiting until his men were settled. He talked to Tebba, Weil, and each of the platoon sergeants, then merely watched. The perimeter was roughly circular, allowing for the terrain. The fire teams stayed close, without much distance between teams. Because the chance of hostiles stumbling on them was so low, Lon did not order the men to dig trenches. *Let them get as much sleep as they can,* he thought. *No need to waste part of their sack time digging.* If the level of danger had been greater, he would have had no hesitation about ordering the work.

Only when most of the platoon had settled in did Lon get off his feet. He took off his equipment harness and let the pack and web belt slide to the ground. Then he sat beside them. He loosened the closures on his boots but did not take them off. After hours of hiking, his feet would swell, and getting the boots back on in a hurry might be difficult.

Lon knew that once he lay down, sleep would come quickly, so he waited before stretching out under one of the low-slung trees. He was tired, his mind slowing already. *I guess we did push it as hard as we could,* he thought. He was certainly no longer the youngest man in the company—far from it—but he was also not among the oldest. Tebba and Weil were both at least fifteen years older, and there were a couple of other men in the company who were even older.

No one called with problems. Everyone was ready to take what sleep they could. After several minutes, Lon pushed his pack and harness farther under his tree, then slid in beside it. He unrolled his thermal blanket, wrapped himself in it, and lay on his back. The padding in his helmet had to serve as pillow. He adjusted his position and almost before he stopped moving, he was asleep.

Here, sleep could not be the total oblivion of slumber in known safety. No matter the exhaustion that occasioned it, sleep was a skittish horse in the field, starting at every real or imagined hint of danger. Lon's mind did not totally abdicate awareness, so there was a disturbed quality to his rest. Sound penetrated, raising his level of awareness until the mind convinced itself that no immediate threat had surfaced. Dreams flitted about the edges, chaotic, incomplete; there was no way to assemble them into a meaningful whole, any more than a jigsaw puzzle could be successfully erected with miscellaneous pieces from a dozen different pictures. "Combat sleep" was what soldiers called it . . . on the rare occasions when one man could bring himself to discuss it with another.

Lon had left instructions to be wakened after three hours. It took only a single word, "Major," spoken over the radio, to bring him out of his less than peaceful repose.

"I'm here," he replied before he recognized Dav Grott's voice.

"Three hours are up," Dav said. "Should I rouse the men?"

Lon glanced at the timeline display on his helmet's visor. "Another fifteen minutes. Just call Tebba and Weil for now."

Lon put himself through a full minute of stretching exercises while he remained on his back, pumping himself up to full alertness, getting his body ready for the demands of another day. There was a damp chill to the night breeze, a promise—or threat—of rain riding the air. When Lon looked out from under the tree, he noticed fog, ground mist, softening the darkness, setting trees up as ghostly silhouettes.

His abbreviated exercises complete, Lon called *Tyre* and spoke to the duty officer in CIC. There were no updates on the position of the raiders, no news on other activities that might affect the mission that Lon and his men were currently on, except for a confirmation that rain might be near. Then Lon called Tebba and Weil.

"Half an hour for breakfast and the necessary," he told them. "Then we get on our feet again. We'll take it fairly easy the first hour, work into our pace gradually."

There were no comments other than acknowledgments.

The fog deadened what few sounds the men of A Company made getting ready for the new day—a "day" whose sunlight would not start for two and a half hours. Dirigenters trained to operate silently, but the fog—which thickened during the half hour Lon had allotted for preparations—would cover any mistakes.

"I hope it lasts well into the morning," Phip said when Lon checked in with him by radio. "It won't hamper us any, and it should put a crimp in how well the raiders can see."

"If it's true that they don't have any night-vision gear," Lon qualified.

"None of the bodies we found at Tuplace had any," Phip said. "I can't see that they'd take time to strip their dead of those when they were in a hurry to get away."

"At least some of them must be able to see in the dark," Lon said. "They wouldn't be so eager to make their attacks at night otherwise. Maybe squad leaders and up. And they *might* take the time to remove any evidence of equipment they didn't want the Bancrofters to know they had. Just don't count on any of them being blind in the dark."

Lon talked to each platoon sergeant, eating while he did. There were none of the problems that could plague a force on the march—leg cramps, blisters, or sprains. The minor aches could be treated with med-patches. Every man was accounted for.

"All right, Weil, form them up and let's get started,"
Lon told the lead sergeant when the half hour was up.

The company had not been on the march more than
twenty minutes when Lon had a call from Corporal Reillor. "Major, the raiders are up and moving. They were
already hotfooting it away when our sentry noticed. The
fog here's so thick we didn't see or hear anything before
that."

"Any change of direction?" Lon asked.

"No, sir. They're still following this valley toward
the southeast. I don't know what got into them."

"Well, at least we know there's no target for them to
raid anywhere close, Taw. Stay with them. We're about
an hour back. We'll catch up to you as best we can."

"They got some kind of bug in their drawers, Major,"
Taw said. "They're moving faster than they did anytime
yesterday, like they suddenly remembered they're late
for a hot date."

"Just keep an eye on them and make sure they don't
spot you," Lon said. "You may have been spotted already and they could be setting you up, so be extra careful."

Lon passed the news to Tebba and the sergeants, who
passed it along to their squad leaders.

"What do you think it means?" Tebba asked.

"I was about to ask you that same question," Lon
replied. "One possibility is that they've spotted our people and are setting them up for an ambush. Other than
that, they could be heading in for an attack on some
mining camp—except that according to the intelligence
we have, there are no mining camps anywhere close—
or they're in range of their base or an LZ and they're
in a hurry."

"We have to trust the intelligence Henks gave us that
there are no mining targets close," Tebba said. "It might
be wrong, but we have to accept it. Since they seem to
be in a sudden hurry, I'd guess that it's either an ambush
of our people or a scheduled rendezvous with air trans-

port. In the dark, they might be able to get a shuttle in and out without our people spotting it, if they've got up-to-date stealth tech. And they were moving shuttles around without notice until we caught them at Tuplace.''

''I'll get on to CIC,'' Lon said. ''Make sure they've started our shuttle patrol again. They pulled in everyone after the raiders bedded down for the night.''

''Shuttle pilots need sleep, too, the same as real people,'' Tebba said.

Lon switched channels to talk with the duty officer in *Tyre*'s combat intelligence center, who brought the officer of the deck from *Sidon* into the conference. Both of *Tyre*'s shuttles were on the ground in Lincoln, next to the militia camp. *Sidon* was just getting ready to launch its first shuttle of the morning. That shuttle would be over the area of the raiders in twenty minutes.

''Assume the raider aircraft have at least the stealth capabilities of our Shrike fighters,'' Lon said. ''I know we have trouble spotting them on exercises, especially at night.''

More things to worry about, Lon thought after he signed off. *Why can't it ever go right according to the plan?*

He asked more speed of his men, picking up the pace. With the raiders on the move again, rendezvousing with Taw and the other scouts before sunrise looked less and less likely, but he wanted to try. If the raiders did plan on luring the scouts into a trap, getting another 130 men into position would turn the tables in a hurry.

The other possibility worried Lon more. Taw Reillor and his companions were alert to the chance of an ambush, and they would not be easy targets. But if the raiders met shuttles and were lifted out of the area before the three platoons of Alpha caught them, the pursuers would be back where they started, with a day and a night of pushing through the forest wasted, and no victory or prisoners to show for the effort.

Forty minutes after the report from Taw, Lon called

the corporal back. "Listen, we still don't know what
those raiders have in mind, but if they rendezvous with
air transport, you and your men are going to have to
stage a delaying action, try to hold them up until we get
there. We're coming as fast as we can, but we're not
closing the gap very quickly. If it comes down to it, hit
them, move, and hit again. Maybe they won't risk putting a shuttle on the ground if they think there's a real
firefight going on."

Taw hesitated for a couple of seconds before he replied. He had no doubt at all what the likely outcome
would be if his handful of men tried to stop the entire
raider contingent . . . and it wasn't something that was
likely to give him a chance to have grandchildren to tell
about it.

"Yes, sir. If they rendezvous with air transport, we'll
do what we can to keep them in place until you arrive,"
Taw said.

A minute later, Lon told the point to pick up the pace
again. "We can't catch up at the rate we've been going."

After another hour Lon could see some of their rush.
On the mapboard, the gap between Taw's men and the
rest of the three platoons had narrowed by more than
half a mile. But the raiders had yet to stop for even a
five-minute break and showed no sign of slowing down.

In the forest, the fog remained, diffusing the first light
of dawn, giving the men a little more visibility. Every
few minutes Lon wiped his faceplate with his sleeve to
get rid of the condensation. He was beginning to feel
the strain of the forced march through the forest. Soon
he would have to give his men at least a short rest, but
he begrudged the distance they would lose stopping even
for five minutes.

The raiders must be in the same situation, he told
himself. *We'll stop when they do.* But he kept looking
at the timeline on his visor. When would they stop? And
why were they in such a blazing hurry?

• • •

"Major, this is Taw." The call came just as Lon was about to concede a break, without waiting longer for the raiders to stop. "They've changed course. They're starting up the slope on the east side of the valley, almost due east. I can't see the lay of the land there clearly. I don't know if this is where they're going or if they're just crossing to the next valley."

"Hold up for a couple of minutes, Taw. Give them plenty of room before you follow." Lon pulled his mapboard from its pocket on the leg of his battledress and unfolded it. "I don't see any sign of a clearing large enough for an aircraft to get in there, not close." He zoomed in to the best magnification the mapboard provided and scrolled his way along that next valley. "Maybe five miles southeast, along the creek that runs along the bottom of that valley. As long as you can see which way they turn, if they do, after they cross the ridge."

Five minutes later, when Taw called again, Lon could hear gunfire over the radio. "They suckered us, Major. We've got raiders on three sides."

19

Lon immediately called the shuttle that *Sidon* had sent down on patrol and ordered a strike against the raiders. The only reference he could give the shuttle was the position of Taw's patrol. "Cover the area around them, in as close as you dare," Lon told the pilot. "We'll need forty minutes to reach them."

Without serious help, Taw and his men would not be able to hold out that long. They might be able to slip away in the fog. Taw had said that there were raiders on *three* sides. There was a chance for escape, but Lon could not count on it.

His next call was to *Sidon,* to get the next shuttle out as quickly as possible. One craft's munitions would not last long. Then he alerted *Tyre*'s shuttles, parked outside the militia camp in Lincoln. "We may need to evacuate wounded, or we may need your weapons," he told both pilots. "Get ready to take off on a minute's notice."

Lon had cut Tebba and Weil in on his conversations, so the news did not have to be repeated. "Tebba, take second platoon and push as fast as you can. The rest of us will follow." He picked second platoon, Phip's platoon, because it was in front at the moment, a few score yards closer to the enemy than the rest of the company.

Second platoon had the fewest men on the march. In addition to its casualties from Tuplace, it was missing the men who were being attacked now. They had all been Phip's men. That would give second platoon an extra incentive to move fast.

"Weil, we'll take two minutes, just long enough to

reorganize and get going again,'' Lon said after second platoon had started jogging away from the rest. ''We can't afford to take more time that than.''

Weil passed the word to third and fourth platoons to rest for two minutes before he replied, ''Yes, sir. Two minutes will help, a little.''

Lon squatted where he was, then slid back until he was sitting so he could stretch his legs. He took a sip of water, then spent the next minute breathing deeply, almost to the point of hyperventilating.

If the raiders are in reach when we get there, he thought, *we hit them and keep hitting them. No more following to see where they go. As long as we get at least one prisoner in condition to talk, that's victory enough.*

Lon called Harley Stossberg and told him to alert first platoon and Colonel Henks. ''Get ready to board the shuttles on two minutes' notice, Harley,'' Lon said.

''We can board now and be airborne ready to come in,'' Harley said. ''We might be able to get there before you can.''

''No clearing near enough. We may have to use our shuttles for their rockets and cannons. But get on to Colonel Henks and tell him it's time to muster his rapid response company.''

Lon got back to his feet before he gave the order for his men to get up and start marching again.

As soon as third and fourth platoons were on the move, Lon switched to the channel that linked him to Taw Reillor. Lon called Taw's name but got no response, only a faint static. He switched channels, to one of the squad frequencies that the patrol had been using.

''This is Zeffo, Major,'' a whispering voice said. ''I don't dare make much noise. There's still raiders close by. They quit shooting at us as soon as the shuttle made its first run, but they haven't gone far. We got hit bad, at least three men dead. I guess I'm the only one still got a working radio.''

"We're on our way, Zeffo," Lon said, also whispering. "We'll keep air cover over you as much as possible. The second shuttle will be coming in as soon as it can get down from *Sidon*. And we'll be there twenty minutes later, maybe less. Second platoon has gone on ahead, pushing. Just hold on."

Lon pushed forward from his position between the two remaining platoons, getting near the front of third, which had the point now. He settled into the line near Dav Grott, who acknowledged his presence with a nod.

"We can't go faster than we are, Major," Dav said on a private channel. "Not and do any good when we get there."

"I know, Dav," Lon replied. "I just . . ." He stopped, uncertain what he wanted to say.

"Yeah, me, too, Major," Dav said. "I know just what you mean." But he did not try to put it in words either.

The fighting was over long before Tebba Girana and second platoon reached the patrol. The attacks from the air had kept the raiders from coming in to finish off the survivors, but only four of the Dirigenters were still alive. Lance Corporal Zeffo was the only one who was uninjured. Corporal Reillor had suffered several wounds. Two bullets had hit his helmet, and though neither penetrated Taw's skull, there were superficial head injuries—and the helmet was a total loss. There were also wounds to his side and one leg. Tebba reported what he had found and called off the air attacks, then posted a perimeter while the medic with the platoon treated Taw and the other wounded.

"Send a couple of scouts out to try to determine which way they went," Lon instructed. "Tell them not to get in sight of the raiders. I just want to know what direction they went."

"Right," Tebba said. He was breathing heavily. After half running the last two miles of forest with full field kit, he had not had time to catch his breath. "I was going to do that. I just had to take care of the immediate situation first.''

"I know, Tebba," Lon said. "The rush is off now. I'm going to give the men here ten minutes, then we'll be on our way. The shuttles will be scouting from overhead, trying to pick up the raiders, but they might not be able to see much."

"We're still going on after them?" Tebba asked.

"As long as they leave a trail we can follow. Have you found any raider casualties?"

"Still looking. At least two dead, one with his front slit open from neck to navel. Zeffo did that. The dead raider was lying on top of him. I guess that's how he managed to escape."

"Do what you can to get Reillor stabilized, Tebba. It's five miles to the nearest landing we can bring a shuttle into, and we've got to get there in force to protect the LZ," Lon said.

"The medic's working. Taw's the only one hurt bad. We'll rig a stretcher to carry him. The others will be able to walk shortly. Lon, if you take the rest of the company on a direct line to the LZ, you'll save time."

Lon looked at his mapboard, drawing lines with the cursor and comparing them; then he emphasized the topographical situation. "Maybe a few minutes," he said then. "Over a hill that rises about four hundred feet over the valley on this side."

"Still faster, I think," Tebba said.

"We'll try it," Lon said. "Try to stay out of trouble."

Lon switched channels to talk with Weil Jorgen, Wil Nace, and Dav Grott. He gave them the change of plans and slaved their mapboards to his to show the route they were going to take.

"It *will* be faster," Weil said.

"I'd like to know where the raiders are," Wil said. "They could be waiting for us when we show up."

"Second platoon is trying to find their trail," Lon said. "Right now, our major concern is getting the wounded to where they can be picked up for treatment. Five minutes and we're back on the move.''

As long as the location of the raiders was unknown, Lon had another worry, the possibility that the enemy might reverse positions and become the hunter instead of the hunted. Every combat veteran in the unit was aware of the chance. The point and flanking men were at their maximum level of alertness, even as they worked to keep the pace of the platoons as fast as possible. Men trod carefully, eyes on the ground as well as on the forest around them. They listened to the sounds, straining for any clue they might have to other intruders in the wild.

Lon kept a radio channel open to Tebba, who relayed information as he learned it. By the time the two platoons with Lon had covered half the distance to the planned landing zone, the scouts Tebba had sent out had followed the trail of the raiders far enough to see that they had started to cross the next line of hills, continuing east rather than southeast.

"Do I keep them on the raiders' trail or pull them back?" Tebba asked.

You mean, do we risk losing another patrol the way we did the last? Lon thought, hesitating—but only briefly.

"If we don't keep some contact with the enemy, we might play hell trying to find them again," Lon said. "Tell your scouts to stay with them, but well back, and to get out of the way in a hurry if they sense anything—*any*thing out of the ordinary. Right now, I'm content as long as we can mark their trail."

Lon waited for Tebba to pass those instructions along before he continued. "We won't try to wait for them to go to ground, Tebba. Once we get the shuttle in and out, we close with the enemy as quickly as we can and attack. We'll deal with this batch. And it'll give the Bancrofters some idea of the location to search for any base, even if we don't take prisoners."

"We are still going to *try* for prisoners, aren't we?"

Tebba asked, a hint of uncertainty in his tone.

"Yes, Tebba," Lon replied. "We stick with regs. We're not looking for a bloodbath if we can help it. We want prisoners, and Henks wants them, too, someone to parade through Lincoln and show the people that their militia is doing its job and that we're earning our pay."

Ten minutes later, Lon decided on a slight change in tactics. He called Harley Stossberg in Lincoln. "Get first platoon and the Bancrofters in the air. There's a good LZ six miles east of the raiders' current location, just south of the last line of march we could mark. You take our men in first to secure the LZ, then bring Henks's men in behind and set up a solid defensive position. We'll use classic hammer and anvil tactics, with us driving the raiders into you."

"Six miles—isn't that going to be cutting things a little close?" Harley asked. He had a mapboard open and was looking at the situation. "You might have trouble catching up with them in time, and I assume you want us all in on this."

"Yes, but we can't risk setting you down any farther away. If they change course again, it could put you too far out of position to reach the fight. If necessary, we can move you back a little once you're on the ground."

"We'll be in the air in five minutes," Harley promised.

The men from the militia camp in Lincoln—Dirigenters and the militia rapid response company—were in the air when Lon received a call from CIC aboard *Tyre*.

"There appears to be a raider attack in progress, just started," Commander Tanner, the skipper of *Tyre*, reported. "Sixty miles west-northwest of Lincoln."

"We'll reroute my first platoon and the Bancrofters," Lon said. "I'll have Lieutenant Stossberg coordinate with you for updates."

"Roger, Major. We'll keep an eye on things."

"Can you spot a good LZ for them, close but not right on the target?" Lon asked. He was still in the process of getting his mapboard out and finding the location of the new attack.

"Three-tenths of a mile out," Commander Tanner said quickly. "A patch of bare rock on top of a ridge, or rather just west of the ridgeline, out of direct view of the village."

As soon as Lon finished his conversation with Tanner, he switched channels to tell Harley about the change.

"Colonel Henks would insist on responding to this, so we start on that basis. Same deal as we were going to run here, Harley. Take our men in first to secure the LZ and bring the Bancrofters in once you have a perimeter established. Use your shuttle's guns for close air support."

There was a very slight hesitation before Harley replied. He had just realized that he was going to be commanding in a combat situation for the first time—*commanding,* not in the middle, as he had been on his other combat experiences—and if things went badly, there might not be time to get the rest of the company in to support them.

"We'll do our best, Lon," he said.

"I know you will, Harley. Keep the Bancrofters in check as best you can. And good luck."

20

Lon and the men with him climbed out of the fog two hundred feet above the valley floor. The sun was out, casting bright reflections off the top of the fog. The sun was not very high above the next ridge to the east. Looking back down into the valley, only the tops of the tallest trees were visible above the layer of fog. Overhead, the sky was nearly clear, with only a few wisps of clouds very high.

"We'll take five minutes," Lon told his platoon sergeants. Lon took out his mapboard as he sat on a rock. He worked at stretching his legs while he checked map positions. His calves were tightening up, and he did not want to risk cramps later. He called Tebba.

"We've got to rethink things a bit," Lon said as soon as his second-in-command responded. "This new attack ties knots in our plans."

"I guess," Tebba replied. "Any word on how many raiders are involved in this attack?"

"Not even a guess," Lon said. "Maybe we'll get some idea once Harley and Henks are on the ground."

"What about the group we've been following?" Tebba asked.

"We find them, we take them out," Lon said without hesitation. "We don't let any of them escape if we can help it. That might not end Bancroft's problem, but it should certainly put a crimp in the raiders' operations. Look, right now there's no point in heading for a rendezvous near that clearing we were going to use as an LZ. Give your men a rest and we'll catch up with you as quickly as we can. Maybe forty-five minutes once we start again.''

''I won't argue,'' Tebba said quickly. ''Hang on.'' The pause was just long enough for Tebba to switch channels and get second platoon stopped and moving into a defensive perimeter. ''I'm still concerned about the people we're following. I don't want to have more men walk into an ambush.''

''I know, Tebba,'' Lon said. ''But we've got to at least know there's a trail we can follow. We can't let them disappear into the forest and pop up somewhere else later.''

''My guess is that we're not too far from where they're going,'' Tebba said. ''That deal with the ambush, and the sudden change of course. It smells as if they're trying to get away from observation before they go to ground. And it might be exactly what they plan to do.''

''Caves?'' Lon asked after only an instant's hesitation.

''I've seen a couple already,'' Tebba said, ''and there's a good chance there are more of them around.''

''Could be,'' Lon conceded, nodding slowly even though Tebba could not see him. ''This country is a lot like where I grew up, and there were scores of caves around, some of them large enough to hide an army.''

Lon gestured to Weil Jorgen, and the lead sergeant got the two platoons on their feet and ready to move again. Lon stood then and put his mapboard away. ''We're starting out now,'' he told Tebba.

Fifteen minutes later, Harley called Lon to let him know that first platoon was about to land and secure the landing zone near the newest raider attack so Colonel Henks and his rapid response company would be able to come in safely.

''We haven't had any additional intelligence about the situation on the ground,'' Harley said. ''Lincoln has lost contact with the village.''

"That might mean we're too late," Lon replied. "They might be gone already—or secure enough to hit you fast after you get on the ground. Make sure the men know they have to get out into a perimeter fast."

"They know," Harley said. "We all know."

"Keep me posted on what you find," Lon said before he cut the connection. He was tempted to monitor the conversations going on in first platoon once it landed, at least the channels that Harley and his noncoms would be on, but he resisted the urge. It would show a lack of faith in Harley's leadership abilities, and Lon did not want to do anything to undermine the young lieutenant's confidence.

Lon knew the steps first platoon would take—straight out of a drill book until events on the ground forced changes. The shuttle would come in hot—as fast as it could safely manage. Even before it came to a full stop, the men inside would be unbuckling their safety harnesses, ready to get out of "the box" as quickly as they could. Lon could empathize. He had been through enough combat landings in his years as a soldier to know exactly what they would be feeling. A soldier felt most vulnerable while he was in a shuttle heading toward hostilities. In the box, he had no way to defend himself. His fate was entirely in the hands of others. Only after the shuttle landed could he get out, in position to take a hand in his own defense. No matter how intense the opposition, a soldier always felt a little relief getting out of the box.

On the march, Lon could not let his thoughts remain entirely with first platoon. He had three others to worry about, and second platoon might run into raiders as quickly as first. It was not out of the question that the two platoons with him might even come across the enemy first, walk into an ambush. When that thought came into Lon's head, he called the fire team walking point and reminded them of the possibility.

He also had to watch where he was walking, and keep track of the men directly in front and behind to maintain proper spacing. In rough country, with plenty of cover, an average separation of two to three yards seemed plenty. That spread the platoons out enough to minimize the casualties that might be inflicted in the first seconds of a firefight if the raiders did ambush them, but they were not so spread out that all of the men could not be brought into a fight quickly.

You've already divided your command in too many pieces, Lon told himself. He took a quick look around, scanning from as close to the point as he could see toward the rear. *We don't have much more than parity in manpower with the raiders we know about. A smart ambush could quickly give them numerical superiority.* He shrugged, an almost invisible gesture. It was too late to worry about the number of slices he had cut his pie into. They were not too far from gathering in one of the separated platoons. That would give him back the three platoons he had allotted for this operation at the beginning.

Lon was startled out of his reflections by a hint of quick movement on the ground, no more than two feet from the path he was following. A snake slid under old dead leaves on the forest floor, out of sight, fleeing from the intruders. "Snake on the right," he reported over his all-hands channel. "Watch for it." Lon kept moving, watching that side of the trail for the next few steps. He could only wonder if the snake might be poisonous. *We know too damned little about the animals here,* he thought. They had been briefed about the more common animals—predators and prey—but not in nearly enough detail. That had been back before the mission had changed, before the rider to the training contract put the Dirigenters out in the field. *Should have followed up on it,* Lon thought, shaking his head. *Too many mistakes here.*

"We're on the ground, in our perimeter," Harley reported. "I don't hear any gunfire. The Bancrofter shuttles are on the way in now."

Lon acknowledged the report, then called Tebba. He

relayed the news about first platoon, then asked, "Any sign of our raiders yet?"

"Nothing new," Tebba said. "Our scouts don't have them in sight just now. They're playing it careful, the way you said. They think they've still got a good line on their trail, though."

"We're getting close. Should be within sight of your perimeter in six or seven minutes. You know the course we're on." It was unlikely that Dirigenter soldiers would make a mistake and fire on their own comrades, but nothing would be left to chance. Lon was not going to make another mistake if he could avoid it.

"We'll be watching for you," Tebba said. "I'll give you a call as soon as we spot the point."

Once rendezvous was accomplished, Lon gave the men who had marched with him a much-needed rest. It was only fifteen minutes, but even that helped. Second platoon spread their perimeter and did the watching for all of them. Lon, Tebba, and Weil met near the center of the defended area to plot out next moves while each ate a meal pack.

"We have to assume that the raiders know the terrain a hell of a lot better than we do," Lon said. "That gives them an edge, and we've already seen that they've got tactical sense. We may have been underrating them from the beginning, gotten a little too complacent. Myself included," he added after a short pause.

"The more I see of their work, the more I think we must be up against trained mercenaries," Tebba said. "There might not be a lot of them, but the people we've seen operating here are not just a bunch of thugs hired in spaceport bars."

"Hitting our scouts the way they did, that gives them a hell of a boost," Weil said. "Makes us slow down, take more care, gives them time. If they're not professionals, they were trained by pros. I'd wager my contract bonus on that."

"When we get started on their tail again, make sure

the point and flankers are on the lookout for booby traps,'' Lon said. ''That extra time might have given them a chance to lay stuff in our path.''

Tebba and Weil both nodded. ''We have to assume the possibility,'' Weil said, ''but my hunch is that they'd leave a plainer trail if they wanted us to hurry after them, and they're not. They appear to be trying to avoid leaving any sign at all—from the reports we've had from our scouts.''

''We're not going to play 'odds and evens,' '' Lon said. ''Right now, I'm more interested in doing this right than fast. They're not going to get away from us.''

''In any case, if this chase goes much farther east, the terrain is going to get a lot better for us,'' Tebba said. ''We're near the last chain of these hills. Two valleys over, there's a fair-sized river that the raiders aren't going to cross without boats. And the one valley left between us and the river eventually peters out and runs into the river as well, about thirty miles south of where we are now.''

It was little surprise to any of them when, three minutes later, the scouts reported that the raiders' trail turned north in the next valley over.

''Time to get moving,'' Lon said after he had finished questioning the scouts. ''We've got ground to cover.''

Reports started coming to Lon from Harley Stossberg. First platoon and the company of Bancrofter militia had entered the mining village called Doreen's Gap after setting up a defensive perimeter around it. The raiders had been and gone, leaving twenty villagers dead and four dozen wounded—many of those critically. The Bancrofter shuttles had returned to the LZ, and the wounded were being given battlefield first aid and a quick flight to Lincoln. The Dirigenter shuttle was circling high overhead, ready to come in to provide close support if that proved necessary.

''Do you want us to try to follow these raiders?'' Harley asked after he had finished his report.

"No, and do everything you can to persuade Colonel Henks not to," Lon said. "Once the wounded and dead have been tended to, tell him you'll send scouts out to determine the direction the raiders took, but don't send anyone too far, and tell them to be damned careful they don't walk into an ambush."

"Lon, I don't think there's one chance in a million of holding Henks back. He's already made it clear he wants to go after these raiders."

"Tell him we've still got this batch of raiders to deal with. Once we neutralize them, we should have prisoners who can tell us where to find the rest of their forces. If he goes off after that bunch alone, he could lose men to no point. If that argument doesn't work, bring me in on the radio and I'll try."

"I'll give it my best shot," Harley said.

The platoons of A Company with Lon did not follow the trail on the valley floor that the raiders had taken once they crossed the ridge. Instead, Lon kept his men on the western slope, eighty to a hundred feet up. The footing was slightly less secure, and the slope made walking less comfortable, but there was, Lon thought, less chance of running into booby traps or ambushes. The raiders were moving too quickly to plant traps clear across the valley and both hillsides.

No one let his guard slip, though. Even twenty men back in the column, Lon watched the ground and trees around him almost as carefully as he would have if he were walking point. Lon would not make the mistake of underestimating the opposition again. Not soon.

The scouts reported at irregular intervals, checking in so no one would think that anything had happened to them. The trail they were following headed northeast along the floor of the valley, on one side or the other of a shallow creek that meandered along the lowest part of the valley.

"They're being more careful about leaving sign," one scout reported. "Can't tell anything about how many there are now, and there's been a couple of places we went a hundred yards or more without seeing anything to say that people had been by."

An hour before noon, a scout spotted the raider rear guard. The Dirigenters stopped and went to cover immediately, then waited for five minutes before moving thirty yards to the side. Lon's orders had been to avoid direct contact.

Lon listened to the report, then checked positions on his mapboard. He stopped the company for lunch, then brought Tebba, Weil, and the platoon sergeants in for a conference.

"We're only three-quarters of a mile from the scouts and not much farther than that from the raiders," Lon said. He slaved the mapboards of the others to his and moved a cursor to highlight the relative positions. "The break now should give the raiders a chance to move away from the scouts, keep us from having to close with them too soon."

"How do we handle this?" Tebba asked. "Move in and attack, or try to get the Bancrofters and our first platoon in front of them again?"

"It's going to be at least a half hour before the others can get airborne again," Lon said. "The Bancrofter shuttles are just getting ready to take off from Lincoln after transporting the last of the villagers." The unwounded survivors had been taken out after the wounded. "Harley's scouts will be back by then as well. The problem is that there's no suitable LZ close enough to get them in place here in less than three hours."

Lon indicated the nearest suitable landing zone on the other side of the raiders. It was north and east of the course the enemy was following, across another ridge. "And three hours is pushing it," Lon added.

"Does that mean we take them on ourselves?" Tebba asked.

"If necessary," Lon said. "I'm going to get the others in the air and moving toward that LZ. After lunch, we'll start moving again. We have to try something, I think, to slow the raiders down long enough for the rest of our assets to get into position. My inclination is to catch up and hit them. If we can pin them down until the others get here, so much the better. If not, we take them on by ourselves. We'll be above them, unless things go drastically wrong, and that should help.''

''We gonna cross the ridge to keep out of sight until we're in position?'' Weil asked.

Lon nodded. ''That's what I'm planning. We can move faster, let a fire team on the flank get them in sight as well as watch for trouble.''

Lon added an extra ten minutes to the lunch break, getting his men back on their feet only after Harley called to report that first platoon was in the air, behind the two shuttles carrying the Bancrofter militiamen. By that time Lon's scouts had been moving for ten minutes, anxious to get back on the trail of the raiders.

Twenty minutes after that, Lon had a call from the scouts.

''We've lost the trail, Major. There was a rocky flat and we can't find any sign of which way they went from there.''

''How far out have you looked?'' Lon asked.

''Three hundred yards past, toward the north, about half that on either side, up the slopes. It's like they just vanished.''

21

Lon turned off his transmitter before he indulged himself in thirty seconds of soft cursing. He took a deep breath and held it for an instant before he opened the transmitter again.

"Don't take chances," he told the scouts. "Head this way, fast as you can. The raiders might be setting another ambush."

"Moving now, Major."

Lon switched channels to give Tebba the news.

"I don't like it," Tebba said. "They're up to something."

Tell me something I don't know, Lon thought. "Let's just get to the scouts first," was what he said. "Once we've got the numbers together, we can worry about what comes next. Harley and Henks will be on the ground shortly. One way or another we should be able to reestablish contact with the raiders and get this over with."

"Maybe they went underground."

"If we don't find a trail somewhere, we'll bring echo gear down from *Tyre*."

"Won't a cave opening be fairly obvious?" Tebba asked.

"Not necessarily," Lon said. "Left natural, some of the caves back on Earth were hard to find, even if you knew where the entrance was. And if these jokers have camouflaged a hideaway, we might search for a week and not find the way in."

The company kept moving during the discussion. Lon

signaled a slight increase in the pace. He was anxious about the safety of the scouts. One group of his men had been ambushed in similar circumstances. He did not want to have that repeated.

It only took twenty minutes to effect the rendezvous. By that time Lon had decided on the next course of action. He briefed Tebba and the noncoms.

"We head to where the scouts lost the trail. The first order of business will be to set up a strong defensive position, to the point of putting snoops out around our perimeter. Then we do a systematic search to find either some indication of which direction the raiders took—or the entrance to any cave they might have taken shelter in. If necessary, we'll keep at that until first platoon and the Bancrofters reach us. I've already alerted Lieutenant Stossberg to the fact that we've lost track of the raiders and that they might be heading toward them." Lon shrugged, though only a couple of the others were close enough to witness the gesture. "It would be too easy, I suppose, to have the raiders walk right into the arms of first platoon and Colonel Henks's militia company."

"Stranger things have happened," Weil Jorgen commented.

"I'm going to have *Sidon* load echo-ranging gear on one of her shuttles, and we'll bring that in if we have to," Lon continued, ignoring the interruption. "And the patrolling shuttles have been listening for electronic emissions right along—radio or anything else that puts out a detectable signal."

"Without luck," Tebba noted. "Part of the paradox. The raiders fight like highly trained professionals, and they're well armed, but they're apparently not using any electronics. We haven't found night-vision gear, sophisticated battle helmets, or anything else on any of the dead they've left behind."

"They must have some way to contact their shuttles," Phip said. "Do they have gear that's so much better than ours that we can't even detect it?"

"We would have recognized comm gear," Lon said.

"If they're using anything, it almost has to be on a very tight beam, maybe even a modulating laser."

"Not very practical if one end of the conversation is aboard a shuttle doing several hundred miles per hour," Phip said. "Be almost impossible to keep a lock on it without some pretty hefty tracking gear, and we know these raiders aren't carrying anything that bulky."

"I know, Phip. I know," Lon assured him. "Now let's get back on the move. We've had all the rest we can afford."

As the company started moving again, Lon caught himself checking the position of the selector switch on his rifle, making certain that he had not left the safety on. If they walked into an ambush, the fraction of a second he would lose learning that his rifle would not fire because the safety was on might be critical. Then he wiped the palm of his hand on the side of his trousers. His hands were sweating.

I haven't been this nervous since the first time, he thought. For just an instant, his mind flashed back to Norbank, the world where he had experienced his first combat—years and light-years away. *At least we knew who we were fighting there.* He recalled Arlan Taiters, the lieutenant who had mentored him through his months as a cadet, waiting his chance to earn a lieutenant's pips the only way possible in the DMC—in combat. Lieutenant Taiters had not survived Norbank. Nor had a lot of other good men. *"We try not to waste men, but there are never any guarantees,"* Taiters had once told Lon. *We've walked into more than our share of hairy ones,* Lon thought. Even though it had been more than four years—before Bancroft—since Alpha had lost any men killed on a contract, it was the other contracts Lon remembered now.

He shook his head vigorously, as if that might help him discard the errant musings of his mind. This was not the time to get lost in thought. Memories were better restricted to the safety of a garrison, with no enemy on the same world.

Watch over the shoulder of the man in front of you. Scan the terrain to either side. Keep your eyes moving. Give the minimum attention necessary to the ground underfoot but don't ignore it. After twenty men have walked the same path, you're probably not going to hit a trip wire, but it's not impossible. Don't let yourself think that it's highly unlikely that a small band of raiders is going to booby-trap the woods just because no one has ever really chased them for any length of time before. They've shown themselves to be smart and well trained. You don't know enough to assume you can predict what they will or won't do. The only surprise will be if there are no surprises.

The thoughts were no distraction; they were scarcely conscious. Lon did the proper things by habit. Years of drilling and field exercises, months of teaching those skills to others ... and more months of using them in combat situations made it all almost automatic. It was a way of life, a way of staying alive.

As a unit, Alpha Company functioned smoothly, efficiently, for the same reasons. Every man knew what he needed to do, and all but a few of them had honed their abilities on combat contracts in the past. Every combat rookie had veterans in his squad to keep an eye on him and make certain that the necessary lessons were not forgotten. Even the veteran had others to look out for them, squad leaders, platoon sergeants, up to the company lead sergeant and officers. Detailed instructions were rarely necessary. Lon felt safe in delegating tasks to subordinates without trying to talk them through routine operations.

Lon's three platoons reached the rocky area where the scouts had lost the trail of the raiders. He gave the order to set up a defensive perimeter. That would not be on the valley floor, but high on one of the slopes that flanked it, with men covering the ridge. On the ground, it was still an axiom of military thinking that the high ground had the advantage.

"The classic example," one of Lon's instructors at

Earth's North American Military Academy had said, *"was the destruction of French imperial forces at Dien Bien Phu in what was then known as French Indochina, later Vietnam. The French, including elements of their legendary Foreign Legion, were in a valley. The Vietnamese freedom fighters had the high ground all around them, and bombarded the French with artillery and small-arms fire until the French were forced to surrender . . . those who were lucky enough to live that long."*

The students in that freshman tactics class had replayed the Battle of Dien Bien Phu on computers, on sand tables, and on their first field exercise. The freshmen, plebes, had assumed the role of the French forces. Upperclassmen and instructors had filled the roles of the besieging Vietnamese.

"We do a methodical grid search," Lon told his noncoms once the essentials had been seen to. The men in each fire team were taking turns watching for the enemy and scraping out defensive positions. The ground was impossible for foxholes, or even proper slit trenches, but some improvements could be made. "I don't care how good these raiders are, they can't go forever without leaving some sign of their passage. It's up to us to find it. We'll put three squads out at a time, work the valley to the northwest and each side. Start by checking out to five hundred yards. If that doesn't produce results, we extend the search, and keep at it at least until first platoon and the Bancrofters reach us."

"I know we don't have any mines with us, but do we plant bugs to let us know if anyone's coming?" Wil Nace asked.

"Yes, but sparingly," Lon said. "We don't want to put everything out—in case we have to move in a hurry."

Lon flirted with the notion of going out with one of the patrols himself, but it did not take much willpower to resist. That was not his job. It might almost be construed as dereliction of duty if he were to indulge himself that way. He had enough other duties to attend to.

He talked with Harley, explaining the way he wanted first platoon and the militiamen to search for traces of the raiders on the way in. He walked around the area the company had ˙staked out, stopped to chat with squad leaders and platoon sergeants, casually inspected the preparations that had been made. Occasionally he shared a few words with an individual or a fire team. There was no need to critique the preparations that had been made. He saw nothing to criticize. He did offer an occasional word of encouragement.

Only after he had made a complete circuit did Lon settle himself in at the makeshift command post that Lead Sergeant Jorgen had established near the center.

"Time you had something to eat, Major," Jorgen said. "Before the others get here or something breaks."

Lon nodded and tilted the faceplate of his helmet up. The lead sergeant already had his faceplate up. Lon sat with his back against a tree trunk and stretched his legs out in front of him. Then he took a battle ration packet from his pack and took out his canteen.

"It's an effort, but you're right, Weil," Lon said. He closed his eyes for an instant and chuckled.

"I could use a good joke if you'd like to share it, Major," Weil said.

"Just an odd memory," Lon said. "Back when I was a fresh young cadet, everyone in the company seemed preoccupied with making sure that I stuffed my face at every opportunity. Made me feel like a tom turkey being fattened up for Thanksgiving." He pulled the tab that started his meal heating and opened it.

Weil smiled and nodded. "Good advice then and now, sir. Eat when you can. In the field, meals can be a long time apart."

The reinforcements arrived—first platoon and the Bancrofter militia—and settled into the defensive perimeter, extending the area within it. The patrols searching for the raiders continued, new squads replacing those that had been out. Tebba Girana coordinated the search patterns, and started overlapping areas so that two different patrols went over each. Much of the terrain was moderately difficult. Some of the slopes were more than fifty degrees. Trees and underbrush alternated chaotically with exposed rock—some of it rotten, fissured, and apt to crumble or break off when weight was placed on it. After the first accident, which luckily did not result in casualties, the men in the fire teams exploring those areas were roped together for safety.

By the time the afternoon shadows had made the forested valley almost night dark, the searchers were certain there was no sign of which direction the raiders had gone within seven hundred yards of the point where their trail had been lost.

"It just isn't possible," Harley Stossberg said. The three Dirigenter officers and Colonel Henks were sitting together a few minutes before sunset. "Six or seven dozen men can't suddenly disappear, and they can't go far in a forest like this without leaving some evidence of their passage. I don't care *how* good they are."

"I agree," Colonel Henks said. "We know they're not ghosts. We've counted the bodies of their dead. And these raiders apparently had wounded to carry along with them."

Tebba had started shaking his head softly while Harley was speaking, so Lon let him handle the rebuttal. "*We* could do it, if we had to. Some of our men *have* done just that, or more, in the past. We stress stealth throughout boot training, and in the practical exercises we conduct to keep ourselves in top form. We've given your men considerable training in the techniques, Colonel. Maybe they've still got a ways to go before they're up to an act like these raiders seem to have pulled, but it's not impossible. Difficult, yes. Impossible, no."

"Major?" Henks asked, turning toward Lon.

"Tebba is right, Colonel," Lon said. "For example, Wil Nace, my fourth platoon's sergeant, could do it almost with his eyes closed. A lot of the others in the company as well." He shrugged. "There is, I suppose, a slight chance that the scouts who lost the trail were mistaken about the exact point, but even so, we can't be far from the place where they last saw the raiders. They were so close they almost fell in step with them.''

Henks hesitated before he spoke again. ''I can't argue the point, Major. But we do continue the search, don't we?''

''In the morning, Colonel. Looking for faint traces of men skilled at hiding their tracks, we can't expect to do any good in the dark, not even with the best night-vision gear in the galaxy—and we *do* have that.''

''But by morning they might be so far away we won't have any chance of finding them,'' Henks protested.

''We can't help that,'' Lon said. ''We are going to keep shuttles out flying patterns overhead and running infrared searches. The raiders we've seen weren't wearing any special thermal protection. At night they should be easy to spot, especially if they're moving. If one of our shuttles spots anything suspicious, I'll know about it within two minutes.''

Lon slept lightly that night, as he always did in the field on contract, and he woke often. But there was no message from a shuttle or from CIC. There was no sign of the raiders.

22

There was an annoying chill to the air in the hours before dawn. Dirigent battledress was an excellent thermal insulator, but exposed skin tingled. Despite a moderate breeze, it wasn't really *cold*. The temperature never dropped below fifty degrees. But the chill was noticeable on cheeks and fingers.

"Good old mountain air—crisp, clean, invigorating," Lon said when Phip Steesen muttered a half-serious complaint about freezing important body parts. Lon had given up trying to get back to sleep about an hour before sunrise. He had heated a cup of coffee—water from his canteen, a freeze-dried portion of coffee crystals, and a catalytic agent to cause it to heat—and sat nursing the brew, waiting. Simply waiting. Phip had come by fifteen minutes later and sat by his friend and commander.

"Why don't we ever get contracts in places where the weather is just right?" Phip asked. "It's always too hot or too cold, or too damned wet."

Lon chuckled. " 'And the baby bear's porridge was *just* right!' " he quoted.

Phip's answering growl would have done Papa Bear proud. "A bear's hide would be welcome. At least bears stay warm."

"Six hours from now you'll be complaining that the sun's too hot," Lon chided.

"And I can't get beer and sausages for lunch," Phip replied in the same light vein. The bantering came automatically, and on contract it could be a welcome diversion for both men.

"Have a cup of coffee," Lon suggested.

"I did, and a breakfast pack besides," Phip said. "It didn't help much." He paused. "Seriously, Lon. What happens next? You really think we have any chance of finding that batch of raiders again?"

"They didn't disappear into thin air. They went somewhere, on foot, on the ground. They had to leave some trace."

"It doesn't look that way. We know they're good, Lon. Maybe they're *that* good. And even though we've been careful, it won't take much before we get to the point where we won't know if the sign we see is theirs or ours."

"You were complaining about the cold. It made me think that this kind of tracking would be a lot easier with snow on the ground. They couldn't avoid leaving tracks then."

"How long do we keep looking?" Phip asked.

"I don't know. If we don't find some trace of the raiders this morning, it's something Colonel Henks and I are going to have to discuss."

The searches started again as soon as the sun was high enough to give the men decent light. One squad of men was sent to the nearest suitable landing zone to pick up the specialized sound equipment sent down from the ships.

"As soon as we get the gear," Lon told Colonel Henks, "I'll start a second search, from the point where our men lost the raiders. This time they'll be looking for cave entrances, and using the sound gear to try to pick up any subterranean activity—just in case there are cave entrances that are too well camouflaged for us to find."

"It's possible you'd miss caves even if they hadn't been camouflaged," Henks said. "These hills are riddled with them. One of the earliest gold mines was discovered by accident. A teenaged boy fell into a cave. He broke his leg and couldn't get out, but he did enough shouting that he was found. The rescuers went into the cave with lights. There was a vein of gold as thick as a man's thigh in the chamber where the boy had fallen. That was within a hundred yards of a village. People had lived around there for ten years or more and no one had ever spotted that hole. It was hidden by tree roots and vines, effectively invisible until someone happened to step in the wrong place.''

''That's why we're bringing in specialized equipment,'' Lon said. ''This gear will tell us if there are caves, and should tell us if there's anyone in them.''

In DMC slang, the sound ranging gear was called ''slap-and-grab.'' A transmitter electronically ''slapped'' the ground. Three receivers, placed at some distance from the transmitter, mapped the pattern of echoes. A series of observations would provide a three-dimensional chart, reaching as deep as fifty yards . . . under ideal conditions. The control panel was linked to a portable comp-link and compiled the information. It was not the most sophisticated implementation of the technology, but it usually sufficed for the needs of the Corps. Every lieutenant and noncommissioned officer took a two-day course in the use and interpretation of slap-and-grab, and many of the privates in Alpha Company had some exposure to the equipment.

Weil Jorgen had more experience with the gear than anyone else in the company. He was given command of the team, and he carried the control panel. Four men from fourth platoon handled the other parts of the system, while a full squad provided security—even though the slap-and-grab search would be conducted inside the area already searched by the company.

''Just in case,'' Lon told Weil. The lead sergeant nodded. He had no argument against caution. ''I think I'll walk along with you. It's better than sitting still.''

They moved down the slope toward the rocky flat in the valley. The raiders had left a clear trail until they reached that area. And none at all coming off.

''We might as well start right in the middle of that,''

Weil said. "I can't see how they could have hidden a cave entrance there, but it'll give us a good baseline for the search."

"Sounds good to me" was Lon's only comment. As much as possible, he stayed out of the way, watching. Occasionally he directed the covering squad to new locations, or had them check out tangled patches of underbrush away from the area that was currently being mapped for underground cavities.

There was no audible noise to the probes, but each time the transmitter "slapped" the ground, Lon thought he could feel it in his feet, a brief vibration that ended before he was absolutely certain it was not just his imagination.

Although Weil kept his crew working steadily, it was a slow process. He would position the transmitter and receivers, run a probe, then move everyone ten or fifteen yards and do it again. The rocky flat that was the starting point appeared to be solid rock, as far down as the equipment could chart. Even where soil started around the edges of the bare rock, there was stone not far below the surface, rarely more than eight to ten feet.

"About what you'd expect in a place like this," Weil commented while his men were moving to new positions after about twenty probes. "We haven't found anything but narrow fissures so far, nothing large enough for humans. Hell, Major, I've only spotted one crack wide enough for a fur midge to crawl in." The fur midge was a rodent native to Dirigent. It was hardly larger than a large bumblebee from Earth.

"We get up on the slopes it might be different," Lon said, gesturing vaguely.

Weil did not reply. His men were ready for the next probe. That one also failed to produce positive results— as did the next two dozen. Lon got tired of standing around and occasionally looking over Weil's shoulder at the latest chart that the series painted on the control panel's complink.

Eventually Lon called Eelen Hoy, the corporal in

charge of the squad providing security for the slap-and-grab. "I want one of your men, Eelen," Lon said. "I'm going to roam around a little and I need a man for backup."

"Sure thing, Major. How about Toby Hastings?"

"Tubby will be fine," Lon said. The nickname had nothing to do with Toby's weight. If anything, he had a slightly malnourished look. But Toby had become Tubby in recruit training, and three years of service in the DMC had not erased it. Toby had resigned himself to it long before.

"What are we going to do, Major?" Toby asked when he joined Lon at the edge of the area being investigated. Lon had the faceplate of his helmet up, so Toby put his up as well.

"We're just going to take a little walk along the slope, maybe toward that low saddle on the east," Lon said, pointing toward it by nodding his head in that direction.

"You spot something suspicious?"

"If I had, there'd be more than two of us going. Let's just say that I need to get a little exercise. All this standing around, my legs might cramp up."

Toby chuckled. "I guess I can understand that, sir. All the hurry up and wait, the old army game."

"Something like that. Just stay a few steps back, and stay alert, just in case there is someone close enough to take a crack at two guys straggling off from the rest." When Lon pulled his faceplate down, Toby quickly did the same.

Once they were away from the rest of the men, Lon moved as carefully as he would have walking point for a patrol into known enemy country. He carried his rifle at port arms, scanned the area around him constantly, and watched where he placed his feet with each step. The terrain was not much different from the foothills of the Great Smoky Mountains he had explored as a child and adolescent. The flora was different, but not markedly so. There had been sizable stretches of those hills that showed no evidence that humans had ever visited them before, although—logically—Lon had known even then that the chances of treading on virgin soil were slim. For more than eight centuries before his birth, the area had been a magnet for tourists, hikers, and campers.

Spring had been a good time to explore the hills back home, when a new year's growth was beginning to make itself visible—the dogwoods and redbuds especially. Lon had found the colors of spring fascinating, and the peacefulness of the hills had always been a welcome retreat.

"I've seen caves you could miss if you weren't looking at just the right spot, from just the right angle," he whispered over his radio link to Toby Hastings. "A crack a couple of feet long and maybe eighteen inches wide. Maybe a quick slide down for a few feet, then a chamber large enough to hold one of our shuttles."

"I'm a city boy, Major," Toby replied. "I'll have to take your word for it."

"Just keep your eyes peeled."

Lon had been looking for the type of low brush that could easily conceal such an opening. There were several candidates along the eastern slope of the valley, even up into the pass leading across the ridge. He was most interested in the sections that would be most difficult to reach, assuming that anything close to an animal trail would have been searched most carefully by the squads that had gone over the terrain before. At one point Lon got down on his stomach and edged his way carefully under a tangle of vines. He got partway into the mess and then started to slide. Behind him, Toby grabbed Lon's ankles to stop his slide, then had to pull his commander back out.

"You'd slid much farther, sir, and we'd have had to cut you loose," Toby said when Lon was back on his feet.

"Some kind of moss under there," Lon said. "Like a water slide, slick as anything."

"Maybe next time you'd better let me do the stunts,

sir," Toby suggested. "Being skinny does have some advantages."

There were no other locations that required such maneuvering. Lon looked at half a dozen places without finding anything. He and Toby worked their way from the flank of the hill to the pass between it and the next one to the north.

"The raiders had been working their way toward the east before," Lon said. "If they planned to go any farther that way, this was the logical way for them to go."

"Yes, sir. I was on one of the patrols searching this way across. We didn't find so much as a snapped branch."

"We'll work our way along this side of the pass, then come back along the other side." Lon pointed. "There's a lot of bare rock, some of it covered with vines hanging from above or growing up the wall." He shrugged. "Not that the direction it's growing in makes much difference."

It was difficult to get close to the steep side of the pass. Thick, tangled vines grew everywhere, obscuring, blocking. It reminded Lon of the kudzu vines that had occasionally threatened large tracts of the area where he had lived as a child.

They had worked their way nearly halfway across before Lon stopped abruptly and pointed. "Look, back there," he said over his radio link to Toby. "You see that chimney?"

"Chimney, sir?"

"That vertical crack in the rock," Lon explained.

"Yes, sir, I see it. What about it?"

"You look back in there when you were searching this area?"

"I didn't, sir, but one of the others in the squad went back there, I'm sure."

"Well, I guess we can check it again," Lon said. "You stay out here and keep your eyes open. I'll see if I can work my way all the way back into that chimney."

"I can go in, sir," Toby said.

Lon chuckled. "Didn't anyone ever tell you not to volunteer for anything in the army?"

"Not more than two or three hundred relatives," Toby replied. "I never was much good at following advice."

"Just the same, I'll go. I've had experience with this kind of thing." *I might even see if I can work my way up that chimney a little,* Lon thought.

He took a couple of steps, then stopped abruptly. He chided himself, *I'm not taking this seriously enough. We're not here to play games. There could be raiders close enough to pick off a careless target.* He looked around, shaking his head. *Don't go looking at this as if it's a weekend lark back in North Carolina. You could get yourself killed in a hurry.* He took a deep breath.

"You okay, sir?" Toby Hastings whispered over the radio.

"Fine, Toby. I just had to collect my thoughts. Keep your eyes open."

Lon took another deep breath, then started to edge through the tangle of vines and scrub trees toward the chimney in the rock wall. It *was* possible to move through the mess without snapping twigs or scraping bark, but it took concentration and a measure of planning—looking three steps ahead, or more. There was bare rock underfoot. The vines appeared to be rooted somewhere above, in the slope, hanging down. Lon spotted no ends. Everything seemed to curl back on itself in knots. Leaves—short, fuzzy things that reminded Lon more of woolly worms than vegetation—grew close to the ankle-thick branches.

Each step Lon took seemed to divert him from the direct line to the chimney. The tangles could only be accommodated; like the Gordian knot, they could not be conquered without cutting. Lon kept moving, always looking for a route that would take him more directly toward the opening he wanted to investigate.

Twenty feet back into the thickest tangle, Lon saw clear space ahead, a sheltered area just at the side of the rock face—kept clear of vines by a slight overhang above. *Almost like a cloister walk,* he thought. The easiest path to the clear area was off to his right, farther away from the chimney.

"Of course," Lon whispered. He stopped and turned to look back toward his starting point. Toby Hastings had moved from his original post, attempting to stay in the same relative position. Lon turned on his transmitter. "I'm going to rest for about two minutes here, Toby. Navigating this mess is like trying to swim through gelatin."

After Toby acknowledged the message, Lon squatted in place, looking toward the chimney, searching for any hint of an easier passage to it. *This is a fool's errand,* he thought. *Eighty-odd men didn't sneak through to that chimney in the little bit of time we weren't following them.* He snorted softly. *All the more reason to keep looking. That's just the kind of thinking that would help them stay hidden.*

He got back to his feet and stretched, careful not to bump into the vines above his head. Another fifteen minutes of steady effort took him through the last section of vines to the clear space below the overhang.

"I'm back," he radioed Toby. "I'm going to look along this clear lane. There could be an easier route through the vines, somewhere that doesn't show any obvious connection with the chimney. You stay put, where you can see into that cleft in the rock."

Below the overhanging rock, he might almost have been walking along a corridor in any well-kept building. There was clear space above his head. The overhang was about ten feet up. The corridor petered out on the west after some thirty feet. Lon noted a couple of places where travel through the vines might be easier, but did not attempt to prove them. Once he was sure that he had reached the end of the cloister and there were no obvious avenues through the vines, he retraced his steps and followed the clear area toward the chimney.

Lon was cautious when he reached the fissure in the

rock wall. He put his back to the wall and edged closer to the break, moving very slowly, watching and listening—as if there might be a squad of riflemen just waiting for him to stick his head around the corner.

"Toby, move around a little, until you can see back into the opening here," Lon whispered. He waited until the private was in his new position.

"I don't see anything back there, Major," Toby said. "But I can barely see you, so it's no guarantee."

"I'm going across to the other side. Watch while I make my move." Lon waited for Toby's acknowledgment, then said, "Now!" and a second later, he virtually jumped across the thirty-inch break in the rock, looking back into the opening as he moved, his rifle swinging into position, ready for use.

He saw no one.

Beyond the chimney, he leaned back against the rock, almost out of breath, not from the effort, but from the adrenaline rush of the possibility of imminent danger. He needed a moment to get his breathing, and his heart rate, back under control, using feedback techniques he had learned as a cadet on Earth.

"I'm going back into the chimney," Lon said once he could speak without effort. "See how far it goes."

He was still careful about exposing himself. He got into position, then moved his head just enough to barely look around the edge of the chimney. The break in the rock went back twenty feet, varying in width between thirty inches and about six feet, mostly in abrupt breaks, with edges jutting out or back. The lines of different strata of rock were apparent in the wall, the layers tilted at nearly sixty degrees from horizontal.

The opening appeared to be a dead end. Lon let his gaze travel up the chimney then, looking at it as he might a climbing challenge, judging the distances across the gap, the difficulty of working up the chimney without ropes or other climbing gear. His rough assessment was that it *could* be done but that it might not be easy.

When he moved into the chimney and started walking

toward the far end, Lon held his rifle at the ready, his finger over the trigger guard, the safety off. It might be overly cautious, but that was the side he wanted to make any mistakes on.

Each place where there was a jagged edge to one side or the other of the lane, he stopped and looked cautiously past, to see the next bit of rock. All the way at the end, there was a gap to his right, two feet across. That ended five feet over.

Just as I expected, a dead end, he thought, and he got ready to move back out of the chimney. Then something on the ground caught his eye, something that did not seem to belong. Lon knelt. It was only a tiny chunk of stone, not much larger than a child's marble. But one side of the sliver of rock was almost white instead of the ocher gray of the exposed rock around him. It had been freshly broken off from wherever it had belonged. Lon turned the stone over. It was roughly pyramidal, but the point opposite the break had . . . a few threads caught on it. Lon brought the stone close to his faceplate and turned the magnification of that up. Thread. Artificial threads.

Somebody came by and got their clothing caught on this, he thought. *They pulled, and this bit of rock broke off.* Lon started scanning the rock around him, looking for a matching section of light, the place where the tiny chunk had been. His heart was beating a little faster.

"There," he whispered when he saw the place, waist high, at the end of the side cul-de-sac. He got to his feet, stepped closer, and noticed another opening. There was a four-foot-high hole in the side of the hill, past a natural baffle.

Lon backed away quickly, then hurried out of the chimney, turning to the right, along the section of clear ground behind the vines that he had not investigated before.

"Toby, be ready for anything," Lon instructed. "I think we've found what we're looking for." He switched channels on his radio then to call Tebba.

"Take a good fix on my location. I think I've found where they went. Get one platoon positioned on top of this hill, bring another into this pass. Have Weil and his slap-and-grab crew drop what they're doing. I want to map the inside of this hill as fast as possible. Talk to Colonel Henks. Have him spread his men out along the facing slopes to either side. Put a squad of our men with each half of his company."

Then Lon started working his way back through the tangle of vines. There was an itch in the middle of his back. He felt as if someone had painted a bull's-eye on it.

23

"You still don't _know_ that the raiders are in there,"
Colonel Henks protested. The mercenaries and militiamen had formed a cordon around the hill. Weil and his
slap-and-grab team were mapping the subterranean
structure. They had two squads of Dirigenters providing
protection for them now. Lon and his lieutenants had
discussed what they were going to do with Henks and
his senior people.

"No, I don't know absolutely for certain, Colonel,"
Lon replied patiently. "And the mapping we're doing
might not tell us. What the mapping _will_ tell us is if
there's enough room that the raiders _could_ be in there,
and it will map any passages and chambers within reach,
maybe pinpoint other entrances as well."

"And then?" Henks prompted.

Lon took a breath and let it out. "Then we go in and
look for ourselves."

Henks did not respond to that except to blink.

"That is going to be the touchy part," Lon said. "But
if your raiders are in there, it's either go in after them
or just seal every entrance we can find. There are two
problems with that. First, if we seal the entrances, set
off explosives to collapse them, you may never know if
there really was anyone inside. Second, you want prisoners to question, to show the people in Lincoln and the
other towns that you've really accomplished something."

"Isn't there any way to force the raiders out?" Henks

asked. "It seems that would be preferable to going in after them."

"Theoretically, you could flood them out, either with water or some noxious but nonlethal chemical agent; or, you could just mark all the entrances and put your militia to watch until the raiders have to come out or starve. But, in practical terms, none of those options is realistic."

"Why not?" Henks asked.

"How many million gallons of water can you force into that cave at any given time?" Lon asked. He did not wait for an answer. "How much appropriate gas could you pump in to allow for dissipation and however much volume it would have to fill? That could be millions of cubic feet. How many months are you prepared to keep men sitting here waiting for the raiders to get hungry? They might have food replicators and enough raw materials to keep them going for a year or more. And before you seriously consider any of those options, you still need to know whether there's any point to it, if there's anyone inside."

"I get the point, Major," Henks said petulantly.

"Believe me, Colonel, if there were any other practical way to handle this, I'd be the first to suggest it," Lon said. "If there is anyone inside, getting to them might be a bloody business, and I don't like putting my men in unnecessary danger. It's bad for business, if nothing else. We value our people, and from what I've seen, you value yours just as much."

"We won't go in blindly," Tebba offered. "Once the mapping is finished and we locate any additional access points, we do some cautious probing and plant electronic bugs. We go in a little ways, wait and listen, then go a little farther."

"Until the raiders start shooting?" Henks asked.

"If it comes to that," Lon said. "But it might not reach that point. It depends on how extensive the caves are, how much of it the raiders actively defend. We'll know more as we go along."

"We do have one very major advantage, Colonel," Tebba said. "To the best of our knowledge, the raiders have no night-vision gear. We do. That means they're going to need lights to do anything, and we can operate almost as efficiently in the dark as in full daylight— more efficiently in some ways."

"And we won't go in until it's dark outside," Lon said. He paused, then added, "If we have to go in at all."

"What are you getting at?" Henks asked. "Didn't you just get done saying that there was no alternative to going in?"

"I did, and there probably isn't."

"You must have something in mind," Henks said.

"I'll know more once the mapping is finished," Lon said. "We might be able to play mind games with the raiders, if they are under that hill, and if there's more than one way in and out. *We* know we want prisoners, proof, but *they* don't know that. The raiders would have to assume we'd be satisfied to see them all dead. If there are other entrances, we can seal off all but one, try to make the raiders think that their only chance of survival is to come out and make a fight of it. It's like bluffing in poker."

"And hope they take the bait," Tebba said. "Otherwise, we still have to go inside."

"They could hide a couple of regiments in there, Major," Weil Jorgen said about three hours past noon. The slap-and-grab team was taking a much-needed break. "The gear can't get to all of it. There are places where we can see passages leading deeper than we can range. We've marked two other entrances, and God only knows how many more of them there might be. Some of them could be miles away."

"Get that hill charted, then do what you can to track any passages that might lead elsewhere, Weil," Lon said. Men had already been posted to guard the additional entrances. Both were on the far side of the hill, one near the valley floor and the other on the slope, halfway up. The squads sent to investigate and watch them reported no sign of anyone having used them. But they had not gone in. Lon had ordered everyone to stay out.

"We're not going to finish this by dark," Weil said. "It could take two or three more days to be sure we've got everything we can find."

"Whatever it takes," Lon said. "We can't try to scare them out until we know where all the bolt holes are. If we miss some, we could be watching the wrong hole when they come out. That could get dicey."

Waiting. Marking time. Running in place. However he thought of it, this was not Lon Nolan's favorite way to spend time. He kept himself busy, and tried to avoid giving his men any indication of how restless he was. The emotions of a leader were contagious. Some of the time he spent with his complink and radios, conferring with CIC aboard *Tyre,* and studying maps and other data about Bancroft. He conferred with Colonel Henks, his own lieutenants and noncoms. He spent a few minutes, now and then, with the slap-and-grab team.

The ring around the suspected location of the missing raiders was improved. Electronic bugs—sound and motion detectors—were placed. A shuttle dropped ration packs and explosives by parachute. The drop was successful, the loads retrieved and brought into camp.

Sunset. A new team took over the slap-and-grab gear and worked for two hours. The job was far from finished, but continuing it would wait for morning.

Mercenaries and militiamen took what sleep they could in the night. In Lon's company, one man in each fire team was on watch at all times. The rest slept, or tried to. In Colonel Henks's militia company, the men were put on half-and-half watches—50 percent awake and on guard at all times. Colonel Henks and his company commander split the time between them. Lon divided the night with Harley and Tebba. One of them would always be awake, monitoring the electronic snoops and alert to any warning from the guards or from the eyes above—the shuttles that were still on rotating patrol and the ships in space.

When he was not on watch, Lon at least made a pretense of sleeping, rolling up in the thin thermal blanket that was part of the regular battle kit for DMC soldiers. But he slept very little. His mind refused to let go, refused to stop searching for easier ways of doing what had to be done—or finding an alternative.

If I have to order men into those caves after raiders, some of them are going to die, was the thought that tormented him whenever he tried to clear his mind for sleep. Too many men had died on this contract already.

When he did sleep, the faces of friends who had died on other contracts came back to haunt him.

At about three in the morning, it started to rain. At first there were just widely spaced sprinkles, but the rain increased in intensity after twenty minutes. There were no tents to shelter anyone. Ponchos gave the men who were on watch some protection. The blankets the sleeping men used also shed water, and most of the Dirigenters slept with their helmets on. The webbing inside made a more comfortable pillow than rocky ground.

Near four o'clock, when he started to hear the rumble of thunder and saw lightning in the sky, Lon gave up his pretense of sleeping. The lightning was not yet close, but it was coming nearer, and there was no escape from it, no place of safety he could take his men to. He did give orders to pull sentries off the crests of the ridges, to get them down far enough that they wouldn't be the nearest target for an electrical bolt. And everyone would avoid—as far as possible—the use of active electronics while there was lightning in the area.

For thirty minutes, the camp was deluged by heavy rain and repeatedly illuminated by lightning. Just south of the defensive perimeter, one tree was struck and burned briefly before the flames were extinguished by the downpour. The thunder was so loud that no one was sleeping any longer—no one above ground, at least. Men huddled under their ponchos, doing their best to stay dry, not moving unless it was absolutely necessary.

The storm passed over and moved on toward the east. The rain lessened and then ended. Lon called CIC and asked for a weather report.

"Looks like you might have more storms moving through," the officer on watch aboard *Tyre* said. "We're tracking several bands. It could go on for the next seven or eight hours. The next should reach you in about forty minutes."

Lon passed the report along to the other officers and his platoon sergeants. "Better tell the men to get their breakfast eaten while they can eat it dry," he added.

He took his own advice, but once the meal was finished and the remnants disposed of, he got up and packed his blanket. It was time for him to start his new day in earnest.

There were the little things—the walk around the perimeter, stopping to chat for a moment with individuals and squad leaders. Lon was comfortable with his open style of leadership. He felt that it added to the cohesiveness of his company. His men knew that he cared.

"Couldn't you at least have picked better weather for this operation?" Dean Ericks asked when Lon stopped to talk with him. "I don't mind a little water, but where there's rain, there's mud, and *that* I can do without."

Lon laughed softly. "Mud's good for the skin, Dean. Ladies pay good money to get mud packed on their faces. Besides, with all this rock around, we shouldn't have too much of it. Just keep your head down so you don't draw a shot of lightning."

"That's bone, not steel in my head. I think you owe Phip and me both a couple of rounds the next time we get together somewhere that has beer instead of just water," Dean said.

"If I bought all the rounds the two of you say I owe,

Lon, Junior, and Angie would have to drink water instead of milk.''

"That's right, pull family on me. Make me feel like a heel.''

Lon laughed again. "Well, if the shoe fits . . .''

Dean growled at the pun and Lon walked on to the next squad.

"You know, Major, we can't use the slap-and-grab while we've got thunder overhead,'' Weil Jorgen said. "Even if we were willing to take a chance of drawing a lighting strike, this gear can't filter out the interference.'' It was near sunrise, though the heavy cloud cover hid the first traces of dawn.

"I know, Weil. We'll just have to work between the storms, do the best we can. The last line of storms should be past us by noon. Thereabouts, anyhow.'' Lon shrugged.

"That's the report now,'' Weil said. "One thing about the weather. It's always subject to change.''

"Do what you can between the squalls, and hope we can finish the work before sunset,'' Lon said. "If possible, I'd like to make our move against the caves tonight. Finish this mission and get back to the barracks in Lincoln.''

"Even without working between the raindrops, I think we can finish by sunset,'' Weil said. "Unless we find some major continuation of the cave system.''

The creek in the valley ran a little higher, a little faster, but conditions stayed decent along the slopes on either side. There was little bare soil in the area. Everything that wasn't rock was covered with vegetation of one sort or another. Mud was at a minimum. Weil Jorgen got his crew to work between thunderstorms. The chart of the cave system improved, expanded. Two more entrances were traced by the time the last storm struck the area. After that storm passed, the rain eased, then ended, and a few breaks started to appear in the cloud cover to the west.

Lon sent squads to check the newly identified cave entrances. One was clearly too small for humans. The other was marginal but possible. It would have to be eliminated.

"Get a few men preparing the explosives for the openings we're going to close," Lon told Tebba. "We're going to take out all but that first one we found yesterday."

"Can I make a suggestion?" Tebba asked.

"Of course." Lon was surprised that Tebba felt it necessary to ask that question.

"Close that entrance. Hit it first and hardest. The raiders might know it's the one that tipped us off. Pick one of the other openings to leave—one they might suspect we don't know about. That might increase the chances they'll try to make a break."

Lon nodded. "You're right. Let's look over what we've got, see which of the other entrances gives us the best fire zones if they come out."

"If there's anyone *to* come out," Tebba said.

"There's always the possibility we're watching a dry hole," Lon conceded. "But I don't think we are."

"I hope not. We're going to look slightly foolish if we've wasted two days and all this effort," Tebba said.

There was still an hour of daylight left when Weil told Lon that his team had finished the mapping operation. "As far as we're ever going to be able to," he said. "There were those spots that went down below the range of our gear. I can't answer for where they might lead."

Lon rotated the view of the final chart on his mapboard through all three dimensions. The flat screen could only approximate full three-dimensional form, but layers could be represented by different colors and boldness.

"It should do," Lon said. "At least we can hope it will. Good work, and tell the men that for me."

"I'd still feel a lot better if there was some way we could tell whether or not there are any rats in that hole before we start plugging it," Weil said. "Hate to waste a lot of explosives if there's no point to it."

"Don't bet against there being raiders in there, Weil. The odds are all that there are."

"I think so, too," Weil said. "After listening to that hill for the last day and a half, I feel them in my bones. They're in there, thinking they've pulled it over on us for sure."

"We'll find out soon enough. We'll have all the entrances set up but the one we're going to watch before sunset. Then we wait for dark and collapse those holes one by one."

"That's a good touch," Weil said. "Space them out. Give the raiders more time to think about what's happening."

"But not enough time for them to try bolting through the wrong hole," Lon said.

24

Lon held few illusions. The sound gear had never picked up any noises in the underground system that pointed—inarguably—to the presence of humans. All of the preparations might be for nothing. The raiders might be scores of miles away . . . preparing for their next attack, perhaps, or just laughing at the way they had escaped their pursuers.

But Lon continued to make his plans based on the assumption that there *were* raiders in the caves and that they would have to come out once the Dirigenters started destroying the exits they would have to use. He chose which entrance to leave untouched, set the deployment of forces around it and the sequence in which the other entrances would be demolished. Nothing was arbitrary. He conferred with his senior people on each step. But once the decisions were made, they were not questioned.

"We give it time to get completely dark tonight," Lon told Colonel Henks once the Bancrofter militia company had been deployed alongside the mercenaries. Each platoon of militiamen had a squad of mercenaries with it, to ensure that any orders or warnings got through without delay or confusion. "We'll leave teams to watch the other exits until each one is closed, just in case the raiders try a premature escape. One by one, we collapse every other opening to the cave system. We'll wait at least twenty minutes after the first one. The raiders will need time to decide what the explosion means. They might suspect it's the prelude to an assault. We let them worry about that. Then blow the next entrance—and the next.''

''You think you can get all of the other exits closed in time to force them to use this one?'' Henks asked, gesturing at the opening the majority of the men were covering.

''That's the plan. We'll leave less time between subsequent explosions than we do between the first and second. I don't think they'll have time to get organized and moving before we blow the last of the ones we're going to.''

I hope, Lon qualified silently.

''They'll come out, Lon. Once we start blowing their exits, they won't have any choice,'' Phip Steesen said over a private radio channel. ''Then we'll have all the advantages.''

''I hope you're right, but it's still all a patchwork of guesses,'' Lon replied. *Things are* really *iffy when Phip thinks he needs to take the positive side instead of shooting bitches at the idea,* he thought. He shook his head. *Don't give yourself more reasons to worry. The worst that's likely to happen is that it's all a waste of time, a dry hole.* He wouldn't mind looking foolish—too much—as long as no one was killed in the process.

''The only possible hitch I see is that the slap-and-grab might have missed an exit or two,'' Phip said.

Lon managed a chuckle. ''I'm glad you've got tunnel vision. I can see a lot of possible hitches.''

''Well, you always were the worrying type. That's why you've got the brass on your shoulders and I've just got these miserable stripes on my arms.''

Dusk settled slowly into dark. After the rain of the previous night and morning, the sky had cleared, and there were plenty of stars visible overhead, as well as a sliver of Bancroft's largest moon. Under the trees the sky would make little difference, and if Lon had to take his men into the caves, the stars and moon would make no difference at all. To put on a show of confident leadership, Lon sat and ate a meal pack in the last twenty minutes before the scheduled start of the night's activities. The fabricated food was unusually dry and tasteless, but Lon ate methodically, making a show of giving the meal his undivided attention. He smiled to himself at one point, recalling how Matt Orlis, then commander of Alpha Company, had advised young Officer-Cadet Nolan to get involved in amateur theatrics to improve his leadership presence.

Just as Lon was getting rid of the remnants of his meal, Lead Sergeant Jorgen came over and squatted near the commander.

"Everything's ready, whenever you give the word, Major," he whispered, lifting the faceplate of his helmet halfway.

Lon nodded, checking the time as he did. "Another five minutes, then we go right into it, the way we planned. What's the mood?"

Weil Jorgen shrugged. "Not bad. Kind of strange, actually. Some of the men think we're wasting our time. Others see it as the operation that gets us back to barracks and that much closer to going home."

"I hope they don't get to thinking it's all a lark," Lon said. "This could turn nasty in a hurry."

"The noncoms will sit on any of that fast," Weil assured him. "All it will take is a single hostile gunshot and the men will all be one hundred percent, and the squad leaders will make sure no one gets too careless before then."

Lon gave the order for the first detonation precisely on the minute he had scheduled. Although he had the volume turned low on the earphones of his helmet, the explosion still seemed uncommonly loud. It was three hundred yards from his position and set several feet back into the cave entrance. The rock and debris that was blown out was directed by the confines of the entrance, and Lon's men had been positioned so that no one would be directly in the anticipated path.

Well away from any of the entrances, the slap-and-grab receivers had been positioned. They would be overloaded at the instant of each explosion, but between blasts, the echoes would allow some refinement to the charts, perhaps even fill in some of the blanks—the areas that had been too deep for the power of the set's transmitter.

"Fifteen minutes," Lon reminded his officers and sergeants immediately after the first blast. He had decided that twenty minutes was too long to allow between the first two blasts and changed it an hour earlier. "We give them a little time to think, time to get worried."

The order in which the openings would be closed was not truly random, though Lon hoped that it would seem that way to the raiders he assumed were in the caves. The second blast was almost as distant as possible from the first. Eight minutes later, the third was positioned closer to the second than the first. Two minutes. Blast. Six minutes. Blast.

Each time an entrance was closed, the fire team that had been observing it waited for the debris to settle, then went as close as was safe to make certain that the opening had indeed been sealed. Then they moved to other positions, either in the perimeter around the opening that was going to be left open, or in the thin outer perimeter that Lon had established against the possibility that the charting operation might have missed one or more exits from the underground complex.

"Major, I think we've got something," Weil Jorgen said after the fourth explosion. "It's not too clear on audio, but the analyzers call this a human scream." He played a few seconds of sound that the slap-and-grab receivers had intercepted.

Lon listened to it, then listened again. "I think that's it, Weil," he said. It was indistinct, muted and mutated by echoes and depth, but the sound did seem to be someone screaming. "Pass the word that we've got something to indicate there probably really are people down there."

It was a relief, the first solid evidence—if far from indisputable proof—that Lon's assumptions were correct. He let out a long breath, almost a sigh. *Someone down there tripped and fell over the edge of panic,* he thought. Panicked soldiers might not hold to whatever training they had received.

"Pass the word to your men that we could have action almost any time now," Lon said, speaking on the channel that connected him with his platoon sergeants. "It seems the folks down there have figured out what we're doing."

Another explosion. There were only two exits left to block. Lon was considering whether he might speed up the final two blasts, set them both off, leave the raiders with only one way out, when he heard gunfire, followed almost immediately by a call from the lance corporal leading the fire team watching one of the remaining holes.

"We've got a breakout, Major. They're coming out shooting."

"How many?" Lon asked.

"At least two dozen. They caught us a bit off-guard. They—"

The transmission ceased. Lon switched his head-up display to find the vital signs of the lance corporal who had been talking. Flat lines. He was dead.

"Tebba," Lon said, quickly switching channels, "breakout at hole number seven. Move two squads to block them." He switched to his all-hands channel, to warn everyone to look out for the raiders. They were coming out.

Lon could feel his mind gearing up, and it was only then that he realized that he, too, had been less than confident that his plan would work, that there was any enemy around. There was no time for him to berate himself over that lack now, though. He concentrated entirely on the work at hand.

"Blow the other opening before they start coming out there, too," he ordered, and the explosion came within

ten seconds. That left just two ways out of the caves—
that Lon knew about. He hesitated for only an instant,
then ordered the demolition of the opening that raiders
had already come out of. First, it might keep more from
coming out. Second, it might put down some of the raiders who were already engaging his men, help the survivors of the fire team that had been watching that hole
until their reinforcements arrived.

Lon started moving toward the area where the fighting
was going on as soon as the last prepared explosion
sounded and the heaviest debris came down. The fact
that there was still gunfire there was heartening. Some
of his men were still alive and fighting. The nearest four
men of his headquarters squad moved with him, fanning
out to put him nearly in the middle of their impromptu
formation.

At a hundred yards he could make out targets. The
raiders were clustered in a fairly small area, to either
side of the gap in the side of the hill where the hole
they had come out of had collapsed. Lon's men were
farther off, on the facing slope. And the two squads that
Tebba was sending as reinforcements were on a con-
verging path.

"At least some of them must have night-vision gear,"
Lon said, not stopping. He was linked to his lieutenants
and sergeants. "That gunfire is too accurate for anything
less."

Before anyone could respond to that observation, gunfire broke out near the final cave entrance, the one that
the Dirigenters and Bancrofters had concentrated their
forces against. Lon was not too concerned with that. The
raiders would have to come out almost single file, into
the concentrated fire of half of Lon's men and three-
quarters of the local militiamen. He concentrated on the
first breakout.

"Get them bottled in, and put the cork in," he instructed. This was not the time to remind anyone that
they needed breathing prisoners.

Lon and the few men with him took cover and started

adding their own rifle fire to the fight. On his own, Lon worked to wound rather than kill, aiming low. *Put them out of action. Hope there are some who live long enough for us to get our hands on them.*

With more of his men moving into position, this part of the firefight would not continue long. Lon monitored the other engagement over the radio but concentrated on the situation right in front of him.

There were only three or four raiders still firing when the final raider counterattack started—the one that Lon and his men were not fully prepared for. Gunfire started coming from behind the main body of mercenaries and militiamen, north of the mapped areas of the cave system.

There was *another exit, one we didn't find,* Lon realized as he heard gunfire coming from a new direction and heard the first radio reports of the attack. The raiders had emerged and had time to form up before entering the fight. They were not seen until they started firing.

The assault did cause confusion. Among the Dirigenters, that confusion was minimal and lasted only a few seconds. Squad and fire team leaders responded quickly, switching part of their forces to cover the new threat. The Bancrofter militia was somewhat slower to react. They didn't have enough training or experience for their response to be so nearly automatic. But nowhere were militiamen far from mercenaries. As much by example as instruction, Lon's men brought their trainees into alignment.

"I don't think they want an all-out fight, Major," Weil said less than two minutes after the latest attack had started. "It looks as if they're just trying to break everyone free."

"Maybe *they* don't want an all-out fight, Weil, but that's what they're going to get," Lon replied. "Our hosts wouldn't have anything less. We'll see just how determined the raiders are. Maybe this last batch will give up and run for it when they see they can't penetrate our lines."

It did not take long. The last group of raiders fought—
with more enthusiasm than skill—for nearly ten
minutes, but then they started to withdraw. On the other
side, the raiders who remained of the groups trying to
fight their way out of the cave exit that had been left
unmolested started pulling back inside. The threat of being entombed alive was now less than the threat of being
killed outright. The few raiders left whose bolt hole had
been destroyed behind them had no option. They tried
retreating up the side of the hill past the rubble of the
explosion that had closed their exit, but that just exposed
them more completely to the gunfire of the Dirigenters
and Bancrofters. That fight was soon over. No raiders
were left to contest the issue.

"Get men in there fast," Lon instructed. "We want
live prisoners now."

"Do we go looking for the exit that last batch came
out of?" Harley Stossberg asked a moment later. "If we
don't find it, the rest of these birds might escape the
same way."

"Not yet, Harley," Lon said. "We've got too many
hostiles in the woods now for that. Hold your positions."

Colonel Henks, accompanied by a full squad of his
militiamen, worked his way to Lon's position. "Some
of the raiders are getting away," he complained.
"Shouldn't we go after them while we can?"

"Not yet, Colonel," Lon said. "Right now, we need
to secure this site. We're going to get your prisoners for
you, and we need to find out just what sort of prize
we've captured. This might be their main base, Colonel,
and we could well be set to recover a fair portion of the
loot they've taken. You'll have your victory, your prisoners, and maybe more."

That possibility slowed Henks's response. He hesitated, uncertain whether to protest again about letting
some of the raiders escape. A sudden increase in the
amount of gunfire near the last guarded opening interrupted.

Lon looked that way. "What now?" he asked on his channel to Tebba.

"I think it's just the ones behind us trying to pull the last of their people away," Tebba said. "We're getting hit hard, but they're not coming *at* us. And more of the ones we had pinned down against the exit are trying to slide out from under us."

"Let them go," Lon said, glancing at Henks even though he was certain that the militia colonel could not overhear the conversation. "Give them room. Don't make it particularly easy, but I'd rather have them on the outside running than back in the hole where we'd have to dig them out."

"Lon, you'd better get to me quick." Phip's voice was unusually tight. There was almost no shooting going on, just the odd shot by overenthusiastic Bancrofters. "It's Dean."

Lon started moving immediately, clicking over the head-up display on his visor to look for the vital signs of Dean Ericks. What he saw was not good. The traces were almost still, almost flat.

"You got a medic there?" Lon asked Phip as he and his headquarters squad ran toward them.

"Yes, but . . ." Phip stopped, and Lon knew why. Dean's vital signs had stopped.

Don't you dare die on me! Lon thought, hoping against hope that the mental order might make a difference. The medic would not give up as long as there was any chance at all. If the slightest tie to life remained, getting a man into a trauma tube gave him a better than 98 percent chance of survival.

When Lon reached them, the medic was getting to his feet. Phip was kneeling next to his longtime friend. Phip's faceplate was up. Lon could see the anguished look on his face, and Lon's mind tried to reject the obvious. *No!*

"He never had a chance, Major," the medic said. "I don't think he knew what hit him. The bullet severed the spinal cord at the base of his skull, then apparently ricocheted and ripped open the carotid artery. If there had been a trauma tube sitting next to him and he'd rolled straight into it, I don't think it would have made a difference.''

Lon dropped heavily to his knees at Dean's side, across from Phip. Phip's eyes showed awareness that Lon had arrived, but he could not speak. He looked at Lon, then looked down at Dean.

At first, Lon felt nothing. His mind did not want to deal with what he saw, what the medic had said. He swallowed hard, then reached up and pulled off his helmet. Unaware of his actions, Lon dropped the helmet at his side.

You've seen death before. You've always known this could happen, to you, to anyone. It's part of the job. It's a risk you accepted a long time ago. Anguished thoughts caromed around Lon's head, unheeded, almost unnoticed. There was an infinite instant of shock, a numbness.

Then the mask of leadership cracked. Shattered.

A tortured sob bubbled up out of Lon's throat. He bent forward, as if seized by a stomach cramp. For the first time in ages, almost longer than he could recall, Lon Nolan cried helplessly.

25

Lon took no consolation from the fact that only two Dirigenters had been killed in the fight, or that fifteen raiders had been killed and a dozen captured. A part of Lon's mind, and more of his heart, remained walled off, numb. After no more than two or three minutes, he put his helmet on again, got to his feet, and moved away without speaking to Phip or the medic. Lon returned to the necessary work of concluding the engagement and dealing with all the casualties.

Tebba Girana and Weil Jorgen took as much of the load as they could, and most of the men around Lon shielded him from any unnecessary interruptions. Everyone in the company knew how close their commander had been to Dean Ericks. The old-timers recalled the four young men who had always been together. And now only two were left in the company—one dead, another long escaped from the occupational hazards of the mercenary life.

A new perimeter was established. Patrols were sent out to make certain that the raiders did not remain close enough to harass the mercenaries and militiamen. The immediate fight was over, but not the danger. Wounded men, on both sides, were treated. Colonel Henks wanted as many healthy prisoners as he could get, both for questioning and for parading in front of the citizens of Bancroft.

The cave entrance that the slap-and-grab team had missed was found two hours after the firefight. It, too, was demolished, leaving—the Dirigenters hoped—only one way in or out.

"We'll wait until morning to go in," Lon told his lieutenants and Colonel Henks. He voice was under tight control, but the men who knew him well could feel the pain he was trying to conceal. "We've got wounded who need trauma tubes to survive." Portable trauma tubes and other needed medical supplies were on their way. A shuttle would drop them in. After first light, the few wounded who were going to need extensive periods of regeneration and recuperation would be evacuated, along with most of the prisoners.

"There might still be raiders in the caves," Tebba said.

Lon shrugged. "We'll deal with it, go in as if we know they're there. We need to see what's inside." His voice was flat, dull. "The men are on half and half?"

Tebba nodded. "For the last hour." Half of the men in each fire team would be awake, on watch, while the rest slept. "We're sharing the duty of guarding the prisoners with the locals." Most times that would be a precaution to make certain that the mercenaries' local allies did not massacre the enemy out of hand. It was probably unnecessary this time, but it was routine.

"When do we start questioning them?" Colonel Henks asked.

Lon stared at him for a moment before he answered. "It will keep until morning, Colonel. They're not going anywhere."

"It makes me nervous," Henks said. "I don't like to take the chance of having anything happen before we get the answers we need about where they came from and who set them up here. We lose the chance to question these prisoners, we might not get another opportunity."

"I want answers, too, Colonel, but it will keep. We've put sleep patches on all of the ones who are healthy enough to cause trouble, and we've got enough people to make sure no one is going to come in and rescue them. We all need what sleep we can get.''

Sleep was a long time coming for Lon, and it was uneasy, often disturbed, less restful than staying awake would have been. There were too many memories that would not be excluded, and they intertwined in bizarre combinations. Lon, Phip, Janno, and Dean. Sergeant O'Banion and Private Green. Lon, Junior. Death in dozens of macabre vignettes. Mourning. When morning came, Lon looked drawn and haggard.

Soon after first light, Lon stood fifty yards from the cave entrance, staring at it. Glaring. Grinding his teeth. The temptation to lead the first squad going into the cave was almost overpowering. There was something very like desperation in his desire. He knew all the reasons why he should not, but that very nearly was not enough. After Dean's death, he felt a compulsion to do *something* active, to look for a chance to get some personal measure of revenge. There *might* be a few raiders left inside the caves, and they might resist. None of the raiders so far had shown any interest in surrendering. As long as they were able to move, they fought, they died, or they fled. And killing one or two himself, preferably at close range, even with his bare hands, would have been—temporarily, at least—immensely satisfying. Even the danger that this job might impose would be welcome.

Lon argued with himself, even though he knew what the outcome would—*must*—be. The men in the company who knew Lon best could guess what he wanted to do. Tebba and Weil had both been part of the discussion over tactics and assignments, ready to object as strenuously as they could if Lon said anything about leading the first patrol himself. And they were both close in the morning as the time for action came.

The seconds, and minutes, slid by on the timeline on Lon's visor. Finally he took a deep breath and repeated the assignments he had decided on earlier.

"Wil Nace will take his first and second squads in on point," Lon said. "Those two squads can leapfrog each other. As they work through a section of cave, we'll bring in more men to investigate any branches and secure the route back out, keep reinforcements close enough to lend a hand if necessary." There was a long pause before he said, "My CP will be just outside the cave entrance. We'll set up an inner perimeter on the hillside and place detachments out farther, along possible enemy approaches—bugs placed to cover the gaps and give advance warning if the raiders decide to come back."

Lon missed the glance that Tebba and Weil exchanged, the look of relief that neither managed to hide completely.

"Colonel Henks, I think you'd like to have at least a squad of your men inside, in the second detachment, following the two point squads?"

Henks nodded. He had been wary in his conversations with Lon since the end of the fight during the night. Weil Jorgen had taken the colonel aside and explained what was bothering Lon, that he had lost one of his closest friends in the firefight. "Once the place is secure, Major," Henks said, "I want to look around for myself. But later. I'm not suggesting interfering with the real work. Let those who are best qualified do that."

"We'll get our chance, Colonel," Lon said.

Lon adjourned the meeting after setting a jumping-off time. Then he took Wil Nace aside. The two men lifted the visors of their helmets and turned off their transmitters so their discussion would remain private.

"Be careful, Wil," Lon said. "If there's even a hint of someone ahead of you, toss stun grenades in first, unless you think there's too much danger of bringing the roof down on your men. And watch out for booby traps."

Nace cranked out half a grin. "I value my skin," he said.

"I'm going to monitor the action through your camera. Maybe I can't go in with you physically, but I'll be with you every step of the way.'' Dirigenter battle helmets had small cameras. Linking through their communication system, Lon would see almost everything Wil Nace did.

"Just don't try to micromanage this, Major," Wil said. "I know how you feel right now. You're not going through anything I haven't gone through a lot of times. But the camera doesn't have the same field of vision I do, and I need to be able to communicate with my people instantly.''

Lon hesitated briefly before he nodded. "It's your show, Wil. You're the best man in the company for this job. That's why I chose you. Just one note of advice: I've spent time in caves before. Trust what your helmet tells you. It's easy to get disoriented, lost, in caves. You'll swear you're going in the wrong direction when you aren't. Go by what your electronics tell you even if you're ninety-nine percent certain they're wrong. They probably won't be.''

It was a slow process. Wil Nace sent two men ahead, often crawling on their stomachs, to the next intersection or change of direction in the cave. There, the point men would extend electronic snoops—the same bugs that were used to provide early warning on a defensive perimeter—past the corner to look and listen. Only once it was certain that the next section was clear would Wil bring up the rest of his two squads. A different two men would scout the next section.

Larger chambers were handled similarly, with great caution. After the first was found, investigated, and secured, Wil passed the word to Lon that the next section of soldiers could come in. That included the other two squads of Wil's platoon and a squad of Colonel Henks's militia.

When Wil reached a major branching in the subterranean system, he had his men probe each of the branches out to fifty yards, then passed the decision to Lon.

"From the charts we have, the branch leading down and right is probably the main course," Lon said. "I'll send your backup people to where you are now. They can guard the second branch while you go on up the first." Another group was sent to cover the first large chamber. "I don't want to put everyone under the hill," Lon said, "but we need to make sure you have reinforcements close if there's trouble."

Sunset was two hours away when Wil's men discovered the cache of minerals and precious metals. "It looks like there's a lot the raiders didn't ship off-world," Wil reported, although Lon was still watching through Wil's helmet camera. "Must be a ton or more here. I can recognize gold. I think I see platinum as well, but I'm not sure what some of the other stuff is."

The company of Bancrofter militia was detailed to carry the loot the raiders had left out of the caves. Lon gave Colonel Henks very little choice. "You've had your victory over the raiders. We've got prisoners. Now you've got at least a nice fraction of what they stole. We get that out of here, then we finish sealing the cave, along with any raiders who might still be inside. It's not worth risking my men or yours to investigate every cubic foot of that system. If you're still curious in two or three years, come back and open it up. There might be other loot stashed somewhere else."

It would be morning before shuttles could come in to pick up the metals, the minerals, and the men. Once everything was out of the caves and the final entrance had been razed, Dirigenters and Bancrofters started the march toward the landing zone five miles away. With prisoners to guard and more than a ton of recovered booty to carry, it was a slow trek. Only when they were camped near the landing zone, with a perimeter in place, did Lon finally give in to Colonel Henks's continuing desire to start questioning the prisoners.

''We'll pick one likely-looking candidate, see what we get out of him,'' Lon said. ''We get a few answers now, that should satisfy both our curiosities—at least enough to hold us until we're back in Lincoln.''

The subject was chosen after Lon and Henks consulted with the men who had been guarding the captured raiders. The guards indicated one of the prisoners who had appeared to be in command, some sort of leader among them. He was taken away from his cohorts. One of Lon's medics administered the drugs that would ensure truthful answers to questions.

Colonel Henks wanted to get right to tactical matters— how many more raiders there were on Bancroft, where they would be, and where they might strike next. But Henks was not doing the questioning himself. Lon was, and there were other questions he wanted answered first.

The process was not particularly fast. The truth drugs did not induce a subject to volunteer information. Each bit had to be specifically requested, and questions sometimes had to be repeated and rephrased.

Arnold Garr was the name of the man being questioned. He was from Earth, specifically Montreal, in the North American Union's province of Canada. All of the raiders were either from Earth or Mars. They had been hired and trained—over a period of nine Earth months— for this job. Their employer?

''The Colonial Mining Cartel,'' Garr said.

''I've never heard of it,'' Lon told Henks in a whispered aside.

''I have,'' Henks replied. ''They've got the franchise from the Confederation of Human Worlds on Earth to import any mining products from any colony world. A monopoly. We wouldn't accept the prices they offered. I guess they decided they weren't going to take no for an answer. We shut down their operation here, maybe they'll think better of it.''

Maybe, Lon thought.

26

The contract came to its scheduled conclusion. The three months of training were completed. Colonel Henks announced his satisfaction. Governor Sosa hosted a celebratory dinner. All due fees were paid, including the percentage on the recovered loot. The mercenaries returned to *Tyre*. The three civilian munitions experts returned to *Sidon*. The ships headed for home.

During the first days of the voyage, before the ships made their first transit of Q-space, Lon spent as much time as he could with his men, talking to individuals and small groups. He ate with them, exercised with them—as he normally did while they were in transit.

After the ships made their first transit of Q-space, Lon went to a section of the ship he had only visited once before, and then just because he had wanted to see every part of the vessel. His destination was far back in the ship, near the main engines and just at the edge of the habitable portion of *Tyre*. He went all the way to a hatch he could not open.

Beyond that hatch, preserved by the cold of space, were the bodies of the eleven men of Alpha Company who had died on Bancroft.

Including Dean Ericks.

The Dirigent Mercenary Corps always brought everyone home—when it was physically possible. When they landed in Dirigent City, the dead would head the procession across town to base. They would pass in review before a regimental formation, be given the salutes of their living comrades.

There were no chairs in the room just outside the sealed chamber where the dead made their final space voyage. It was just an open space, little more than a glorified airlock, used only when the cold chamber was heated enough to allow loading and unloading.

At first Lon leaned his forehead against the sealed hatch. Although there was sufficient shielding, the metal bulkhead felt cold.

"Good-bye, Dean," Lon whispered, his eyes closed. "We'll miss you." He remained motionless for a couple of minutes then, as if he were listening for a reply. Then he sat on the floor, his back against the hatch.

Now, finally, there was time for him to work through the grief. He had days and light-years. It would not be enough to eliminate all the pain, but it would give him a chance to move on. Silent tears fell freely.

When the first flood of grief had passed, leaving Lon feeling drained, exhausted, he made the slow trek back to his cabin. With the door locked behind him, he sat on the edge of his bunk, portable complink on his lap. For a time he merely stared at the blank screen. Then, very carefully, he wrote out his resignation from the Corps. He spent an hour at the task, going back and rewriting, revising, editing, trying to get every word exactly right.

Lon did not date the letter. When he had polished it as far as he could, he encrypted it and filed it in a private, locked directory on the complink. There was no rush. It would be another ten days before *Tyre* and *Sidon* reached Dirigent, and there would be no rush to submit it even then. He could take more time to think, time to talk it over with Sara. *Maybe it is time to take up pulling pints,* he thought. *Or maybe emigrate, move to a world where boys don't grow up to be soldiers and die. A world where men like Kalko Green don't end up in jail for protecting family.*

Epilogue

It was the last week of February on Dirigent. There were a few traces of snow on the ground, not yet melted despite several days when the temperature had risen a few degrees above freezing. Bare trees stood sentinel around the cemetery where the dead of the Corps rested. Two hundred yards to the east, just beyond one of those lines of trees, were the nearest barracks.

Each regiment had its own section in the cemetery, noted by its regimental flag. Flat stone markers identified every grave. Embedded memory modules could be linked to to hear more information than was provided on each headstone. Name, rank, unit, date of birth, date and place of death.

Two taxis waited at the curb of the lane next to 7th Regiment's portion of the graveyard, their drivers waiting inside their heated vehicles.

Eleven new graves were grouped together. The soil over the caskets had not yet completely settled. Near the foot of one of those graves, people stood silently, staring at the headstone.

Phip Steesen stood a little apart from the rest. Lon stood holding his son's hand. Sara held Angie, who really wasn't certain what this outing was all about. Mary Belzer stood next to Sara. Her husband, Janno, was at the end of the line, and their three children were between them: the oldest was nine, the youngest just a few months older than Angie Nolan.

After a few minutes, the children started to get restive, though the older ones did know why they were there. They remembered Uncle Dean and knew that they would not see him again. Lon, Junior, tried to keep from crying, though he wanted to. *It happened to Uncle Dean; it could happen to Daddy.*

The adults also worked to keep their emotions from showing. There had been little talk since they had met at the Nolan house for this pilgrimage.

Lon's thoughts were disturbed by increased pressure from his son's hand. He glanced down at the boy and nodded. Then he looked to the headstone again.

"Good-bye, old friend," Lon said softly. "We'll miss you." Phip and Janno also said farewells, then the group moved back toward the taxis. The women and children got in one, to head back to the Nolan house. The three men took the other. Before they joined the others, they had one other duty to perform for their lost friend.

At the Purple Harridan, they ordered four beers. Each man drank one. The fourth was left on the table, a coaster placed over the top.

Lon's letter of resignation remained hidden in his private files. He had not reached a final decision yet.

PENGUIN PUTNAM INC.
Online

Your Internet gateway to a virtual environment with
hundreds of entertaining and enlightening books from
Penguin Putnam Inc.

*While you're there, get the latest buzz on
the best authors and books around—*

Tom Clancy, Patricia Cornwell, W.E.B. Griffin,
Nora Roberts, William Gibson, Robin Cook,
Brian Jacques, Catherine Coulter, Stephen King,
Jacquelyn Mitchard, and many more!

**Penguin Putnam Online is located at
http://www.penguinputnam.com**

PENGUIN PUTNAM NEWS

Every month you'll get an inside look at our upcoming
books and new features on our site. This is an ongoing
effort to provide you with the most up-to-date
information about our books and authors.

Subscribe to Penguin Putnam News at
http://www.penguinputnam.com/ClubPPI